ABSOLUTION
ROAD

ABSOLUTION ROAD

rachel blaufeld

Edited by
Pam Berehulke
www.bulletproofediting.com

Cover design by
© Sarah Hansen, Okay Creations, LLC
www.okaycreations.com

Images
© 4X6, © Vadim Kozlovsky

Formatted by Tianne Samson with E.M. Tippetts Book Designs

www.emtippetsbookdesigns.com

Warning:
Content contains explicit sexual content and crude language, and is intended for mature audiences. Parental/reader discretion advised.

Dedication

*For Pam, not only my editor, but also my fairy godmother,
true friend, and confidante.
Thank you for all you do from lending an ear to cleaning up my messy
messes. And most of all, thank you for believing in me 365 days a
year, even on the days when I don't believe in myself.
This one—book five—is all for you.*

Author's Note

Absolution Road is the second book in the Crossroads series, an emotional story following the life of Jake Wrigley and his path to finding absolution and love. If you haven't read the story of Lane, Jake's twin brother, in *Redemption Lane*, reading it first will enhance your enjoyment of *Absolution Road*.

PROLOGUE

B LOOD was everywhere, all over my skin and clothes. Dark red liquid spilled onto the dirty floor as my head spun like the Tilt-A-Whirl at a carnival. My vision blurred and lightness faded in and out, but I wasn't sure if it was a dream or reality.

Was I dead? Wait . . . would I never live? Shrieks bubbled up in my throat and barreled out through my vocal cords, desperation fueling my cries.

My eyes kept drooping from the hurt and the shock; I'd never been in so much pain. I didn't know where I was or how the hell to get help, but I wanted it, wanted to live. I didn't want to just survive, but I needed to breathe *his* air, live with him side by side.

But like the blood seeping from my body, the chances of him finding me were slipping. Fading. Everything became darker, and then the light came again.

"Help!" I screamed, but it came out more of a ragged whisper since my throat was now completely raw. "Help!"

My voice bounced off the wooden walls. I squinted around me, realizing I was in what looked like an old barn. I didn't know where, though. How would anyone find me?

I'm going to die here.

CHAPTER ONE

jake

THE metal door clanked shut, the sound of its lock slamming into place echoing off the cold wall I currently leaned against. As I pressed my back against the coarse cinderblock, reality hit me smack in the chest like a bullet train barreling through my heart.

Christ. After a whole goddamn year of trying to get my life in order, to heal past wounds and move forward, look at where I landed.

Shit.

Did they hold mass in the slammer? Not that I was religious, but I would need someone like God on my side, because there was no way in hell Lane was coming to get me. Actually, for the first time ever, I told myself I wasn't calling him. I'd leaned on my twin brother for two decades too long. I'd only deserve whatever wrath he served up if I called him from the clink. *Again.*

Forget it being fucking Christmas, he had a gorgeous wife and a cute little baby daughter, a big house in the country, a huge career, and lots of cash. He deserved to be left alone.

Me, I deserved this. I'd get to make one phone call, and it looked like it was going to be to that little wench—the same woman who landed me behind bars.

My frayed jeans tightened around my thighs as I slumped to the floor. I tilted my head back against the wall, rolling my neck. Taking a long breath, I noticed the guy opposite me—he was big, tattooed, hairy, and snarling at me.

I could fucking take him. Let him just try to approach me. *I own a gym, for Chrissake.*

"Jake Wrigley?" the guard yelled as he approached the holding cell. "Which one of you fools is Jake?" He shoved his key in the keyhole, eyeing me up and down. Nothing like a big-as-fuck black dude with his biceps bulging through his polyester uniform looking at me like he was thoroughly pissed.

Who shit in his eggnog?

I stood. "That's me." I ran my hand along my buzz cut and smoothed out my beard. "Time for my phone call?"

"Nah, man. PD's here to see you."

"Oh, good. Maybe he wants to go home to his family, and I'm gonna get out of here in time for the holidays," I said, then chuckled to myself.

"I wouldn't hold your breath, my man," the guard said, shoving me toward the next set of locked doors.

"Thanks, Paul, I've got it from here," a soft feminine voice called out from behind us.

Sweet . . . a female guard.

"That's okay, Ms. Road. I'll make sure he gets to the interview room. This one here's a live wire," he said, keeping his hand on my arm as he escorted me forward, not allowing me to turn around.

Paul gave me a little shove inside the dank questioning room. "Sit down over there, hands up on the table, and don't try no shit. I'll be right on the other side of the door, you stupid prick," he said, nodding his chin toward a chair.

I pulled out the metal chair and silently wondered whether it would hold my weight. At least the guard was being lenient and I wasn't cuffed. I might have beaten the shit out of that neo-Nazi asshole in the bar, but I wasn't a threat to society at large.

"What kind of dumbass gets into a bar brawl on Christmas Eve?" Paul muttered to himself as he made his way out of the room.

The door swung closed, leaving me in complete silence. While I waited, I stared at my calloused hands, listening to my own breathing as I wondered how everything went from getting a little better to complete shit. Again.

I was so deep in thought, I didn't hear the door creak open or notice anyone had entered the room until I was enveloped in a fog of perfume or body spray, or whatever that vanilla-and-toasted-almond smell came from.

"Good evening, Mr. Wrigley, and merry Christmas. Looks like I have the pleasure of celebrating with you."

The leggy female pulled out the chair across from me and dropped into it, crossing her legs and rolling her silver pen along her lip as her gaze skated over the notes in front of her. I felt totally inadequate sitting across from the beauty in my worn-in jeans, beat-up boots, and Henley. *Not to mention it's obvious I'm a shit-for-brains with a short-fused temper. I'm here, aren't I?*

The woman was seriously all legs and tits. Hell, she could be the X Games Best All Around Chest Winner, if that were an actual category in the sporting event. *Damn, it should be!*

At the moment, her boobs happened to be right across the table from me. Those puppies were perfectly round and mouthwateringly delicious, even through her tight forest-green sweater. I wondered idly if the sweater was in honor of the holiday or to match her big green eyes.

Then there was her hair, all fiery red and secured in a ponytail that was way too neat. All of a sudden, my cock was rising to the occasion, and not for the birth of Jesus Christ. I imagined setting that ponytail free so that red mess would fan around her face, or maybe over my hips as she lowered her mouth . . .

"Excuse me, Mr. Wrigley," Legs said, interrupting my fantasy with her silky voice. "I hate to interrupt your deep thoughts, but it *is* Christmas Eve. You opted for public representation, so I'm here. In fact, I'm the only one here, thanks to my lucky draw of this shift, so I'd appreciate your not wasting my time."

Most women's voices annoyed me, but not hers. This woman's words were breathy. Not exactly husky, her voice sounded more like she was recovering from a bad cold and talking for the first time in days. She didn't need to raise her voice; her quiet demeanor was dominating in some odd way.

And she wasn't just curvy body parts as I'd thought. She had brains too.

I frowned and my ears pricked at this idea. I was usually the dominant in any situation, the guy in charge, and here was this gal taking over with minimal effort. Strangely, I liked it. I nodded in response as I took in the striking bird of prey in front of me. Silently, I willed her to pick me as her new victim. I could pretend to let her chase me a little before capturing me and bedding me down.

God, I'd fuck the stiff pole right out of her ass, and then she'd know who was really in charge.

"Alyson Road," she said, offering me her hand. It was creamy and dainty next to my dark skin, roughened from hours in the gym.

"Allison Road? You've got to be shitting me? Like the song?" I couldn't help but burst out laughing while still grasping her hand in mine. I hated that stupid song. Fucking pussy song. "Did your parents write that song? God, I hope not."

My gaze followed every one of her moves, watching intently as she crossed and uncrossed her legs, her tight black pants doing little to conceal her curves or the knee-high boots she wore underneath, before she pulled her chair more snugly underneath the table. No longer extending her hand, she said flatly, "No. They did not."

"Thank fuck! That is the worst song I've ever heard. God, every time the Gin Blossoms perform on Howard Stern, I want to take his fucking man card away."

She cleared her throat. "If it's okay with you, we'll move on to why you're in here. I've heard all the jokes before, so you're not impressing me with your quick wit or humor, Mr. Wrigley. And it's A-L-Y-S-O-N, not A-L-L-I-S-O-N, for your information." She spelled out the letters of her name, each one rolling off her tongue with a confident ease.

Leaning my chair back on its two rear legs, I couldn't help but laugh again before trying to contain myself. This chick and her soft demeanor were all business. Of course, she would be. Who else would work on Christmas Eve? I was pretty certain she could have made me wait until the day after Christmas to post bond, but here she was defending the public on the most holy night of the year.

Add a big heart to the brain, tits, and long legs I'd already noted in her plus column. Maybe I didn't want to bang her, but rather cherish this sweet thing? The reality of that seemed slim, seeing as the smart, good girls didn't go for me. Nor did I expect them to. I was the bad boy, and I had the guilty conscience to back that notion right the fuck up.

"Of course, Ms. Road. It's Jake, by the way. Just J-A-K-E. Full name is J-A-S-O-N, but I haven't been called that in twenty years." I mocked her spelling with my very own rendition, teasing the schoolgirl, looking for a reaction like I was in the third grade. "So, let's get down to brass tacks and get my ass outta here so you can head home to your . . . husband? Boyfriend? He must be waiting for a gem like you to come home to start the holiday, right?"

No harm in trying.

As I spoke, she narrowed her eyes and glared daggers at me. "Are you done with probing into my personal life, interrogating me? I'm pretty sure I'm not the one in jail."

Obviously annoyed, she followed that volley with another few leg switches. Left over right, right over left. I wanted to grab her knees and spread her limbs and dive in, let my tongue dig deep into her folds, make her let go of all that stuck-up bullshit she had going on while screaming my name. She probably tasted like sweet honey.

I got lost in another wave of thoughts . . . was she bald down there? Or did she have a fiery red landing strip? She didn't strike me as the full-bush kind of girl; probably had a regular waxing appointment. Yeah, she most definitely kept that area tight and groomed. She was way too uptight to let it go all jungle.

Being detail-oriented wasn't all that bad. This was the type of woman who remembered birthdays and anniversaries. She'd never leave her kids with the wrong babysitter.

"Mr. Wrigley! Can you please focus? I really do want to go home and have some hours to myself this holiday."

Herself? Hmm . . .

"In addition to not seeking or calling a lawyer, I understand you still haven't made any calls? Is that right?"

"Yeah. I don't want to bug my brother. It's his first Christmas with his new family and, well, he's always been the more responsible of the two of us. This would just give him more ammo against me. Basically, Ms. Road, I'm still one huge disappointment even at thirty-one years old, so I didn't call him. I guess I could call Camper, but she's the reason I ended up bashing that asshole's skull into the wall, so I don't really feel like seeing her right now. So, yep, no call. Looks like I'm spending the holiday in the slammer."

I leaned forward on my elbows, bowing my head between my arms as the severity of my situation returned. It wasn't the time for hitting on the hot public defender or thinking about eating her pussy. I was in jail, and this was extremely bad.

Frowning, she asked, "Why did you bash that *asshole's* skull?"

The word *asshole* sounded so funny coming from her pale-pink painted lips. She said it like she wanted to rinse her mouth out with soap afterward, as if her lips had never spoken such an obscenity and now she was forced to while quoting me.

This was a spectacular woman who had everything—smarts, looks, and passion. If my heart hadn't been painted black, I'd hand it over to Ms. Road to do with it what she wanted. Or someone like her, but I never imagined that for myself.

Lane got that. Not me.

"Mr. Wrigley?"

"Fucking neo-Nazi. He was spewing some shit to Camper earlier in the evening, running off at the mouth over 'her nose not looking like a Jew girl' and 'she should keep herself bald because her dark pubes gave her away.' I guess she had a night or two with him, and he didn't like that she was Jewish. He kept going, running off at the mouth over his other lady freaking over him hitting someone Jewish on the side. Can you believe that crap? Guy was downright disrespectful. I mean, if you're sleeping around with a bunch of women, you don't go bragging in public. Anyway, she's a good friend and she works for me, so I let my emotions take over. She had already gone by the time it happened." Frustrated, I let out a long breath.

"Did he say anything to incite you? Or you just acted on earlier emotions?"

She was scribbling notes on her legal pad, her slender fingers wrapped tightly around the pen. For a moment, my thoughts wandered again, visions of her hands wrapped around my cock skipping through my raddled brain.

"Cocksucker got all up in my face and said, 'I know you're tapping her and you should scrub your dick because she's nothing but a dirty Jew.'" I felt my Adam's apple bob in my throat, as if trying to clear away the rising emotion. "I really don't know why I cared that much. I'm a fucking atheist, and it's not like I'm some protector of the Jews. Yeah, I tap . . . I mean, Camper and I have an arrangement. We hang out together when we aren't seeing someone else. She's not dirty, and my dick doesn't need a scrubbing. I never even realized Camper was Jewish."

"I hear you, Mr. Wrigley. No need to discuss your manly digit or who you're *tapping* anymore. Although the next time, I may recommend getting to know who you're seeing or dating a little better. At least know their religion." She actually blushed when she said *manly digit*. Then she sort of scowled as if the mere thought of my dick disgusted her.

Maybe she's a lesbian?

"So after the man you assaulted, um,"—she looked down to check her notes—"after Mr. Cameron insulted your body and your friend, you did what?"

"I grabbed his big, fucking ugly bald head and bashed it into the brick wall until it was bloody. Oh, and I coldcocked him in the nose, which also happened to get very bloody. I would've done more damage, but the cop was right on me, and now here I am with you on Christmas Eve."

"I see you've been arrested one other time?" She had flipped through a folder, her green eyes concentrating as she used her pen to trail the line she was reading.

"Yeah. Some other ass started spewing yo-mama jokes at me at some rinky-dink frat party back in college. My mom's dead and I don't take kindly to that shit, so I pummeled him, left him with a concussion and a broken arm. He didn't press charges. Apparently it was more important that the stupid fraternity not get into trouble for serving alcohol to minors and passing drugs than it was for him to get justice. Lucky me, I guess."

She nodded while I talked, her eyes intently focused on me as if I was the most fascinating man on earth. And at that moment, I wanted to be. I also wanted to see her head nodding in my crotch, if I was being completely honest.

My semi had yet to subside; Ms. Road had done little to entice it to do so. Not only with her looks, but her eyes that consumed each of my words and her willingness to listen pulled confessions of the truth from my lips. But I knew her intent interest was all part of the gig; she listened for a living. It had nothing to do with me.

Or did it?

"I'd say. Looks like you're in luck again tonight because when the police went to question Mr. Cameron, they found some very interesting stuff going on in his apartment. Let's just say, he won't be pressing charges either. You're free to go, Mr. Wrigley. Merry Christmas."

"What the fuck? What were all the questions for?" I stood abruptly, my erection now fully deflated. Here I was thinking this was a pretty cool chick, even though she was nailing my balls to the wall, and she played some mind game with me.

"Had to make sure I wasn't releasing a full-time scumbag back into the world just in time for the holidays," she said, barely glancing at me as she shuffled her stack of papers, gathering them into a neat pile.

There she went again, being all stand-up and earnest. And gorgeous, to boot.

She unfolded those long legs and stood, holding out her hand to shake mine again, but I couldn't move.

I could leave? Just like that? Oh well, who the fuck was I to complain? Except I'd just admitted more to this woman than any other woman in my life.

What a fucked-up night, especially when I realized it was all because of the absurd sexual-favors arrangement I had with Camper. I got a lot of pussy over the years, so I wasn't sure how I ended up so deep with her, especially since she works for me. Yeah, the responsibility probably fell on me. I'd been in a bad place, desperate for some TLC, and she gave it without strings—mostly. I knew I'd never have what my brother found, but everyone needs a little love, right?

Bottom line: this was on me. I'd fallen down the rabbit hole with Camper, so I'd beat the shit out of this dude when he insulted her, and now I was paying the price. Or not, or whatever the fuck this was.

Following Ms. Road's lead, I stood, practically jittering on my feet as the adrenaline rush slowly came to a halt.

Finally convincing myself to calm down, I shook her hand and looked straight into her big green eyes. "It's been a pleasure meeting you, A-L-Y-S-O-N. I'll never be able to think of that song the same. By the way, do you work out? I own a few gyms around town . . . maybe you'd like a complimentary membership?"

I rambled as I stalled, not wanting to part ways with this chick. Now that I was a free man, I wanted to see her again. She ignited something inside me, a desire to protect and care for her, or some weird crap like that. What was this—Oprah?

"Thank you, but I must decline," she said, her voice polite but with no hint of regret. "The whole lawyer-and-client thing—it doesn't look right. But you have a good New Year, Mr. Wrigley."

And with that, her boots clicked against the floor as Ms. Road walked toward the door and slipped out, leaving Paul to handle the rest of my details, and me wondering what the hell just happened. And I don't mean being released from jail.

CHAPTER TWO

aly

two months later

I JUMPED off the bus in Oakland and slowly made my way toward the center of Pitt's campus. Students rushed by me as the ringing of church bells hung heavy in the damp winter air. My mind empty, I was focusing on nothing but the sound my boots made crunching along the snowy sidewalk as I headed toward my happy place, when my phone vibrated in my pocket. I tugged off my glove with my teeth and reached in my coat pocket to grab it, then swiped my finger across Answer Call. My heart fell when I saw who was calling, and for one fleeting second, loneliness enveloped me until I shoved it away, forcing myself to replace it with cheer.

"Hil, how's the new city?" I said, greeting my law school buddy with a smile brightening my face. She couldn't see it, but I knew she could hear it. Hilary was one of only a few outsiders I let in. The petite Asian woman understood how hard I'd worked to get where I was. The daughter of Chinese immigrants, she was also the first generation in her family to attend college. Originally named Hui, once she started school she'd demanded everyone call her Hilary, wanting to fit in.

"It's good. Cold when the wind whips off the water downtown, but my job is pretty cush, and I found a fabulous studio apartment near the nightlife. I'm trying to get out, meet people."

A genuine grin transformed my face as I heard this. Hilary was always more social than me, and she deserved to make a great life in Cleveland.

"Sounds incredible. How's your caseload?" I slowed my pace as we talked, wanting to savor my few minutes on the phone with her before hitting my destination.

"Oh, Aly, you should think about leaving the PD office. I have an assistant who basically does everything I don't want to do."

My heart pinged at her laughter that tickled my ear—not because she was teasing me, but because I missed having her around. She'd left her government job for greener pastures, and I was truly happy for her. The only problem was the big hole in my already bleak social life with Hilary gone.

"Ha! Maybe someday," I said wistfully. "In fact, the current case I was assigned may do me in. I got a real ass to defend."

Hilary gasped. "Aly! I never heard you talk that way before about a client!"

I smiled as I envisioned her throwing her arms up in the air, mocking me. "I know, but this guy says he didn't do it, but gives no reason. He's a nasty one. For the first time, I sort of wish I did contracts or something cut-and-dried like that."

Hilary let out a little snort. "Babe, don't make yourself sick over it. Nothing we do is set in rock . . . or whatever the saying is."

"Stone," I said, gently correcting her. Although Hilary's English was perfect, she could be forgetful when it came to small details. "It's true. I know."

"Look at us. My parents own a dive Chinese takeout place, and your mom worked hard to raise you. By the way, how is your mom?"

"Eh. Hanging in there, but not really herself."

"Ugh, Al. I'm sorry."

"I know." Not wanting to dwell on the negative, I said brightly,

"So, do you have big plans for the next few weeks or what?"

"Actually, I have a ton of work, but of course, I'm going to check out some of the local hot spots. You should come visit for a night!"

I reached for the door to the Cathedral of Learning, the epicenter of Pitt's campus, and said, "You know what? I think you're right. When this case is over, I'll come visit."

"Plus there's a fabulous outlet here," Hilary added in a singsong voice.

I laughed. The girl knew me well. "I don't need any more enticement than to see you, Hil. Listen, I just got to the Cathedral and I have to change. Let's make a time to FaceTime so I can see your place."

"I'll text you, okay?"

"Absolutely! 'Bye, honey."

She said, "Talk soon," and I ended the call and headed toward the ladies' room.

After I tossed on my leggings and T-shirt and toggled the Do Not Disturb button on my phone, I plugged in my earbuds and headed for the deserted stairwell. I took a deep breath, closing my eyes and letting go of everything in my brain before I began to climb the stairs. One foot after the other, I picked up speed at each landing as "Lovin', Touchin', Squeezin'" blared in my head and sweat beaded at the nape of my neck. This was Pittsburgh, after all; listening to Journey was a birthright, practically a local religion.

Before long my legs quivered and burned, and my lungs worked hard as I climbed higher toward the top of the Cathedral of Learning. Once I reached the top, I'd head for the bottom and do it all over again and again and again. It was quiet and deserted, but I felt safe. I'd been doing this same workout since I began law school at the University of Pittsburgh. It didn't matter that I'd graduated four years ago; I still ran the steps three times a week.

The dark, cavernous cathedral walls, the stone facade, and the musty smell all felt like home to me. When I used to sit and study over coffee, poring over legal briefs and memorizing case numbers, I'd get lost in the fact that I was actually there, in this legend of a building where the likes of the Carnegies and the Mellons once roamed.

Me, the daughter of a cleaning woman!

Even now that I held down a decent-paying job, I couldn't shrug the feeling that I was less than everyone else—except when I was actually doing my job. The notion that I was inferior had been pounded into my head since I was my mom's "little lady" and would sit in the corner of the houses my mom cleaned.

"Here, little girl, this toy is for you," the woman of the house would say to me, shoving some outdated broken toy into my hands. Her own kids would be baking in their Betty Crocker mini-ovens and shaving ice with their Snoopy snow-cone makers, a mess my mom would clean up for nothing pay. "Go on, you can ask to play with them," my mom would whisper to me, and I would just shake my head and remain firmly in my corner.

I never wished for that kind of life. I didn't need opulence or riches, but I could use a tiny dose of getting over my past. Just like Hilary. She was all about moving forward.

"Aly! Hey, Aly!"

I was making my way down the stairs for the second time, wallowing in my self-loathing as my quads strained to keep me upright while I flew down on the balls of my feet. I grabbed the banister to slow my pace and looked up to find Drew Burnes, managing partner of a big law practice downtown, the one and only firm I interviewed at and quickly decided wasn't for me. Too many river views, expensive lunches, and shifty defenses offered up for my undistinguished, play-by-the-books, get-to-the-bottom-of-everything palate.

I'd "risen above it all." That was what my last lover said to me about my childhood while sipping drinks together one evening after work. He was "so very impressed by me," but really his compliment was poorly disguised pity. I never saw him again after that night. I didn't want to be on the receiving end of that pitiful stare.

"Hey!" I yelled back at Drew, my voice booming through the empty stairwells as I pulled out my earbuds.

I liked Drew, though. He was nice enough to back down when I turned down his offer, stayed in touch after recruiting me, and was one of the few people who didn't look at me like some dirty ragamuffin.

"You started without me? I'm hurt." He put on a phony pout and pretended to massage a broken heart. He also liked me, and I wasn't really sure about what to do with that.

"I didn't really believe you were coming."

"I never back down from a challenge," he said as he ran up the stairs, closing the gap between us.

Last week, we'd bumped into each other at the coffee place near the courthouse. While we shared a table, I'd told him about my obsessive stair running, playfully teasing he couldn't keep up.

"Well, you ready?" I asked. "I have a few more laps up and down in me."

"Beat you to the top!"

He took off in front of me, giving me a chance to take in his perfectly styled short brown hair, not to mention the outline of his firm leg muscles showing underneath a pair of designer LuLu Lemon track pants.

"No fair, I've already been up and down a couple of times," I yelled after him.

"You're warmed up and I'm not. You should be whipping my butt."

I pushed my legs to catch up with him, and we stayed shoulder to shoulder for the remainder of the workout, huffing and puffing, not talking other than an occasional, "Keep it up!" or "Let's do one more!"

"Shit! That was a lot harder than the elliptical at the gym," Drew admitted as we cooled down and walked toward the main hall. "By the way, I don't think you should traipse around here on your own all the time. It's pretty deserted."

"It's fine. Don't worry about me. Can I say 'told you so' yet? No need for fancy equipment when you have the stairs." I nabbed my bag from the lockers situated near the elevators and slipped on my sweatshirt.

"So, you want to grab some dinner or something?" he asked as

I was pulling the sweatshirt over my head. When I could finally see him, I raised an eyebrow and gave him the stink eye.

"I know, I know. You got me locked in the *mentor zone*, but I don't want to just give you professional advice. Come on, one casual dinner? We're all sweaty . . . it can't be that formal or painful of an experience. A salad or something?"

"Okay."

"Okay? Really? You're giving in? You're saying yes?"

"I'm saying okay to salad." I pulled my coat on, zipping it up tight. "I'll take it."

We made our way into the night. It was late February, and the bitter cold slapped me hard in the face as we made our way outside. It should have been a reality check, but Drew wasn't that bad. What else did I have to do? I didn't even have a dog waiting for me at home.

Drew flipped my hood over my head and tossed his arm around me, pulling me snug and knocking me out of my thoughts. "Just salad," he muttered, then asked, "You have a car with you?"

I shook my head inside my big puffy hood. "I took the bus from town straight here."

"Mine's right over there." He pointed toward a shiny black Porsche. *Of course.* "I'll drive and then bring you back home."

"Okay."

I slid into the soft leather seat, rubbing my hands together to stay warm. There was no sense in pretending that I didn't live in a shitty apartment. Drew had seen my job application; he knew exactly where I lived. And yet he still wanted to have dinner with me, which was a far cry from sticking me in the corner.

Drew suggested a small strip of restaurants in a neighboring suburb. It sounded great to me; dining out for the heck of it was new to me. We didn't do it much growing up, and I tried to reserve it for special occasions these days.

I was a bit dazed as we crossed a bridge, Drew's fast car barreling over the steep incline, the river below us, the skyline of stadiums on the right and murky water on the left—evidence of the 'burgh formerly being a steel town. We sped on through the tunnel cut through a mountain and entered the freeway, or the parkway as we Pittsburghers called it, exiting for the suburbs.

The street we parked along was quaint with its lantern-style street lamps and dimly lit storefronts and bistros. Suddenly, I felt insignificant. I'd never been here, really anywhere, and this was way more than salad.

"Thought we could both use a break from town," he said as he opened my car door.

"You sure we can go like this?" I gestured to my black leggings and sweatshirt covered by a big bulky coat.

"It's cool, the owner's a friend of mine. He ran into some trouble a while back, and I took care of things. Plus, the place is super casual."

Swinging his arm back around me, he guided me to the door with the name Roman's etched into the frosted glass, its frame trimmed in white twinkling lights. As soon as we walked inside, the scents of garlic, fresh basil, pungent tomato sauce, and fresh-baked bread assaulted my nose. My belly growled for Italian food, yet another Pittsburgh staple. If you grew up in this city, you had to love Italian food. My mom was Irish, and yet she'd made it a point to cook Italian specialties as I was growing up. Her neighbors taught her, and the ones before showed my grandma. The memory of her cooking made me a little sad, knowing she wouldn't be cooking for me anymore. Parkinson's disease had made cooking difficult for her, long before the dementia kicked in.

"Hey! My hero." A guy dressed in chef whites called out from the open kitchen. "Good to see you, how many tonight?"

Drew held up two fingers as Roman—I presumed—wiped his hands on his apron and made his way out. The two men shook hands, and Drew handled introductions.

"Chef Rome, meet Alyson. Alyson, meet Rome."

"Aly," I said, correcting him gently with a small wave.

Rome winked at me, his light gray eyes crinkling around the corners. "Good to meet you, doll."

"Don't get too friendly; she's one of the *honest ones*. I tried to get her to come my way, but she has morals." Drew was smiling, lending a sense of lightheartedness to his words, but they weren't light to me. I believed in a fair trial for those accused, but also justice for the victims.

"Public defender, I take it? You'll change your mind soon enough." Rome slapped Drew on the back, causing his own jet-black hair to fall over his forehead, and gave me another wink. "Come on, sit down. I'll send over an appetizer on me."

After we'd settled in a booth in the back corner, a large platter of roasted vegetables and a bottle of sparkling water appeared before us, and the waiter asked if we wanted wine.

"No, thank you," I answered politely. Nowadays I dined out way more than we ever did when I was growing up—which was like never—and I still couldn't get over how much people spent on wine and food. "I'll have the small salad with grilled chicken and portabellas, vinaigrette on the side, and also, can I have extra cucumbers?"

Drew ordered some gigantic Italian salad with meats and cheeses, and a bottle of beer. While we waited for our dinner, we made small talk. Despite what he did, Drew was a nice guy. He was funny and sweet, and it was obvious he liked me. Even though we did the same thing, he made fun of my altruistic career choice.

I knew he was mostly joking. I'd told him during my job interview that I really couldn't do what he did. I was honest . . . my dad was the victim of crime although it looked like it was his fault. I'd given Drew my party line, telling him earnestly, "In my mind, criminals should be punished only if they deserve it. Too many times we pin the wrong guy."

The difference in opinion was mostly why I held back from Drew. That, and the money factor was intimidating, but he truly didn't seem to be affected by the vast divide between the two of us.

"Roman, baby! How are you?" A shrill feminine voice rang out through the small restaurant.

My head whipped up and I saw a head of blond curls nestled against Roman's broad chest. How did the guy get anything cooked? All he did was come out and talk—and flirt—with customers.

"Hey, get your dirty paws off my employee," came from the direction of the door.

The familiar voice sent a shiver down my spine and back up again. Hearing it was like slipping into soft pajamas after a long hot bath. I'd only met the owner of the voice once, and it took every fiber in my body to keep from crossing a professional line and a personal vow.

With two arrests for assault on Jake Wrigley's record, he would normally be classified as violent, but when I'd heard why, I'd become sympathetic to the criminal with the velvety voice. He'd spent the better part of being detained by the police hitting on me. Well, he actually had been free to go, but I kept him a bit longer, questioning what happened, curious about his motives.

That was a mistake. I should have just accepted at face value that the gorgeous man in front of me on that bitterly cold Christmas Eve was a criminal, but I'd asked for it. If the charges had stuck and I'd been tasked with representing him, I would have gone for the jugular and gotten him off.

Jake Wrigley was a protector. Did he have the strength to hurt someone? God, yes. Rippling with muscles and nearly bursting through his tight-fitting clothes, I imagined he could take Rocky Balboa down with one blow.

"Jake, you can't hoard Camper all to yourself!" Roman tossed back toward the door while he spun around the female in question, breaking out into an impromptu dance in the middle of the restaurant.

She giggled and laughed at the attention, batting her eyelashes and feigning embarrassment. Her loose-fitting cropped sweater hung off her shoulder, revealing a thin black lace bra strap, and when Rome spun her, her tight butt came into view, encased in form-fitting jeans.

Camper. She must be the girl Mr. Wrigley was defending that night.

Drew was talking, saying something about his firm taking on a big national case, but I didn't hear a word he said. I was fascinated by the woman in front of me. Her curves were round and perfect, her hair was wild, shiny and free, and her skin was a golden brown. No freckles in sight. She was just like the girls who would bake in their mini-ovens while I sat in the corner. She was perfect, and I was not.

Amazing how I could be incredibly confident in an interrogation room or a courthouse, but not in my own skin. I believed in the law and giving my clients a just defense, but not myself. When it came to me, I didn't know what I deserved.

"Yeah, yeah, Rome. She works for me and answers to me first." Jake came up behind the two and tugged Camper away, guiding her toward the bar and pulling out a stool.

"You two eating here tonight?" Rome asked them as he headed back toward the kitchen.

"Yep. Left the new girl in charge, giving her some space, and I owed Camper here a meal for all she's done this month."

"Aly? Hello? You okay? Where'd you go?" Drew's voice drew me out of my bout of voyeurism.

I shook the cobwebs from my head. "I'm good. I just got distracted for a moment." I took a sip of my water and plucked an asparagus spear from the plate in front of me. "So, you were saying?"

"Well, this national case, the guy who went on a multi-state shooting spree? We got it, and I'm representing the guy. At least, I'm one of the lawyers on the case. He's got like five or six. Two or three are definitely in it for the spotlight. I'm not sure, but we'll be dealing with multiple jurisdictions, so it could mean some travel, but definitely a ton of hours."

"Wow! I guess," I said. "You know I get conflicted with the way you handle matters. Of course, he deserves a strong defense—I don't know what his motives were or if he's been wrongly accused—but it's all the witnesses paid on the side and expert testimony you bring in. I can't help but think they're people for hire and just plain dirty."

Drew ran his hand through his hair, and I noticed there was a tiny bit of gray appearing along his temple. "You know what? Let's talk about something else."

"Sounds good." I smiled at the thought of being let off the hook. After all, this was just salad.

"Any big weekend plans?" Drew asked.

"Not really," I mumbled, my attention drawn to Jake and Camper in my peripheral vision.

Jake's arm was flung around the back of her chair, and he was leaning in and whispering in her ear. She, of course, was laughing like he was the funniest, wittiest guy in America, and he probably was. His thumb ghosted across her bare shoulder and back again as he leaned in and hung on her every word.

I'd had to try so hard that night in the interrogation room to remain professional and not laugh when he teased me about my name. Yeah, it was annoying, and I'd heard it all before, but the way he said it was the *worst song ever*. His honesty was hilarious. I wanted to welcome more of it, beg him to continue to chat, to spend the holiday with me.

Camper ran her hand down Jake's cheek and placed a soft kiss on his temple. He ran his hand down her slender arm that was now bare. She'd removed her sweater, leaving her in a sleeveless black tank. It was the dead of winter, but she probably wasn't cold cuddled up next to him. He'd gone to jail for her, and even though he played it off that he only was "tapping" her sometimes, it certainly looked like more.

Lucky girl. *If you want a bad boy, that is.* Although, he didn't look so bad at the moment.

Thankfully, our food arrived. Drew and I finished our meal in comfortable silence, only interrupted by a few mumbled declarations over how good the food was. He tossed Rome a thumbs-up when the check came, then paid and helped me from my seat.

For a second, I wished I'd considered dessert because we were going to have to walk right past Jake on our way out. As we stood from the table, Drew helped me put on my enormous parka. I busied myself with zipping it and fastening the waist belt, keeping my head low as we walked toward the door.

"You gonna be back, Aly?" Rome bellowed as he pulled out a

pizza from the brick oven.

I waved and muttered a quick thank-you, desperate not to call attention to myself.

Rome wasn't having it, though. He tossed the pie on the rack and hurried out. "Was it all good, babe?"

He winked and pulled me in for a hug. No one could accuse this chef of sticking me in the corner. Prying myself out of Rome's arms, I tripped over my own feet, overwhelmed with the unexpected display of affection and suddenly flustered with all the attention. Of course, my hip dipped right into Camper's bar stool before I stilled myself with my hand on the back of the chair.

"Excuse me," I whispered, then turned and addressed Rome quietly. "It was awesome. Thank so much. Good night."

Pivoting toward the door, I heard Drew saying good-bye to Rome. When a loud, "Hey!" rang out, I walked on as if I hadn't heard it.

"Hey, you! Ms. Road?"

I stopped in my tracks but didn't turn around.

"Aly?" Drew raised his voice from behind me. "Someone's calling you."

Running my hand along my sleek ponytail, I swiveled around. "Mr. Wrigley."

"Jake. Remember, just J-A-K-E."

I nodded. There was nothing else to say; I wasn't about to mention we met in jail or that I'd fantasized about him a few times since. Both were against the rules and were considered inappropriate conduct.

"Drew Burnes." My dinner companion smiled and offered his hand.

"Jake Wrigley, and this is Camper." His lips pressed tight, Jake poked the bubbly blonde on the shoulder, but she couldn't even be bothered to turn around when he tried to introduce me. Her curls bounced like a shampoo ad on TV, making me wonder what type of conditioner she used.

"Camp, this is Alyson Road."

"Shut up! Like the song? That's hysterical." Camper now whipped around in her seat, gawking at me. "That's the dumbest song. I can't believe you're named for it."

Jake's mouth turned down into a formidable scowl, and although he was trying to be discreet, it was hard not to notice him give the overzealous Barbie a pinch on the arm.

"Well, not exactly. It's just a coincidence," I said, not entirely sure why I was gracing her with an explanation. "And I go by Aly," I felt compelled to add, which was strange since I usually only allowed those who were close to call me by my nickname.

"I never thought of the coincidence," Drew said in an attempt to join the pointless discussion.

I rolled my eyes and wasn't entirely sure, but it looked like Jake's scowl deepened.

"Probably why I stay friends with you. It's an age-old joke that I've been hearing for over the last decade." I threaded my arm through Drew's down-coat-padded elbow. "Well, it's nice running into you, Mr. Wrigley."

I tried to walk away again when I saw the wheels turning inside Camper's head. Her gaze was pinging wildly between Jake and me, her brow scrunched tight. She was chewing on her lower lip with such fierce concentration, I thought she was going to eat right through it.

"How do you know each other? Is this the new investor for the third gym?" She waved a hand between the two of us.

Jake shook his head and a loud laugh rumbled through his chest. He was nothing like the anxious inmate I met in jail.

"Nah, why in the hell would you think that?" He turned an eye Camper's way, and it wasn't an overly friendly eye. Something dark lurked behind its blueness.

"Because she keeps calling you Mr. Wrigley." Camper trailed a territorial finger down Jake's bicep, placing some type of primitive ownership in her touch after she realized I wasn't a work contact.

"Ms. Road was the lawyer on duty when I got arrested for beating up your boy toy."

"Ha!" She burst out laughing, almost doubling over in her seat. "I almost forgot about that! God, I can't believe I slept with that Nazi prick," she said, shocking me by discussing what I believed to be private matters in front of the whole restaurant.

Her cavalier attitude about Jake's sacrifice annoyed me, and out of nowhere, I felt compelled to defend the man. "Well, Mr. Wrigley went to jail for it."

"You let someone out of jail after committing a crime?" Drew feigned being flabbergasted, drawing in a deep breath and bringing his hand over his chest.

"From what I recall, he was defending this young woman's honor," I explained. Why, I had no idea, but I felt compelled to stick up for Jake.

"Fuck right," Jake said. "No one insults Camper—or any woman— in front of me. No fucking way."

"Wait, you didn't tell Bess?" Camper pulled on Jake's sleeve. He shook his head and murmured, "Later," but didn't elaborate any further on *Bess*. I was clueless as to what that was all about, but it wasn't any of my business. Yet, somewhere in my gut I wanted it to be.

"But you should learn to use your words, Mr. Wrigley and not your fists." I couldn't believe we were standing here having this conversation in some suburban Italian bistro. The hilarity of it hit me in a quick swoop, and I had to hold back my giggle. "Listen, it's been lovely running into you, Mr. Wrigley, but we really have to go."

"Wait! Thank you." Jake held his hand out to shake mine. "And yes, I know. I've been working on using my words." He winked as I slid my hand into his, his fingers wrapping around mine in an easy handshake. It must have taken a great deal of effort to be that gentle because Jake Wrigley was a big, strong man.

"It's my job, just doing my job," I reminded him, and allowed Drew to lead me out of the restaurant and drive me home to my small, run-down apartment.

CHAPTER THREE

jake
Two weeks later

I was shifting into fifth gear as I came out of the tunnel when the Bluetooth rang through the car, interrupting the Led Zeppelin pumping through the speakers. There was finally a hint of spring in the air, so I'd decided to ditch my Hummer and chase the blue skies in my BMW coupe this morning, and didn't want to be disturbed.

Emotionally, I'd made limited progress over the last year, but I was killing it business wise. One of the reasons being I finally dug my head out of my ass and started listening to my millionaire mogul twin brother when it came to running my two—soon to be three—gyms. Even though his shit advice did take away from my goofing off (a.k.a. fucking around) time.

"What's up, bro?" I answered the call after seeing it was Lane on the screen.

"I'm heading down to Pittsburgh later this week. Want to grab a beer?"

"Yeah, sure. When?"

"Looks like Friday. I hate to be away from Bess and my baby girl over the weekend, but one of the head honchos from the new big hotel conglomerate building downtown is going to be there Friday afternoon, and he wants to meet. This deal would be serious money, so there's no way I'm saying no. I'll meet him on Friday, and then meet up with you, spend the night at the hotel, and head back on Saturday."

Flicking my turn signal to head up the ramp toward Oakland and my original gym, Fizzle Fitness, near the University of Pittsburgh campus, I asked, "You sure?" I knew he really didn't like being away from his wife and daughter, let alone on a weekend.

"James is coming back to visit on Wednesday, and—"

I smirked to myself. Leave it to my brother to fall for a girl whose best buddy was a gay-blade hotel concierge she met in South Beach.

"She wants you to check up on me," I said, finishing his sentence, forgetting James and the paces he put Lane through for a moment. I knew my sister-in-law, Bess, had a soft spot for me, the bad twin brother. Lane was always the responsible one, the good one, and me? Well, I was the fuckup.

"Jake, she cares. You know I don't really give a fuck. I know you're doing better and going to be fine after I make you an even richer son of a bitch, but you know Bess. She worries, so yeah, she wants a report."

What the hell did he know? Lane had it all, and probably thought that me making money was going to fill the hole inside my heart, or lighten the darkness in my soul.

I ran my hand along the steering wheel and took a calming breath. "I'm still in therapy, what else does she need to know? I'm doing it for her. Ever since I saw the tears in that girl's eyes when we pulled that last bait-and switch routine, taking advantage of being twins. Shit, when all the truth came out and Bess realized you were there the night she hit rock bottom, I knew I needed to grow up and stop playing games. It's all thanks to Bess that I realized how important the truth is. Tell her that."

Christ, Bess could be so infuriating, but she meant well. Yeah, she'd been a major druggie and a drunk in college, but she didn't need us to tiptoe around her these days.

"Jake! Are you listening to me? You know she doesn't like secrets, and she won't be happy unless I sit you down and check in with you," Lane shouted through the car's speakers.

"Yeah, yeah. Friday. I assume the Tap Room?" *Only the best hotel and beer joint for my fancy bro.* He might be pussy-whipped and moved out to rural Pennsylvania, but he was still as cosmopolitan as they came.

There was no fucking way I was getting out of it. Bess was a determined little bird. She was the one who held it together when Lane had some type of breakdown over our secret, the one we'd never told anyone. Bess blew the whole fucking thing wide open, making it all right in the end. For him, anyway.

"The Tap Room. I'll text you when I'm done," Lane said, closing the discussion as if it ever were one, and hung up.

Led Zeppelin's "Kashmir" filled the car when the Bluetooth disconnected, but I was no longer feeling it. I turned down the volume as I turned the car into my spot behind the gym. I got out of the car and slammed the door behind me, my Timberland boots thudding heavy on the ground as I stalked toward the back door of Fizzle, still knee deep in regret. *Fucking Bess.* But she was right; I still needed help.

"Hey, Jakey!" Camper hollered at me over the 50 Cent blaring from the gym area. She was waggling her fingers, trying to be seductive, but her eagerness killed the whole effect.

"What are you doing here today?" I demanded. "How come you're not in the burbs?" It came out a little gruffer than I expected, but I was moody after my little walk down memory lane. Lane could be such a pain in the ass.

"Nice to see you too, boss. I have a meeting with Rosie here for our combined marketing campaign. How's the new site coming?"

"Fine. Fucking contractor is screwing me big-time, so I'm going to have to haul his ass outta there and get someone new soon, but yeah, it's fine."

I stomped toward my office, running my hand through my hair.

It was longer again. For years, I'd kept it buzzed, other than those few months when I kept it real long in the front like Lane. Lately, I'd come to terms I wasn't the cocky D-1 baseball player I'd been in college, and grew my hair into a "style." My hairdresser convinced me one night after blowing me in the back of her salon.

"Want to see the new billboard ads?" Camper called after me.

"Nah, I trust you. Don't forget to send them to Bess for the website." My voice carried through the hall until I was finally in my office and about to shut the door. Yeah, Bess worked for me too because the meddling wench had infiltrated every single facet of my life.

"Sure you're okay?" came a whisper from the doorjamb.

I nearly jumped a foot, grabbing my chest as I caught my breath. "Shit! Camper, don't sneak up on me like that."

Camper was a case in point; she'd been Bess's neighbor and partying mate in college. In fact, she was one of the few to bear witness to Bess's downward spiral, and then Bess cut her off when she went to rehab. Lord only knew why she let Camper back into her life, but she did. Somehow I had tangled myself well and good in their web.

"I mean it," Camper said. "You seem upset. Still mad at the way I made fun of that lawyer?"

"No, not that, but that was a shit thing to do, Camp. Bess is on my case. She's sending Lane down to check on me."

I sat down on my desk and sifted through the mail. Invoices and more invoices for the new construction and equipment for my newest venture, Fizzle Cubed. I pulled on my hair, breathing deeply, and considered changing and jumping on the treadmill.

"Who made Bess the Godfather?"

Lifting my head, I gritted out, "What did you just say?"

Camper narrowed her eyes at me. "Bess. You all jump every time she says jump. She's an ex-junkie who wooed your brother. So, what gives?"

"Are you fucking serious, Camper? She's your friend and my sister-in-law." I stood up, and my height loomed over her petite figure.

"Yeah, I am. I sit around here all day, doting on you, waiting for you to notice me—for more than sex—and you only cater to Bess."

"Where the hell is this coming from?"

Apparently Camper had worked up a head of steam, because now she hooked her hands on her hips and spewed fire. "Well, I ask you how you're doing and it's always *fine and good.* I ask you to open up to me, and you go about business as usual, flirting and shit. Bess threatens to send Lane, and you're totally bent out of shape."

"Get out!" I roared, and whirled to face my window, trying to rein in my temper.

"I quit!"

"Good! I went to jail for you, Camper. We've been doing this on-again/off-again bullshit for too long. I know I'm no saint, but for Christ's sake, I'm sick of you letting any muscle-head dip his cock in you, and then I have to pick up the pieces. And yeah, you had no fucking right to make fun of the lawyer. She was there in jail with me, and you weren't." Slamming my hand on the desk, I finished with, "I'll consider this your notice. Don't report back. I'll be happy to give you a decent recommendation. You did do a good job when it came to marketing."

"Jake," she said on a whimper, her eyes welling with tears.

"One piece of advice, Camp. Don't fuck your next boss."

And just like that, I needed a new marketing person for my two currently up-and-running gyms and the third on the way. I was fucked.

I grunted, lifting the weight bar and catapulting the heavy piece of shit over my head.

"Ten," Anthony shouted from the corner. "Two more, baby doll, and then you can take a rest."

I slammed the weights down on the rack. "Shut the eff up, Tony. I'm still your boss. Don't you have any clients coming in?"

"Nah. They're lunching. You know I only train the pretty ladies, and my girls do lunch . . . or salads . . . or their husband's partners. Whatever it is they do, they do it at lunchtime." The son of a bitch winked at me before walking away.

Oomph. I lifted the bar again. I couldn't get any work done after Camper left, so I decided to lift and clear my head. It wasn't working.

The gym was getting crowded with the lunchtime rush. Our location bordering several colleges, the medical center, and close to downtown combined with our high-end locker rooms made us popular with professors, doctors, and lawyers looking for a midday workout.

This was my cue to get to work. I didn't like to take up equipment when there were paying customers waiting. I hit the main locker room quickly, stripping down in front of my general locker before sauntering off buck naked to the shower. Hey, I owned a gym and had been working on my body long before that. I was stacked, and I knew it. Plus, I needed to make sure the facilities were all being maintained; no better way than to use them myself.

Stepping out of the shower and wrapping a towel around my waist, I heard Billy from the front bringing someone on a tour.

"This is the general locker area complete with extra-wide showers and a changing area. In the back, we have a VIP locker area where there's a steam and sauna, whirlpool, rainfall showers, and an attendant."

"That sounds about like what I'm looking for," the dude answered him as I rounded the corner. "I'll be in town two or three times a week meeting with clients and interns, researching a case, so jumping in here at lunch is perfect."

I made a quick escape to my locker to toss on my clothes, but not without grabbing a better look at the prospective member. He looked so familiar, and I was still trying to place him when I headed back into the gym. Billy was waving a hand, pointing out all the equipment options as he sold my hard work. I'd built this brand, and yeah, I fucked up more often than not, but it was coming along.

As I sneaked a quick glance at my watch, I remembered who

the hell the jerk was. He was the guy with the lawyer. *My lawyer, Alyson Road. Legs.* I hadn't been able to get that redheaded siren out of my head for days. I chalked it up to it being Christmas and I'd been lonely, but Christ, if she wasn't on my mind. I'd beat off close to a dozen times to my memory of her and those long legs. Girl was a ball-buster in that interrogation room, but she was so different when I ran into her at the restaurant. Shy, almost timid, but you could see her intelligence. It shone through like a bright light.

I'm becoming a full-on sap.

She had let me off the hook that night. Pretty sure anyone else would have made me sit in jail while they enjoyed their holiday. Not that one, though. I'd thought about that more than I'd whacked off to her.

She's a good person.

Well, she obviously had a boyfriend and he was about to be a client of mine, so I mentally scrubbed her out of my brain. I'd stopped fucking other guys' girls a year ago. The whole Camper thing was a stupid mistake, a clusterfuck, and I needed to make some improvements in general about who I slept with. Period.

My thoughts were interrupted by my phone vibrating in my jeans. When I plucked it out of my back pocket and saw who was calling, I mumbled, "Fuck this day," under my breath.

As I connected the call, I didn't bother with hello or any other formalities. "Doc, sorry, I got distracted with work. Shit! I'm coming now."

"Jake, I don't reserve a whole day for you."

"I know, I know," I said as I headed toward the back exit. "Come on, Doc. I've had a super shitty day. Can you go a little easy on me?" I asked, shamelessly flirting with my shrink.

"Jake, don't try that with me. You're in luck today. You were before my scheduled lunch, so we can push your appointment a bit. Next time, I won't go easy." She didn't chuckle. I knew she wasn't lying. She was one tough bitch.

"I'm getting in my car. On my way." I slid my finger across the End Call button and started up the Bimmer, not the least bit interested in enjoying this day now.

I was five minutes away from my shrink's office. Dr. Wells had been my psychiatrist ever since Lane and I had a come-to-Jesus meeting and finally sat down to discuss what had happened when our parents died—and who was really responsible. Both Lane and I had let our own guilt affect our lives since our parents died, but we were only children at the time. It took some soul-searching on both my part and Lane's to come to the conclusion that we weren't at fault in our parents' deaths. It was Shirley, our negligent drunken babysitter, who was responsible.

Stubborn and reckless, I'd gone on a one-man mission to bring Shirley down. I'd sort of lost it for a while, chasing and berating the woman who'd ruined our family.

Of course, when Bess caught wind of what I was doing, she went into action. Bess had just moved to Florida to live with my twin brother and was surprised to learn she was pregnant. A day or two after this, Shirley had called her, trying to make amends with what was left of our family, and Bess hadn't wanted to hear from her—ever. Hearing from that awful woman was like drinking a bad cocktail on an empty stomach.

I remembered when it happened.

My phone had rung as I'd been finishing up a run and was cooling down as I walked through some graffiti-lined alley, lost deep in my muddled brain.

"Hello," I'd said, panting a little as I got my breath back.

"Jake! How could you?" Bess screeched through the phone.

Whoa. This was totally unlike Bess. She was normally easygoing and chill; she never screamed.

I stopped in my tracks. "What? I don't even know what you're talking about," I lied.

"Jake . . ." My sister-in-law practically growled my name, a no-bullshit tone in her voice.

"I wanted justice," I admitted in a low voice, as if I were ashamed for wanting something so basic, so primal.

She breathed out a noisy sigh. "Listen to me, Jake. The only justice you're going to have is the knowledge that life has been shit for Shirley ever since she convinced you guys not to rat her out. You know damn well the statute of limitations is up, and she'll never be prosecuted for her role in your parents' deaths. Heal yourself, Jake, and forget Shirley. She's not worth it."

I braced myself against the damp cement wall, glancing up as heavy raindrops started to fall from the sky that had turned as black as my heart. Kicking my feet out in front of me, I leaned back my head and blew out a frustrated breath.

"Bess, she was in charge. I was the one ultimately responsible, but she was the adult. I need you to give that to me."

"Did you hear me? I know that. But it's time for you to heal yourself," she said, her exasperation clear in her tone.

"Yeah, I heard you, but I'm not Lane. He harbored all this guilt for nothing, and now he has you, so cut me a break. I got no one."

"Jake," Lane said, somehow breaking into the conversation.

"What the fuck are you doing on the phone?" I roared.

"I grabbed the phone from Bess. It's enough. She's pregnant . . . she doesn't need to hear from Shirley. Let it go, man," he said earnestly, punctuating each word.

I hung up and began jogging back, catching a graffiti tag out of the corner of my eye that read Graffiti God.

It had hit me hard, and I'd realized then and there. No one was God. Not Bess or Lane. Not Shirley, and certainly not me. I'd fucking killed my parents—even if I was a young kid—with Shirley's help. But no one was God, and for some fuck-all reason, God wanted my parents dead and Shirley to get away with it all. Why the hell else would she reappear in our lives right when the statute of limitations was up? That wasn't a goddamn coincidence. That was God playing a joke—one in bad taste.

The rain had pounded down my back, soaking my shirt, as my thoughts clogged my throat. I wanted something, anything, more.

That was a year ago, and I still pretty much believed that shit. God had a cruel and sick sense of humor. I did leave Shirley alone, but only after ripping her a new asshole about contacting Bess.

There was no appeasing me. No amount of success, and no dirty fucks or heavy workouts were going to absolve me. I was still constantly seeking *more*, but I was clueless as to when it would be enough.

Buzzing the bell outside the doc's office, I realized I didn't even recall the short drive over or walking up to the building. Doc—as I liked to call her bony ass—beeped me in, and I collapsed onto her uncomfortable couch. The whole room was a sea of puke pink, the furniture dainty and not built for a man my size. Despite the blatant femininity of the room and lack of comfort, I found some relief within these four walls.

"So, what's up?" she asked, peering at me over the top of the moss-green-framed glasses resting on the bridge of her freckled nose. "You're late, exhausted, and obviously wielding a short fuse. It's been a long time since I've seen that behavior from you, Jake."

Dr. Wells cut right to the chase, sitting in front of me with her legs crossed primly at the ankles, her brown hair scraped back in a bun. She was cute, but so not my type. Too straitlaced and sensible. Although I knew someone else like that, didn't I?

"Fuck!" I bellowed.

She didn't even flinch. Doc was used to my outbursts. After all, I'd had plenty in her office.

"Major shit storm at work," I explained. "Camper quit, which is fine with me. The contractor is flaking out on the new place. And I have this dipshit of a new member."

Doc narrowed her eyes on me. "Dipshit of a new member? Since when do you judge who pays the dues to use your place of business?"

I leaned back into the sofa, its hard edges digging into my

shoulder blades, and let out a long breath. "He's just this prick I met a few weeks back. Rich guy, hair all perfect, thinks his shit doesn't stink."

"That doesn't tell me much. Why is this guy so upsetting to you? You make good money now, enjoy your business, and stay in shape yourself."

"That's all fucking Lane. Ever since he bailed me out with the deal I fucked up with that smoothie company, and then became a silent partner, I'm doing well. He's backing half the new gym, and shit . . . I just want to do something myself."

I breathed deeply as I swept the hair out of my eyes. It was getting shaggy, and I couldn't have cared less. It hid the fear in my eyes; no way I was buzzing it off.

"We've discussed this before," Doc said in that cultured monotone of hers. "Your brother may know business and have funds available to help you grow your business, but he doesn't know fitness machines or personal training, how to design layouts of gyms, or what gym rats want in a locker room. You're the idea person and the executor; don't short-change yourself. Now, tell me about this other guy."

"Don't forget the smoothie incident where I agreed to buy protein from the girl I was sleeping with for a two-hundred-percent markup."

She raised an eyebrow, which meant she knew I was avoiding her question. "Well, that was a while ago, a year or more maybe, during a time before you made a conscious decision not to have sex with 'everyone on two legs with a vag.' I think that was the way you put it."

A loud guffaw erupted from my chest. "Yeah. So, I've just been fucking my marketing director instead. Some resolve that was."

"The man, Jake, the customer you mentioned. Tell me what bothers you about him." She took a sip of her tea, looking at me over the rim of the delicate floral teacup. It was probably full of sunshine.

"Remember when I landed in jail? Over Camper?"

"Yes, we discussed being more professional when it came to her. Sounds to me that problem is solved as of today."

"Well, there was this PD in jail, the one who let me off the hook, but not before interrogating me. She was a vixen. Sort of. Gorgeous, but you could tell she had a softer side. Anyway, I lied to you. I tried to charm her. *In jail.* I'm such a cocksucker, I know. My fantasies went a little wild while I stared at her, but my damn heart beat faster at the way she handled herself, all confident and tough. Tough with a heart, you know? A couple of weeks ago, I ran into her again. She was with this dweeb, the new guy."

"I see." Doc tapped her pen onto her pad. "So you liked a girl? Not just for her looks, but her brains too?"

"I don't know." Leaning forward, I dropped my head into my hands. "I just want something good in my life. One thing, that's it. Not a Hummer or a BMW, or some dumb girl to blow me when it suits me. Something genuine. Will I ever be free of my memories? The one on constant replay where I'm responsible for my parents' deaths?"

Doc set her pad down and leaned forward. "We've talked about this before, Jake. You were a kid playing outside, imitating your dad. You had no idea that pretending to fix the car would result in the wheels coming off and your parents dying an untimely death. That's why your parents left you with a sitter, to watch over you. That's on her, not you."

"Shirley! I hate her!" I stood, roaring like a lion at mealtime. I wanted the woman dead since it was too late to put her behind bars.

"I know you do," Doc said calmly.

"Why does she get to live and love? Be absolved but I can't?"

I roamed toward the window and looked out at the quiet neighborhood, breathing hard. Down below, I saw a couple in love, walking hand in hand. It reminded me of what Lane had now and was a jab to the heart, reminding me of what I would never have.

"But she doesn't, Jake. As I recall, you told me she fights addiction and thrives on controversy in her small town. If I had to guess, she lives with a heavy heart. Plus, this is about you. You have to let Shirley go."

"That's what Bess says, but . . . fuck. I want her good and gone." I banged my wrist into the wall.

"Sit down, Jake," Doc quietly demanded. "Let's look at this, really look at it. You met a woman, albeit under unlikely circumstances, but you liked her. I will remind you, she's not a girl or a chick, but a woman with a postgraduate degree, if she's a PD. Perhaps this is what you liked most? She was different from the young women you meet at your gym, even Camper. From what I gather, this woman shot you down and it hurt. May I remind you, you were in jail for beating up another man while defending a different woman. You see where I'm going?"

I shook my head. "I'm a loser. A fucking low-life piece of shit. All I have is my gyms, which I almost lost last year over a girl . . . a woman . . . and now this guy. Yeah, he was another reminder of what I want, what I need. Love. I never had it. Even with Lane, he'd clean up my messes, but he kept himself ice-cold until Bess. She cracked him wide open, and now his heart pours out like hot lava from an angry volcano. It's annoying as hell. Christ! I'm even talking like a poet."

"Jake, this is normal. You want love, a life, perhaps a partner and a family. You're thirty-one. It's time to stop goofing around and settle down; that's a natural feeling."

I glared at her as I paced her office. "Well, no one is gonna want me back."

"Would you try something for me?" Doc asked.

I stopped to take in her pleading eyes, and shrugged. "Sure."

"Don't go running home with the first woman you meet this weekend. Do something on your own—go visit Lane and Bess and the baby in the country, anything to not sleep with just any available woman. If you don't see your own worth, Jake, no one will."

My gut churned; I'd been getting laid since I started high school here in Pittsburgh. My grandparents were our guardians back then, and they were dumb as dirt when it came to girls and me. By the time I graduated, I'd fucked half our female classmates in the small bedroom I'd shared with Lane in their little suburban home. After that, my D-1 baseball status and my impressive muscles pretty much guaranteed constant female company—a revolving door of cheerleaders, sorority girls, and fitness instructors.

"I'll think about it. Looks like our time is up," I said as I bolted for the door, not leaving any room for discussion on the matter.

When I hopped in my car, I decided to head back to my gym in the suburbs where there was less chance of seeing the guy. *Dumb prick with money.*

I'd bet he couldn't make Legs come if he tried.

CHAPTER FOUR

aly

HEFTING my bag up on my shoulder, I walked out of the county courthouse armed with enough reading for a year. I had all weekend to cram it all in, but I needed to visit my mom in the nursing home too. She suffered from dementia and Parkinson's disease. I wanted to care for her myself, but it wasn't possible. Sadly, I had to check her into a full-time care facility two years ago. Some days, she remembered me. Others she didn't.

It was a toss-up as to what I was least looking forward to over the weekend—visiting my mom or doing the reading for my current case. I was twenty-seven years old and single; neither option seemed like how I should be spending my weekend.

With Hilary now in Cleveland, I was trying to branch out with my social life, but it didn't come naturally to me. Connecting with other women wasn't easy. For most of my life, it had only been my mom and me. She'd work, and then I'd help her with the chores at home and do my homework, so I'd never had a big social circle. Recently, I was making more of an effort with the women at work, meeting for coffee or walks.

In fact, it was the fault of the gals from work that I was now rushing to some young-lawyers mixer. I wanted to go and socialize as much as I wanted to have my legs waxed, but even my head boss had been nagging me to get out more. Laura, the woman who ran our department, was somewhat of a mentor to me. She was also one of the women I grabbed coffee with from time to time, and her concern about my lack of a social life was sweet, but annoying. She kept pushing me, claiming she'd met her husband at one of these events.

As I entered the back entrance of the William Penn Hotel, I swept my hair over my shoulder. It was down for a change, and I considered heading to the ladies' room to put it up, but the department's administrative assistant had said I needed to look my age. "Don't look like a brittle, dried-up lawyer," she'd said with a disapproving frown. "Lighten up, Aly. You're fun when you want to be, and you're gorgeous. Stop trying so hard to be a mature adult. You do that all day at work."

I took a deep breath as her words rattled in my head, then told myself one cocktail and a little conversation, and I'd hop on the first bus home. To no one.

Winding my way to the bar inside the hotel, I broke out in a sweat. I hated these meet-and-greet things because I always felt like the outsider, just like I did when I was growing up. More often than not, I'd end up in the bar sipping on some strange drink while everyone else made small talk. I tried to convince myself to bottle up the confidence I had when it came to work and sprinkle it into my everyday life, but I couldn't do it. Hiding behind my law degree and fancy attaché case was one thing; trying to be popular and a slave to expensive fashion trends like my colleagues did was another.

"May I help you?" the hostess asked, interrupting my private pep talk.

"I'm here for the young-lawyers event."

The attractive young woman gave me a fake smile, then tossed her blond hair back dismissively as she recited in a bored voice, "All the way through the bar, in the back, through the brown door." Then she perked up as she focused on the two young bucks who'd lined up behind me.

Like I said, I hated these events where I felt inadequate. Even my choosing to work as a public defender was inferior in the eyes of those who'd headed to the private sector.

I took off my jacket, tossing it over my bag as I made my way toward the back, then paused when I spotted Jake Wrigley seated at the bar.

Maybe it wasn't him? This guy was wearing a suit, and his hair, longer than I remembered, was professionally styled. The scruffy shadow covering his cheeks was new too; it was an actual beard when I'd seen him last. Sipping a lowball glass filled with amber liquid, he divided his attention between the television hanging above the bar and the door. When his gaze flitted over me, his eyes didn't flicker with recognition, but that didn't mean anything.

Unless I was in a courtroom or a jail's interrogation room, I was pretty much indistinguishable. I was like Superwoman cloaked in my law degree, but an everyday dweeb in plainclothes. It figured that after Jake saw me out a few weeks ago in my workout clothes, he quickly dismissed me.

Trying not to pout, I made my way to the back room when I heard a familiar voice boom out apologies. "Sorry, bro!" The voice was apologetic, almost remorseful, and right behind me. Instructing myself not to respond, I turned around anyway, catching the back of Jake's ass rushing over to his clone.

He's a twin?

As I shook illicit thoughts of gorgeous twins out of my head, I continued to the lawyer mixer, trying to convince myself it was better that Jake didn't see me. I bellied up to the bar in the back and climbed onto a stool, and was shoving my bag underneath when some jerk approached.

"Hey, I'm Rick. Can I get you a drink? You look like you could relax."

"Um, I'm not even sure what I want yet, but thanks for the offer." I picked up the drink menu in front of me and studied it like it was the United States Constitution, hoping he'd take the hint.

"I can wait," Rick the jerk persisted. He hadn't even asked my name or anything.

"Listen, I'll get my own drink, but again, thanks for the offer." I wasn't going to be beholden to this schmuck.

"I got you." He nodded knowingly as he claimed the stool next to me. "You're an independent woman, women's lib and all."

No, he didn't *get it*. Turning slightly away from him, I crossed my legs and gave Rick the cold shoulder. Finally, he moved.

"What can I get you?" an adorable, shaggy-haired, well-built bartender asked.

"Vodka and soda, whatever your house vodka is."

He winked at me and strolled off to the other side of the bar to grab a glass and some ice. After fixing my drink, he set it in front of me with a small bowl of peanuts.

Taking a long sip, I surveyed the room. Lots of lawyers, most of them men all suited up with their ties loosened around their necks after presumably a long week, and a few women all stylish in wrap dresses.

I stared down at my pale pink sweater and brown slacks. Yeah, my outfit was stylish and fit well, but it wasn't worthy of the other women in the room. Mine was from the sale rack at Macy's, and their clothes were from Bergdorf Goodman in New York. How did I know? From years of perusing piles of hand-me-downs thrown at my mom. The ladies she worked for thought she'd wear them. Instead, she sold their castoffs at consignment shops and put the money away for my college.

"You good?" the cute bartender asked.

"Yeah," I said quietly.

"Not your crowd?" He tilted his head toward the room full of stuck-up lawyers.

"Well, I'm one of them, but I'm not. I guess that doesn't make any sense, but that's the truth."

"I got you. I can tell just by looking at you, you're better than all of them."

"What? No, that's not what I meant." Embarrassed, I stared back at his knowing gaze.

"I know, but look at them. All fake and phony, laughing and gaggling and gossiping while you sit here classy and calm, *Red*."

"Please, I'm anything but calm. My boss made me come to this, but I'm not feeling it. How much for the drink?"

"On the house."

After tossing a ten-dollar bill on the bar and mumbling my thanks, I grabbed my bag and left. Of course, I'd forgotten all about Jake being in the main bar as I headed toward the exit, struggling to wrestle on my tight leather jacket while I juggled my bag. I'd almost cleared the doorway when I heard my name.

"Alyson? Hey, Alyson!"

As I stopped short and turned around, Jake Wrigley ran straight into me. Colliding with a wall of solid muscle, I teetered a little and braced my hand on his chest to steady myself, surprised at the heat radiating from him.

"Um, sorry for grabbing you," I murmured as he wrapped a calloused hand over mine, stilling my frantic movements. His hand was so large, so rough, that my hand felt almost dainty in his.

"No worries. This is getting pretty silly, running into each other in the strangest of places. Do you come here a lot?" His brow furrowed and he looked at me as if I were a five-hundred-piece jigsaw puzzle and he was trying to put the pieces together.

Digging for composure, I cleared my throat, pretending I was in an interrogation room. "Not really."

"Me either. It's a bit stuffy."

"I was here for a legal event. In fact, I should be going."

One corner of his mouth lifted into a lopsided smile. "I could see how that would be the case. Not much but suits and secretaries here." He tilted his head toward the bar and some of his black hair flopped over his forehead, definitely longer than when he was in jail. "I was having a drink with my brother. My twin brother," he said, correcting himself.

"Oh, wow! That's cool." I wasn't sure how I played off my surprise, but I did. Must be all those years of playing dumb at work.

Like I did with Jake when I knew they were going to release him, but questioned him anyway. It wasn't really my job to make certain he wasn't a threat, but I'd have kept him locked up if he were. As we talked that night, I could see through his armor, that heavy metal casing made of bravado and flippant flirting. The truth was that Jake Wrigley was a little boy deep down inside. Problem was, he was a strong, gorgeous man on the outside.

"Well, I guess . . . good seeing you. I don't want to keep you." I pointed toward his brother, who was busy pounding away on his smartphone.

"Nah, I'm leaving. One drink with Lane is enough for me. He's the more serious brother," he said with a smirk and a wink. "Where you going? Somewhere more exciting?"

"Actually, home. This is about as exciting as I get."

"You were pretty serious that night in jail. You ever let loose?" Jake took my bag from my hands and said, "Come on, I'll walk you out."

"I don't need you to carry that for me, Mr. Wrigley." Definitely needed to get control of the situation. One minute, I was leaving with my reading, looking forward to a mug of hot tea and a throw blanket waiting for me at home. The next, Jake Wrigley was walking me out and carrying my briefcase.

"It's just a bag, not a marriage proposal, Ms. Road. Let's go." He slipped his hand over the soft leather of my jacket, guiding me by my elbow toward the door.

"Where are you parked? Here in the garage?" he asked, wrestling through his pockets to pull out a valet ticket once we were outside.

"I take the bus downtown, so if you'll just hand me my stuff . . ." I gave him a small smile as I forced down the lump of regret stuck in my throat.

Why couldn't I be exciting, especially with Jake Wrigley? Because I was boring, for starters, serious rather than flirty and fun, and for one defining moment, Jake Wrigley had been in jail where I'd served as the public defender. According to the rules, that moment had to set the tone for any ensuing contact between us, and it infuriated me.

I didn't want to go home, and I definitely didn't want to go back to the bar to all the "Ricks" drinking their Scotch on the rocks. More than anything, I wanted to go with Jake to wherever he might be having more fun; although whatever that was, I didn't have a clue. If Hilary were here, maybe she could have been my wing woman, or whatever it's called.

"Well then, I guess it's good that we ran into each other again. Now I know why—so I could give you a ride home." He handed his ticket to the attendant while I tried to manage an excuse, but all my words were stuck in my chest, shaken and scrambled. For someone who talked for a living, my tongue had never been so tied.

"It's just a ride, you know."

His hair lifted in the wind, but his solid frame withstood the stiff breeze whipping through the city. All the while, my heart plunged to my feet and my hair got stuck in my lip gloss, my fingers shaking like the leaves overhead while trying to pull the strands free.

"I don't know. We don't really know each other, other than—"

"Please don't say other than *me being in jail*, okay?" he said, interrupting me. "It wasn't a shining moment for me, and I was protecting someone else, as you know. I'm not all bad."

His eyes pleaded with me, the moonlight reflecting off the big pools of blue. "I can't put you on a bus in good conscience. It's dark, and it's not safe," he explained, pleading his case.

"Okay," I said just as a black BMW pulled up front. As I watched Jake tip the valet, I glanced at the expensive car and began to second-guess myself all over again. I didn't take Jake for the show-off type. Of course, he was all man complete with flirtatious one-liners, but he wasn't a status-obsessed type one like Drew. At least, that was what I had imagined.

"Miss?" The valet's question knocked me out of my thoughts. I refocused to find Jake standing there, holding the passenger door open for me.

With an apologetic smile to Jake, I slid into the already heated seat and folded my long legs beneath the dash. The red leather was a tone or two deeper than my hair, the dash all lit up and perfectly cleaned. Some type of hard rock filtered through the speakers on the lowest volume.

Jake jumped into the car with ease and shifted into first. "Where to?"

"Oakland. You know the area?"

"Yeah, I own Fizzle Fitness. You know it?"

We whipped out of the drive and into the alley. At the red light, I tried hard not to stare at Jake's profile, at his firm jaw, mussed hair, and five o'clock shadow. Or his larger-than-life biceps.

"I know it," I said, forcing myself to look out the windshield. "I don't go there, but I know of it, I should say."

"It's a living. Been doing it for over a decade, since I graduated from Pitt with a degree in sports management. My brother is helping me expand. He's really the brains; I'm just the brawn."

"I remember the gym from when I first transferred to Pitt from community college. It used to be small and has moved once already?"

"Yep." He smiled with barely disguised pride. "That was when it was just me. When I finished school with a useless degree and a washed-up D-1 career in baseball, I didn't know what to do. My shoulder's pretty much done with, not even the minors would take a look, so I rented this basement shithole and started buying used equipment, got some cheap insurance and opened. People liked my music and the Pitt spirit around, so it grew fast. I moved to the spot we are in now after about two years, and then I bought the building next door after a while, making more room for locker rooms and shit."

"Sounds like you may have some of the brains too." Why I felt compelled to compliment him, I wasn't sure.

"And you, all lawyer and legs?"

"What?" I choked out, shocked at his blatant flirting.

"You got one hell of a pair of legs. Couldn't help but notice when we first met, and a few weeks ago when you had those leggings on . . . wow! Legs for days."

Heat crept up my cheeks. Since I'm so fair, I imagined my cheeks were a rosy pink well on their way to fire-engine red. Thankful for the darkness hiding my silly embarrassment, I stuttered, "I-I'm not sure that's a good thing."

"Having long legs? Or me noticing." Jake turned slightly to face me, his expression curious.

"Either. Both." Nervously, I wound my hair around my hand, knotting it in a bun at the base of my neck. Refusing to meet his gaze, I watched him from the corner of my eye.

"Sorry to interrupt this much more interesting conversation, but where in Oakland?"

"You know the small convenience store near the museum?"

He nodded.

"Right behind it, one street back. In fact, you can drop me at the museum."

"Not a chance," he huffed out. "Now, back to your legs. What's wrong with long legs?"

I turned and studied his Adam's apple bobbing in his throat with each word, and strangely wanted to run my hand over his skin, maybe kiss his neck.

Blinking a few times to force the fantasy out of my head, I found myself admitting, "I grew up pretty poor, a tall, gangly redhead who tagged along with my mom to her jobs. She was a cleaning woman for the rich, and their little girls were always petite and small. I was neither, but I wanted to be."

I'd never really spoken about my past with anyone. Drew knew I came from limited means, but didn't know the details of my life growing up. I typically kept that in a tightly sealed box inside my heart. My throat tightened again, this time with tears.

Jake shot a wry glance my way. "Well, shit, I'd like to see those petite little girls now. They're probably all round and plump."

Surprisingly, I laughed. Actually, I burst out into a full-on fit of laughter, which was something I'd never done when wallowing in the memories of my childhood.

"Please!" I begged him, holding my stomach

"I'd know. I own gyms. Believe me, long legs are an asset."

"Okay, enough," I said, trying to compose myself. "You shouldn't even be looking."

"Why?"

"Well, you asked me not to mention it, but the way we met, and well, if I recall, you were protecting another woman. One who you were involved with . . . Um, take a right here."

I breathed out a sigh of relief that we were close to my place, and the end of this strangely comfortable, yet awkward ride.

I pointed up ahead. "There, over there. First building on the left."

"Here?" He raised an eyebrow.

"It's not much, I know, but I've been here since law school and it's home."

A tear welled up in the corner of my eye. I should have taken the bus and not let this man drive me home in his BMW and see the dilapidated building I called home. *It's affordable and warm. What else do you need?*

"It has cable," I said weakly, feeling strangely compelled to defend my home.

"Hey." He grabbed my arm as I yanked at the door handle, trying to slip out of the car. "I didn't mean it like that. It's just that it's not safe. It's dark and there are no outside lights, and I just saw someone go through the front door without a key or being buzzed in. I wouldn't judge you on this," he said, gesturing toward the run-down apartment building.

"Thanks for the ride and saying that, but I've got to go." Acutely embarrassed, I wrenched my elbow free and opened the car door.

"Alyson?"

Climbing out of the car, I froze, but refused to look back at him. "Yeah?"

"The girl I was protecting isn't around anymore, so is it okay for me to like your legs? And the body and brain attached to them?"

"Good night, Mr. Wrigley." After slamming the car door, I turned and ran toward my apartment.

CHAPTER FIVE

jake

"WHAT's the holdup with the construction?" Lane had asked me at the bar earlier tonight, swirling the ice in his drink so the cubes clinked against the glass. He'd taken a big swallow, a small moan escaping his lips when he released the tumbler from his lips.

"The fuck I know? The guy's a crap contractor, costing me money." He'd chuckled into his glass.

"What the hell?" I had leaned forward, catching his gaze.

"I just like seeing you all serious about your business. Almost as much as I'm loving this Scotch. Christ, this is good."

"You miss the booze when you're home?"

"Nah. Not even one bit. I got my beautiful wife and baby . . . my naked beautiful wife. It's a small price to pay to have Bess in my life. She tells me it's okay to keep a bottle for myself. Tells me she'd be fine, but it's not worth it. She's so strong in her recovery, and that's enough reason for me, bro."

He slapped me on the back and returned to the real reason for his visit. "Enough about me. How about you? I see your head is way out of your ass when it comes to the gym expansion, but you know Bess. She wants to know if you're forgiving yourself for past demons? It's time, Jake."

"I don't know. I feel good, almost normal sometimes. But then I get so pissed off that Shirley is just living her life. She was the adult there that day. She was the one who put that all on us to keep what I did a secret. It just doesn't seem fair."

"Gotta let it go, man. We looked into it, the statute's up. She can't be tried for it now. And you know, she's got a shitty life."

"That's what my shrink says," I said in a low voice, leaning in close when I mentioned my dirty secret. "You two talking?"

Shaking his head, he raised his hand to signal for a refill. I'd been absently watching his finger circle in the air when I caught a flash of red hair walking out of the bar.

"Hold that thought," I'd said, then jumped up to chase the mysterious vixen of my dreams through the bar.

"Alyson!" I'd called out until she finally turned around, and I forgot all about Lane.

I ended up driving her home, and now like a twisted dick, I waited inside my luxury car while she ran up her front steps and into her crappy apartment building. The woman was an attorney, for God's sake, and she lived in a college tenement. What the fuck was I missing?

I'd gone to school at Pitt for four years and owned a gym in the area for over a decade, and I'd never known anyone who lived over here in this ghetto. Lane had some posh on-campus suite for four years, thanks to his academic prowess, and I'd lived in athletic housing. Who the hell lived in this shit? Especially after law school?

Staring at the building, I waited for one of the apartment lights to turn on so I could see which unit was hers and be somewhat assured that she was home safely. Suddenly, one came on in the front. As I shifted my car into gear, I realized she lived on the second floor, too close to the entrance and only one flight up. In a piece-of-shit building like that, it was probably dark and desolate in the hallways.

Anyone could break in and do . . . I didn't know what. Bad shit like rape and muggings.

My car purred to life as I revved the engine and tore out of the decrepit neighborhood before I did something stupid like jump out and climb the fire escape to rescue the girl. I was savvy enough about women to know Alyson was bound to be pissed if I tried to rescue her. And why would I want to do that anyway? She was a stuck-up, do-gooder lawyer who toyed with me in jail, but then she was this nice woman who smiled at me at Roman's place. Her split personality, going from ornery to demure and back again, was giving me whiplash.

Why did I keep running into her? And why did I even care? I was a free man since Camper was gone. My gyms were booming and I was making lots of dough. So, what the hell was stopping me?

Guilt, anxiety, and grief rattled through me like the gearshift grinding beneath my palm as I shifted into fourth. I pushed my speed as I sped out of downtown, across the bridge to the north side of Pittsburgh where I lived along the river.

If I didn't already have beer in my belly, I'd go back to the gym and lift. After all, pushing my body had been my way of dealing with my emotions for the last two decades. First there was Little League with my dad. Then the Pony Leagues, Amateur Athletic Union baseball, and college ball became my coping mechanisms, a way I could not only feel close to my dad after he was gone, but also a way to take out all my aggression. Lifting and training had been my saviors since I was sent to my grandparents as a little boy. Back then, I'd known what I had done, and to deal with it I would tire my body with endless push-ups and sit-ups, and running suicides. Because tiring my body would quiet my overactive brain riddled with guilt.

I was well aware that Lane knew too. We didn't have that identical-twin brainwaves shit they portrayed in the movies, but I could see equal parts pity and anger every time he looked at me since we were ten years old and living in our grandparents' attic.

That's why I'd fucked women—screwing hard and long helped stop the pain, and took the edge off my anxiety. Sex and working out was the only combination I knew that worked for me. When I got older, I'd turned that focus into a business, building the gyms and filling them with a constant stream of willing women.

And now I found myself obsessing over a lawyer—a public defender, of all people. Even if she liked me, once she learned what I'd done she would probably throw me back into the same jail where we met.

I hit the button for my garage and watched the door climb, then pulled my BMW inside and parked it next to the Hummer. As I walked between the two vehicles, I stopped to kick the front tire of my truck in defeat. Here I stood in a garage full of expensive foreign cars worth more than several years of Alyson's rent, yet she lived in a tenement. I needed to get her out of that place to somewhere safe. Not my arms, because those definitely weren't safe, but at the very least, I could make sure she moved.

After punching in my alarm code, I went straight to the fridge and grabbed a light beer before walking out onto my deck. Murky river water lapped underneath me as I tipped my head back and took a long slug, taking in the star-filled sky that loomed overhead. This had been my city since I was ten, but I'd never really belonged. I deserved to be an outcast, but not Alyson. Ever since she stepped into that interrogation room, there was something about her . . . I just didn't know what.

Now I did. The whole tough, lady-lawyer thing was an act, a facade she hid behind that felt comfortable and secure. But inside she was lost, a young girl still trying to find her way. All you had to do was see her away from the justice system, like outside her apartment or out at a restaurant, and the real Alyson was revealed.

How the fuck did I know this? As sure as the moon was shining down on me, I knew it because we were one and the same. The only difference was I was a little boy stuck in a man's body. I might not even be able to help myself or get over the shit I did, but I sure as hell could help Alyson Road.

With renewed vigor, I stepped back inside my townhouse, then dropped and did a set of push-ups, followed by a ridiculous number of sit-ups. As my body worked, my mind cleared and worked out a plan.

I woke up a new man with a purpose. My phone buzzed while I was downing a smoothie and getting ready for the gym. I snatched my phone from the kitchen counter and grimaced when I saw Lane's name on the screen.

"What happened to you last night?" he said, without even saying hello.

Thinking fast, I answered, "I ran into an old friend. Sorry, I should've texted you." I crossed the kitchen while tucking the phone in my neck, grabbed my wallet and keys, and headed to the door.

Lane continued bitching in my ear. "I wasn't worried. Figured something caught your dick's attention."

"Stop baiting me, Lane. I'm doing fine. You saw yourself, I'm making progress. Tell Bess, and kiss the baby. Maybe I'll pop up for a night in the next few weeks. I could use some country air, but not when James is there. He's way too much woman for me."

Lane laughed into the phone. "Got you, buddy, but you know I can't forget how good he is to Bess. Speaking of my lady, I'm on my way back home, but I'll be back in town soon. The hotel CEO wants my software, so don't miss me too much. Also, I texted Jax, the foreman who rushed the job on my house. He's used to large projects, so he's going to call you to see what he can do for yours. It's up to you, but I think you should get rid of the current guys and put Jax on this."

"Yeah, yeah, I hear you. Current dudes have gotta go," I muttered.

"And Jake, I'm here for you."

I swiped my finger across the screen, ending the call before it got mushy.

That was exactly what I needed to avoid. Lane had been covering my ass since we learned how to talk, and I needed to cut the cord. When we were little, Lane would take the fall for spilled milk and messes in the yard. In college, he played along with my duplicitous games of bait-and-switch, pretending to be me with the ladies, and he'd rescued my stupid ass way too many times as an adult. Money here, negotiations there. It was enough.

I might never be able to repay him for his ultimate sacrifice and cover-up, but as of today, I was on my own. It was time to stand on my own two feet and do some good, something to absolve my soul of the blackness I felt there.

Unfortunately, I wasn't able to keep the good vibes going when I finally arrived at my gym. As soon as I walked out of the locker room, I spotted Camper on the treadmill, her big bushy ponytail flapping around as she ran at a grueling pace. I made a quick detour at the café for a bottle of water, then crossed the gym at the front to get to the weights area without walking past her. I guess we never discussed her giving up her complimentary gym membership, which was a big mistake on my part.

Starting with some pull-ups, I let my mind relax. Breathing in, puffing out, I let my brain go still as the veins bulged and popped in my arms. This was my happy space, when my breath came out ragged, my pulse twitched, and a slight pang of pain coursed through my taut body.

Working out and sex were the only two ways I found relief. As I pushed my reps, my flaccid cock brought to mind how long it had been since the latter. A good week or two . . . or more?

Since I'd cracked the guy's skull on Christmas Eve, Camper had been letting me hit it pretty regularly, at least up until the day she quit. I thought it was guilt or some shit like that, but I guess she wanted more. Commitment was the one thing I didn't do. Not ever. Who the hell would want a fuckup like me?

I'd just moved over to the stack of free weights and grabbed the heaviest ones I could find when I heard her.

"Hey, Jake!"

There she was, pretending to be coy, twirling her finger around a damp ringlet that had fallen free from her ponytail, chewing on her sugar-free gum, her tits practically popping out of her sports bra.

Ugh. She disgusted me, and I'd been sleeping with her for a long while, which showed how little I thought of myself.

"Hey, Camp, how you doing?" I asked as if we hadn't run our tongues all over each other.

"Good! Hope it's okay if I still come in and work out?" She ran her tongue over her upper lip, catching little beads of sweat.

"Of course," I said. Sadly, I didn't mean it, but the girl had been there for me, worked hard for the gym, and I was being a better man and all. "You worked here for almost two years, built the brand out in the burbs."

"So, what are you up to this weekend?"

I grabbed a dumbbell and did a few arm curls while we chatted; I needed to feel the burn, needed the distraction. Otherwise, I was going to let her talk me into what she wanted. For me, it would only be a good, hard fuck. For her, it would be me conceding to more. Even I was smart enough to recognize that.

"Lane was here yesterday, and I need to make some decisions with the third location. I'm actually gonna do some work this weekend, maybe even take a ride up to see Bess and the baby tomorrow," I lied.

"Bess. It's always Bess."

"I don't know what crawled up your ass with Bess. She was your best friend in college, and then when she and Lane were apart, the two of you were taking girls' trips and all that shit. Now you fucking despise her?" I switched the weight to my other hand and repeated the curls on the other side.

"She always gets her way," she hissed through a fake smile. "Now she landed the rich guy and has a baby, and I've been waiting a long time for you to take us seriously."

"Camp, babe, all this jealousy isn't becoming on you. You had to know I was never gonna get serious. I can't. It's not in the cards for me. Let's not rehash this, okay? You're a good girl and you deserve a nice guy. Just not me."

Not sure I believed that last part, but I needed to get rid of her. This whole jealousy thing was tiring. I had to admit, though, she was right. Bess was living the dream. But that was never going to happen with me.

"Have a good weekend, Jake. Hope you find peace one day, asshole," Camper muttered and then she stalked off, leaving me to my workout.

I breathed a long sigh of relief and searched for heavier weights.

CHAPTER SIX

aly

"MORNING," I called out to the receptionist as I wound my way to my tiny office in the back of the county justice building.

My mom's rapid decline currently filled my heart with a strange combination of sorrow and peace as I walked into work on Monday. Perhaps this nightmare would be over soon. As sad as that sounded, she deserved better than to rot away in some state-funded nursing home.

I'd called Kathy on my way to work, the lovely nurse I paid on the side to spend a few extra hours with my mom each day. As long as I needed Kathy, I'd have to stay in my lousy apartment, unable to afford better. A chill of shame swept over me as I remembered Jake dropping me off in front of the run-down building.

Why did I even care? I'd been embarrassed about my home my whole life. I'd never really been able to have people over or enjoy company, and it wasn't as if I was going to start now.

Opening my door with one hand while balancing my bag and coffee mug in the other, I found an enormous hydrangea plant on my desk. Its big blue puffballs brightened the room, their smell pungent, their beauty sensational. It was the type of plant the ladies my mom cleaned for would gasp over and then tell my mom to take care of it.

I dropped my pile of stuff into my chair and before taking off my coat, reached for the card tucked into the holder stuck jauntily in the pot.

Ms. Road (A-L-Y-S-O-N) –
I never officially thanked you for your kindness at Christmas time, so these are for you. Hope they brighten your week.
J-A-K-E (J-A-S-O-N) Wrigley

That was it. Nothing more or less said. *He never officially thanked me for my kindness.* I wasn't sure I would have called it kindness, but he did and I wondered why. Had no one ever been kind to him before? I didn't really do anything. In fact, I'd tested the limits with him, playing with his emotions and assuaging my own nerves about not pressing charges on someone who may have really deserved to be punished.

A knock on the door interrupted my thoughts. "Want to go over the case?" my immediate supervisor asked as he popped his head in around the door.

"Sure, Barry, I'll be right down." I stood in front of the plant, trying to conceal the evidence of my inappropriate client interactions. Shit, I wondered who received them and put them on my desk. Did they peek at the card? I slipped the plant under my desk, hiding it from view, and went to meet with Barry.

"This is going to be a big case, Alyson," Barry said as I entered his office. "Super big. Lots of press. Are you ready for the spotlight?"

I nodded, afraid to speak. He was right; this was definitely a high-profile case. I gave myself a quick mental pep talk, telling myself I was ready for what it would mean for my career and my personal goals, as well as for the department.

"It's in the paper today, right here." He folded the paper into quarters and pointed at the right corner above the fold on the first page.

Taking the paper from him, I stood in front of his desk as I scanned the article. The headline read Another Big Break in Racially Fueled Violent Gang Crime, and the article started off with recent arraignments made thanks to evidence recovered earlier in the year. The story was vague, thanks to very few leaks about what the police department had on the gang in question. It did state the police got a "lucky break" on this case, "serendipitously discovering key evidence when investigating a separate unrelated crime."

When I glanced back at Barry, he said, "Well, we knew the press was going to be following the case closely. Luckily, the judge from the arraignment—Fern Baker—appears to be following the rules and not revealing anything of importance to the media, which will go a long way in not affecting public opinion and tainting the jury pool. But I don't think this ends pretty for our guy. Crap, we've got to think on this one."

I sat down in one of the worn leather chairs across from Barry. He looked his usual disheveled self, his shirt rumpled and hair tousled, but not in a sexy mussed way, and I detected the remnants of cigarette smoke that always clung to him. If he put forth a little effort, he'd be half decent-looking, with his tanned skin and dirty-blond hair, but Barry was driven, dedicated. He was married to his job, defending criminals, and I couldn't blame him for that—apparently, so was I.

But this case? I didn't want it. It was the first case I'd ever tried to pass on, but I'd been overruled and couldn't dwell on that now. The case was mine, whether I wanted it or not, so I needed to prove myself. And I would.

"I'm going to try to meet Judge Baker for a drink," Barry said, interrupting my thoughts. "Make our wishes known, keep as many details out of the paper as possible."

"Sounds good." I sat back in the chair, resigning myself to digging into this case.

"In the meantime, what did Cameron say when you spoke with

him last week?" Barry asked with one eyebrow raised, his pencil at the ready to take notes.

"He was vague, but still maintained his innocence. He said he didn't like Jews, and that was his right. He agreed he could be a bit outspoken about it, but continued to argue that he wasn't violent."

"And?" Barry waited for more, testing my competence. And patience.

"I asked who he thought may be involved, who was violent enough to perpetrate the hate crimes pictured on his walls, and why he had the pictures if he didn't do it. He said he didn't know who was violent enough, claimed he wasn't close to many people. He maintained the only thing he's guilty of is being a fan of the handiwork because he believes in their racial cause . . . which is why he kept the photos and taped them up in his living room. My gut churned the whole time I met with him, Bar. Something is so off here. I hate the taste of this case."

I took a long breath. "Oh, I also asked if he was in a relationship, and he said he had an on-again/off-again thing going. When I asked if I could question her and politely asked for her name, he clammed up. Said he was done for the day."

"So, nobody? No other leads in his defense?"

"He made out like he was a loner, other than hanging in bars and sleeping around with this part-time mystery woman. I don't know . . . something doesn't add up. If he didn't do it, he's covering for someone."

"Who do men cover for?" Barry asked, looking up from his notes.

"Women, but he's not budging about sharing."

"Power of pussy," Barry said with a smirk.

My gaze glued to my notes, I abruptly changed the subject. "Now, what do we need to do this week?"

We spent the next twenty minutes strategizing, going over the rest of my notes from visiting our client in jail. I'd spent some time chatting with the guards and learning what our client had been up to on the inside, and that too had left me feeling irked. I was told he'd gotten in tight with some of the other white supremacists in the jail population, and I didn't like how much swagger he seemed to have developed since then. I needed to spend some time later in the week investigating what was going on with that.

"Pretty sure he's going to post bail," Barry said. "The judge didn't deny it, and I think his neighbors started a defense fund for him, which is crazy since he's relying on public defense. You're probably wondering why wouldn't they pay for some hot-shot attorney instead? Believe me, I've seen it all—"

"Unless he has some other grand plan?" I interrupted him, anxious to get the whole case wrapped up and finished.

Wishful thinking.

"No, I don't think so, just thinking aloud. He did live in the crappy apartment and had no job, so he really may not be able to afford anything else. I don't think anyone wants to take it on pro bono. They know the police must have some tight evidence. But still, the whole thing reeks of something foul, but we'll do what we're paid to. Provide a fair defense."

"But why does he want us?" I asked. "I think you're on to something,"

"Eh, I've seen these types of pricks. They think they're going to get a made-for-TV movie or whatever, and wait around for some fancy defense attorney to take their case pro bono. He's biding his time, fixing his story, making friends and cleaning out his enemies. In other words, glossing shit up, Aly. He thinks he's going to be a movie star, letting everyone in America hear his gospel." Barry rolled his eyes and turned back to his newspaper, dismissing both my train of thought and me with a chin lift.

Walking back to my office, I debated mentioning my concern to Barry, but decided against it. I was competent enough to handle this on my own. As I slid into my desk chair, my foot bumped against the hydrangea. Its scent reminded me of the man who sent it, sending waves of an unfamiliar feeling up and down my spine. Want? Need? Hunger?

God, Aly. You're losing it.

Jake Wrigley was one step above a criminal, and I was a public defender who believed in justice. He drove a fancy car, and spent Christmas in jail for a bar fight. Honest to God, something was messed up there. But what did he mean when he said, "The girl's not around anymore"?

And what did that have to do with me? And my legs?

The way he looked at me that night in jail, I felt like he was a giant mountain lion and I was his prey. A kitten falling for a big cat, and I was pretty sure that didn't end well. Yet I couldn't stop myself from Googling "Jake Wrigley and Fizzle Fitness" under the pretense of getting a phone number and leaving a message to thank him for the hydrangea.

What I didn't expect was to have several pages of results come up on Fizzle Fitness. Like Alice falling down the rabbit hole, I couldn't stop from clicking on each and every link. There were two locations plus a third on the way, and review after review about how Fizzle was the "it" place to work out.

Apparently they had state-of-the-art locker rooms and equipment, the best staff, and the hottest fitness instructors. *Is that even a thing?* Yelp loved Fizzle, the Pitt students claimed it was the place to be seen, and even out in the suburbs, the stay-at-home moms couldn't get enough of their superstar trainer, Anthony. Photos of "Toned Tony's" wicked gleaming smile and bulging biceps littered the page.

Geez, their Facebook page had some thirty thousand likes. Did everyone in Pittsburgh work out at Fizzle except for me? I'd heard of it years ago, but it was like a cult or something now.

I scrolled through the About Us page on their website.

Owner Jake Wrigley, a highly regarded baseball player while studying sports management at the University of Pittsburgh, has always been into fitness.

That pretty much jibed with what he'd told me. What he didn't say was that he employed a half dozen trainers at each location, plus a fabulously fit and peppy front desk staff, and a small army of spinning, yoga, and Zumba instructors. Bess Wrigley was listed as the company's web developer, and I was curious how she was related to the man in question. I felt like I'd heard her name before.

Then right there smiling at me from the center of one page was a photo of the ever-present bubbly blond cheerleader, Camper Shure, their marketing director. The girl's photo mocked me, her affluence and perkiness evident in her perfectly straight white smile. Her eyes told me she was a satisfied woman; by her boss, no less. But he claimed she was "no more."

My God! I dropped my head into my hands. How could he be ogling my legs when he spent all day around fit, gorgeous women? I ran stairs and jogged around the track. I didn't do Zumba or even know how to work an elliptical.

My manners urging me to call and say thank-you warred with my insecurities. There was no way I could compete with the beauties who paraded through his life, day in and day out, and I didn't even know if I wanted to. I felt myself reaching for my cell phone despite my heart pounding out a staccato beat against my silk blouse, and my head aching from thinking too hard.

"Fizzle Fitness, city location," a perky voice said. "Are you ready to get pumped today?"

I imagined it was the tall, lanky one with shiny, straight brown hair I'd seen in the website photos who answered the phone.

"Hello, I was hoping to leave a voice mail for Mr. Wrigley."

"Um, hold on one sec!" Ms. Pep-in-her-step said.

I sat there listening to the Katy Perry blaring in my ears while I was on hold, chiding myself for being an idiot, and urging myself to hit End Call.

Peppy Girl came back on the line. "Mr. Wrigley doesn't use his voice mail, and he's over at the new site. Is this important? Can I help you?"

"It's no big deal, perhaps I'll try again—"

"Oh, wait!" she blurted, interrupting me, then it sounded as if she put her hand over the phone, but I could still hear her clearly. "Jake! Phone's for you, wanted to leave you a message. I didn't tell her you didn't know how to work your voice mail or even set it up." She laughed, her voice going all breathy, and even through the phone I could tell she was flirting with her boss.

In the background, I could hear Jake say, "Cut it out, Chloe. This is a business, not a sorority house." Then his rumbling voice was in my ear. "Hello?"

He'd just told poor Chloe off and grabbed her receiver. I pictured him standing at the front desk of Pittsburgh's Most Popular Gym for the last three years running, waiting for me to respond, and all of a sudden the hilarity of what I was about to do hit me. A tiny giggle bubbled up my chest and I pushed it down, clearing my throat as I reached for some decorum.

"Hello?" he said again.

"Hi, Mr. Wrigley. It's Aly Road."

"Excuse me?" The phone receiver rustled as it was moved. "Can you all quiet down? I can't hear the phone."

"It's Alyson Road . . . from jail." I whispered the last word, instantly regretting that I chose that as how to describe myself.

"Hey, it's Jake. What can I do for you? Did you decide to take me up on my offer for a free membership? It still stands."

I gripped my forehead with my palm. Calling him was such a mistake. "I just wanted to say thanks for the plant. It really wasn't necessary."

"Oh, it was. But you don't need to thank me for a thank-you gift, Aly. Is that okay? For me to call you Aly?"

"Um, sure. Okay, so thanks," I said, injecting finality in my tone as I tried to end the stilted conversation.

"Hey, can you hold on one sec?"

"Okay . . ." I drawled out the word uncertainly, but what I really wanted was to hang up. What else was there to say?

I was back on hold, this time forced to listen to some crazy hip-hop that pummeled over the line. I was trying to tune out the constant blaring of what sounded like "pop that pussy" when Jake came back.

"Hey, I'm back. I'm in my office now. Sorry for all that mix-up. Listen, good thing you called, saves me a trip to the county building. I was going to ask you to dinner. So, what do you say?"

"Um, Mr. Wrigley—"

"Jake, remember? I'm not in jail anymore, and you're no longer an attorney on my case."

"Jake, I don't know. I still don't think it's appropriate." My palms were so sweaty, I ran them one by one along my skirt to dry them, having to shift the phone from hand to hand while I did, but it was futile.

"It's just dinner. We started out on the wrong foot and we keep running into each other, so that's got to mean something, right? Let's get together on purpose, Legs."

"You just like my legs." Holy shit! Where did that come from? I was flirting with him, egging him on.

"Well, yes, definitely that too. Why do you think I offered you a membership the first night we met? We need more of those legs in my gym."

I felt the blush creep up my pale skin all the way to my forehead. Forget my face, I was seriously burning all the way down to my core. What the hell was I doing? I was supposed to be preparing for the case of my career, and instead I was flirting with a guy I met in jail—who did happen to look amazing in ratty jeans and a tight Henley.

"I'm sorry for bringing that night up again," I said hesitantly. "That was really inappropriate of me. You weren't charged with anything, and I shouldn't hold it against you. Professionally, I mean."

"Aly, we're on the phone. I'm a man and you're a woman. We're not discussing business or law, or any of that shit. I'm trying to ask you out on a date. Drop all the professional stuff. So, how's Thursday?"

"Well . . . "

"No well. Say yes."

"Yes. Okay."

I was going to hell. With one quick phone call, all my promises to put my career first and never to get involved with the cool kids went out the window because clearly Mr. Wrigley was already interrupting my work. And according to the Yelpers of Pittsburgh, he was most certainly a cool kid.

"Great! I'll pick you up at seven. I already know where you live, so don't come down. I'll come up and get you. What unit?"

"Not going to be that easy, Jake. I'll wait in the vestibule."

Vestibule? More like an ant-filled hole-in-the-wall.

"Just wait inside safely then. And here's my direct number . . . "

He rattled off his cell number, and like I did it all the time, I gave him my number. With that, we hung up with a plan all set for Thursday.

The cool kid and me!

Poor, dirty, geeky, stuck-in-the-corner Aly Road.

CHAPTER SEVEN

jake

"DUDE, get off my site. We're done, you got me? Fucking done." My biceps flexed under my thermal shirt, ready for a rumble. This ass was testing my patience. He'd defaulted on every item in our deal, and Lane wasn't here to negotiate or sweet-talk him off the property, so I was handling shit the way I normally did. With brawn and a few threatening dirty looks.

My soon-to-be ex-contractor glared at me. "That's bullshit. Fuck you. I'm building your muscle house as fast as I can, dude."

"Not fast enough."

When I puffed out my chest and got up in his face, he shoved me backward. Good thing that my new foreman, Jax, was standing behind me. He caught my aggressive ass and held me in a lockdown.

"You're through," I told the piece-of-crap contractor, and kicked some dirt up with my foot to emphasize my point.

"I should call the cops," he shouted as a little spittle ran down the side of his mouth.

"But you won't," I tossed back. "You got a record a mile long, so get the hell out."

Lucky guess. Took one tough guy to know another. I watched the loser kick the door of his truck before climbing in, and then he tore out of the parking lot, kicking up gravel as he did.

Jax and I had visited the site the night before and he was up-to-date with what I needed, so I headed out and left him to it. I had another project to attend to; I was a regular businessman now.

The thought made me laugh to myself as I rumbled down the highway in my Hummer. The Bimmer was gone, and I was now the proud owner of a new venture. Another step toward ridding myself of the heavy burden on my back that I was chipping away at bit by bit. I didn't deserve full forgiveness, but at least I could salvage a small piece of my heart.

My phone rang, interrupting my pride fest.

"Yo, Bess, what's up? All good?"

Without even a hello, she went right for the jugular. "I told you not to get involved with her, didn't I?"

I was an idiot. Rather than punching the dash and veering my car into oncoming traffic, I slapped my hand against the steering wheel. I should have known Camper would go to Bess and play the poor victim. I was so damn angry with myself for ever starting with the bitch, and of course my sister-in-law was right to say *I told you so.*

"Bess, babe, she's cray—the crazy kind of cray—and she knew what she was getting into. I'm not a commitment man like my brother."

She laughed. "He wasn't a commitment man either, if I recall. All it takes is the right girl. But Camper wants it all on a silver platter, and I told both of you to let it be."

"Well, it's not within Camper to listen. That girl can be so freaking fake. You don't even know the half of it. She's pissed at you now too, by the way."

"I know. She called me with her pity-party-for-one, wanting to know how I ended up happy and she didn't."

"Because she's always trying to trade up, looking for an edge. You need to cool it with her. She's not a good friend, Bess." I flicked on my turn signal and took the next exit, veering right toward my destination.

"I hear you, Jake. But you didn't listen either. I've got your best interests at heart, not because you're my brother-in-law but because I love ya. Who rescued me when everything went south with AJ? And who got Lane and me to see clearly? You."

"Bess, don't get all mushy on me," I said while sitting at a stoplight.

"Seriously, what about you? You doing okay? Lane said you're still in therapy. Are you feeling any better?"

"I'm good. Better than ever. Honestly. In fact, I gotta go because I got something new going on."

"Come visit soon?"

"Yeah," I said before ending the call.

As far as sisters-in-law went, Bess could be nosy, but her heart was in the right place. At the very least, it wasn't covered in muck like mine.

At a few minutes before seven, I pulled my Hummer up to the curb in front of Alyson's building and hopped out. Running my hands through my wet hair, I ran up the steps and threw open the door to find my date leaning against the banister at the back of the hallway.

"Hey, Aly," I called out, feeling like Rocky Balboa when he yelled, "Hey, Adrian!" He was a stupid jock, his only asset his strength, and she was a gorgeous, classy specimen of a woman.

I loved the way Alyson's nickname rolled off my tongue like an ultra-smooth Scotch after a long day at work. It coursed through my body with the satisfaction of sliding deep inside a woman splayed out on silk sheets.

The girl was too good for me, but Jesus Christ, I couldn't help but want her anyway. I had brute strength and power, but I didn't have a heart worthy of giving to a girl like her. I'd have to settle for doing something worthwhile for the lady, and if we ended up with a little time between the sheets, who was I to say no?

I took a glance around and said, "Let's blow this joint." Her apartment building was even seedier on the inside than on the outside. I needed to get the hell out of there quickly because if we stayed there one more second, I was going to throw the chick over my shoulder and never bring her back.

"Okay," she said softly. The tough lawyer from jail was gone, leaving behind a woman who looked extremely nervous. If I had to guess, this lady was married to her career. Dating took a backseat—the way-back row—to the initials after her name.

I held the door open and Legs walked through, her dewy scent tickling my nose as I took in her curves, and just like that my cock joined the party. *Down, boy*, I instructed, but it seemed as though my dick had a mind of his own. Before joining Aly outside, I turned back toward the building and adjusted myself, pretending to be careful not to slam the door closed.

"How do you feel about sushi?" I asked, my words tumbling out faster than I wanted as I ran past her down the steps to open the truck door for her. My grandmother taught me that move.

"I like it," she said with a small smile. "I'm not as adventurous as most, but I can make my way through a few rolls." She slid her legs into the Hummer, barely needing any help to hop inside, and I leaned over to buckle her in. "I can do it myself," she said as she batted my hand away, and her feistiness made me smile.

I walked around the front of the vehicle and hopped inside, threw the transmission into Drive, and asked, "All set?"

My heart was beating faster than during any workout. After all, I'd never been much of a "dater." I was more into friends with benefits and one-night stands, but Alyson wasn't that type, and I didn't want her to be.

"All good. New vehicle?" she asked, stroking a finger along the leather interior.

"Nah, this is my regular ride. In fact, I unloaded the other one this week."

I pulled away from the curb and headed back toward town,

thinking the sushi bar at one of the local luxury hotels would be both romantic and fun. What the fuck did I know about dating?

"Oh," she said, then looked out the window without saying anything more.

There was a brief silence, and I needed a filler. It was too soon to toss out what I planned to say later in the evening, so I went for plan B.

"I got a little surprise for you." I hit the touchscreen for the radio and hit CD. The disc dropped into place and skipped to track three. The drumbeat kicked in and the lyrics followed behind.

"I've lost my mind on what I'd find, and all the pressure left behind on Allison Road," blared through the interior of the truck.

I caught Alyson pursing her lips out of the corner of my eye, and at first I felt as if I'd fucked up, but then she burst out giggling.

"I thought you hated this song?" she said, mocking me with a raised eyebrow.

"It's my new favorite," I teased back, and soon there was no more awkward silence.

"Turn it off," she said with a dramatic, yet good-natured grimace. "What do you normally listen to?"

"Rock, some hip-hop, and Miley Cyrus."

"Stop!" She let out a belly laugh, clutching her stomach.

Her smile was wide, and her glossy lips tempted me. If her laughter didn't sound so fucking great, I would have shut her up with my own lips. It had been a long time since I'd heard honest-to-God real laughter.

"Go ahead," I told her. "Put on whatever you like."

Her finger trembled a little as she pushed the button for XM station twenty-five, and "Beast of Burden" by the Rolling Stones filled the truck.

"Good choice." I nodded in approval.

"What did you do with your car?"

Her question caught me off guard. Not yet. It still wasn't time to explain.

"I made a better investment. And you, where do you park your car back at your place?" I asked, looking for a quick change of subject.

"I don't have a car. I can drive . . . I mean, I know how and have a license, but no car. It's part of the reason why I continue to live in Oakland. I usually take the bus. I used to borrow my mom's car up until a couple of years ago."

I glanced at her to find she was staring at her lap as she spoke, as if she were ashamed of her own words.

"That's cool," I said. "Probably better for the environment than this big hunk of junk, but lots of neighborhoods are on the bus line."

"Yeah, I know. Someday soon, I'm going to move. I have some expenses I can't control right now."

I nodded as if I understood, but I didn't. Lane and I grew up middle-class and comfortable, and now he was a millionaire mogul who up until recently had bailed me out of all my mistakes.

Now I was doing well on my own, and wasn't wanting for anything. Except maybe for love.

As of a few months ago, I didn't even know I wanted that—someone to love me. But now there was this woman in the passenger seat, a woman I barely knew, and I'd made up my mind to grow up, not to let Lane cover for my sorry ass anymore. I wanted to be good—no, *great*—not just for myself but for Alyson. Prove myself worthy of managing my own life, and then maybe I could take care of her. Because from the look of things, she could use a little help.

Although I had no clue where this sudden inspiration was coming from, I was in for the whole ride. I'd never been one to back down from a dare or a bet, and I was betting it all on this lady.

The truth was, I wanted Alyson in every way. I wanted to slide my hands up and down her long limbs, run my calloused palms along her curves while I buried my face between her thighs.

Was she a natural redhead? God, my cock sprang to life again at the thought. What was it about redheads? It wasn't just their fiery hair or famous tempers, but the creamy skin that usually came along with their vibrant coloring. Aly probably pinked up in a matter of seconds. I imagined a blush would spread all over her body as I sucked on her nipples or ran my tongue down her stomach, dipping into her belly button before grazing her clit, and the thought of it almost made me come in my pants. My breath stirred at the thought of my red handprint on her ass, and I had to force myself to think of the accounting reports on my desk at the gym.

But that's not all I imagined. With this girl, I wanted something I'd never wanted before. To be a better man. For her. For me.

I wanted to get down on my hands and knees and pray to a God I didn't believe in for forgiveness for my past transgressions. If need be, I would beg for a second chance to be deserving of some goodness, even if it only was for a short while.

The city slipped past our windows, and as the skyscrapers came into view, I veered right toward the hotel valet. A giant sign for the Fish House hung above us as we got out of the truck, the red and blue neon reflecting off Alyson's faded jeans and beat-up leather jacket.

She looked stunning dressed casually tonight, so different from when I first saw her in the jail. The jacket covered a white T-shirt, and layered necklaces wrapped around her neck, mingling with her long hair that was loose and blowing in the breeze. She was so real, and I was such a shell of nothing. I wanted to warn her, tell her to run away fast, but I didn't. Couldn't.

Throwing caution to the wind, I slung my arm around her and guided her into the hotel, tossing the keys to the valet. I came here often, usually by myself, but now as I walked into the lobby with Aly by my side, I regretted the few times I'd brought other women.

Aly's mouth dropped open as we entered the fancy lobby. "Wow." The single word came out hushed and breathless.

"You've never been inside here?" I asked.

She shook her head. "It's stunning."

"I like it okay. Food's good. Hotel's a client of my brother's, so they treat me right."

Aly stopped walking and took a moment to take it all in, spinning around, her eyes wide and her expression enraptured. Glass ceilings soared high overhead, and a cascading waterfall trickled through the middle of the lobby.

Her reaction surprised me. "Where you been hiding, girl? You were this cocky, brazen lawyer in jail. Is that the only place you go?"

I regretted the words the minute they left my mouth, but I couldn't help it. I didn't understand. She'd sat across the table from me in jail, all formidable and full of herself, and now she was timid and intimidated, as if she'd never been anywhere before. What the fuck? I felt like shit. Obviously I was missing something.

Aly deflated in front of me, the awe she'd been enjoying now gone. "I grew up poor," she said in a low voice, not meeting my eyes. "I assumed it was fairly obvious, and now that I have some money, I don't really spend it."

Relief flooded through me. This I could handle.

"Well, good thing I don't believe in going dutch or ladies paying, so let's go eat and enjoy, Aly Road." Snatching her hand, I led her toward the sushi joint with a smile playing on my face for the first time in . . . a long time. I was already doing good for someone else.

Me, Jake Wrigley, who only had ever done wrong, was spreading a little happiness.

CHAPTER EIGHT

aly

JAKE took me to the hotel attached to the convention center, the big fancy one I always stared at while I waited for the bus. It wasn't the stuffy William Penn where I ran into Jake at the Tap Room. This place was chic and oozed modern opulence. I'd never even stepped inside, and now I was letting all my innocence and poor upbringing hang out with my awestruck stare and eyes as big as Bambi. Jake acted like it didn't bother him before he snatched my hand with his, leading us to the sushi place.

My body sizzled everywhere he touched me, my shoulder on fire from when he tucked me into his side. Now my hand felt as if it was scorching, heat fizzling between our palms. I wanted to squeeze his hand tightly and never let go, which was a rarity for me.

"How are you this evening, Mr. Wrigley?" the manager asked as soon as we entered the dimly lit restaurant.

I looked around, noting the sushi bar lining the back wall and the busy bar with high-top tables at the front of the restaurant. As my eyes slowly adjusted to the darkness, I took in the main dining room.

Pale pink tablecloths and bud vases were on each table, and classic Tom Jones's "She's a Lady" piped through the speakers. The place was packed. Chairs and bar stools were full of yuppies out for the night, older married couples having an intimate dinner, and a few singles, presumably travelers.

"Great, Blake. You got a table for two?"

When Jake let go of my fingers to accept the manager's outstretched hand, a chill immediately washed over me until he brought me back into his side. This was ridiculous. I was an independent young woman who didn't get all melty over a guy.

"Not really, but for you . . . always. How's your brother? I saw him for a minute when he was here signing up the new guy coming to town. Kimpton is trying to make a go of it here in the 'burgh, and they're salivating over what Lane does for us and the guys down the street."

Jake chuckled. "Yeah, his software's all over the place. You know Lane and his big, bad domination. He's traveling less now that he has the wife and kid up in the country, and yet he's still doing as much business. But enough about him. This is Alyson. Aly, this is Blake." He squeezed me tighter each time he said my name.

"Nice to meet you, Alyson." Blake held out his hand and I accepted it, giving him my firm work handshake. I didn't want to be known as a wet noodle, even if I'd never been inside the Fish House before.

"But if it makes you feel better, Blake, don't say I said it, but I know your place is Lane's favorite joint to eat," Jake said with a wink.

Blake grinned and shook his head. "Except for the Tap Room."

"He does love his drinks at the Tap Room. Now, what about our table?"

"Sure, how about one next to the window?"

And just like that, we were led to what I assumed was a primo table with an impressive view of the city and an over-attentive waiter.

"All good?" Jake asked me as he sat across from me, giving me a big smile that made small crinkles form next to his blue eyes.

"This really wasn't necessary." It was too much for a girl like me.

"Oh, stop. Let it go, and let's have fun, okay? We're here, we have a great table, and I'm starving and sharing a table with a beautiful woman."

Heat licked its way up my neck, not stopping until it settled in my cheeks. Certain I was pinker than the tablecloths, I focused on the menu in front of me. I was so out of my league, only having had sushi a few times before at the food court with the girls from the office.

"You feel like wine, beer, or sake?" Jake asked, pulling me from my perusal of the menu.

"Wine would be great. You?"

"Why don't we get a bottle? Do you like red or white?"

"Both. I'm an equal opportunist when it comes to wine." And I was, thankfully, because I really needed a little drink, although I was certain this wine was going to be nothing like the bargain bottles I grabbed at the grocery store.

The waiter was already back after filling our water glasses as soon as we sat. "What can I get you to drink?" he asked.

Jake eyed the wine list, scanning the pages while biting his lower lip. For the briefest of moments, he looked unsure of himself, a little nervous and out of place, and I wanted to reach across the table and run my fingers along his forearm. His uncertainty made me want to be a better woman, a caring soul, a girl who allowed herself to fall in love.

"Let's go with the Double T," he said, tossing a quick glance at the waiter before bringing his eyes back to me. "And how about an order of crispy rock shrimp and the spicy edamame?" He raised an eyebrow and asked, "That sound good?"

"Definitely." Just like that, I began to relax. Inside the big brute of a flirt across from me was a gentle soul, and I felt at ease, more so than I had in a long time. I took a sip of my water and asked, "So your brother likes this place?"

"Yeah, he's the real deal, pretty big-time. During college, he worked on this software project helping hotels gather data and analyze it in a million different ways. I was busy drinking and playing ball and fighting and generally fucking up, and he made a name for himself. He's the more impressive of us, and it certainly shows." A small hint of sadness filtered through the brotherly pride in his voice before he cleared his throat and added, "But he's not here, so let's talk about you and me." With a tiny flick of some unknown switch, Mr. Cocky was back in the room.

"Well, I'm a lawyer and you own a gym. Apparently, you get into the occasional fight, but always with some social mission in your back pocket. As for me, I'm a rule follower. Definitely not a rule-breaker." This got me a huge laugh, a guffaw that rose all the way from the bottom of Jake's belly and out his mouth, reverberating around the room.

"What?" I asked just as the waiter arrived with our wine. Jake held up a finger and said, "One sec," letting me know we were definitely not done with the embarrassing conversation.

"Just pour," he instructed the waiter when the man tipped a sip's worth into the glass waiting for Jake to taste it. "I don't need to swirl and smell it. It's wine . . . it'll be good."

We were now left to our privacy again, each of us with a full glass of the burgundy-hued liquid in front of us.

"Cheers!" Jake lifted his and clinked it into mine still resting on the table.

"Cheers." My response came out in a muted half whisper, since I was somewhat unsure of what we were toasting.

"I must point out, Aly, you being here is a bit of rule-breaking. The whole fighter and PD thing? You said you wouldn't have fun with me, and look at you . . . out to dinner with me. I like it!"

The seriousness of what I was doing came crashing down on me like a million-ton elephant, the big gray one sitting in the room. Jake had been in jail, and I'd been sent to release him. If the other guy hadn't opted not to press charges, I would have been in charge of defending Jake. And now we were out for sushi as if none of that had happened.

"It's not right. I shouldn't be here, but you were extra convincing. And pretty demanding, if I remember correctly," I said, laying it all out there. "But after tonight, you'll go back to your life and I'll go back to mine. This really can't go anywhere."

"I call bullshit." Jake leaned forward, the blue of his eyes turning almost metallic, sparkling with silver spokes of anger and determination as he delivered those three quick words.

The moment was broken by a food runner delivering the appetizers, and I breathed out a silent sigh of relief. I picked up my fork and Jake ripped apart his chopsticks, and I thought he was going to let it go, but no such luck.

"Total bullshit, Aly Road. One hundred percent crap. Because no one is going back to their life after this night. Everything, and I mean everything, is going to change."

He clipped a shrimp with his chopsticks and stuck it into his mouth, chewing it with tenacity. I watched his chapped lips work, the slight dark stubble along his jaw moving as he swallowed the morsel before taking a long sip of wine. All the while, I didn't dare move. I didn't eat or drink; I wasn't even sure if I breathed.

"You can't threaten something like that, Jake," I said, finally finding my voice tucked inside my aching belly.

"You bet I can. There's a lot I can't tell you, but know this." His eyes darkened as he pinned them on me with all seriousness. "We were meant to meet in that jail on Christmas Eve. There's a reason you were on duty and responsible for me. All you need to know is I've gone through life with a ton of shit on my back—and it's bad shit—and meeting you was the first time I breathed easy in decades. And why is that? Because we were meant to meet . . . it's why we were both at Roman's and then the Tap Room. It's why you don't have a car and I had two. I was meant to take care of you."

His declaration stunned me. I breathed out his name, my wavering voice begging him to stop, but he went on.

"Yep, I know you hardly know me, and I don't know you. But I know this . . . I was meant to care for you. I wasn't good until I met you. I couldn't focus until I met you. Life meant nothing until I met you. And I know I'm laying this out there over sushi and you're in shock, but life isn't going back to normal after this dinner, Aly."

I took a sip of my wine, allowing it to flow down my throat all the way to my belly, hoping it would take the edge off. Even if I guzzled the entire glass, my nerves would still be humming.

"Jake," I whispered again, searching for the right words. Painful words, words laced with rejection, but I couldn't make them form.

In front of me was a burly man full of enough strength to beat the shit out of anyone in his way. He was an extremely virile man, oozing sex and promising a good fucking, but when I looked deep enough into the crisp blue pools of his eyes, I saw a little lost boy.

And I couldn't hurt him. Either the man or the boy. So I said nothing.

"Eat some shrimp and relax," he said with an understanding smile. "I'm not asking for a lifetime commitment. And I'm not trying to tie your good name to my shitty one. I know I'm a bad apple, but just give me a little of your goodness. I may never get anything like that again."

His Adam's apple bobbed in his throat while he waited for me to . . . respond? Eat? I didn't know. I did know this: I was going to give him some goodness.

And quite possibly break my very own heart in the process.

I lifted my glass—channeling my inner Hilary—and tapped it to his. "I don't know where this can go, probably nowhere, but I can't deny our repeated running into each other felt somewhat serendipitous. So, let's have some fun. No promises of anything more. I don't have the luxury of thinking of the future. I'm trying to survive the moment."

He beamed at me with a broad, delighted smile, and the small crinkles around his eyes made a welcome reappearance. I wanted to reach across the table and smooth the hair out of his eyes, but he captured my hand on the table under his and gave it a squeeze.

"Shrimp, come on," he commanded and I obeyed, spearing a shrimp on my fork. "Next one, you have to try to use the sticks."

I giggled. "No way. I've never used those before."

"Well, you know what they say. It's never too late to learn how to eat with chopsticks."

"Oh, really? I've never heard that saying before."

The music changed and the soft, sweet voice of Taylor Swift wafted from the speakers.

Her words struck me as the lyrics flitted through my head, and I realized that here I was actually living life for the first time. In the worst possible scenario for someone in my position, with red flags raining down all over me, I was living. And there was nothing I wanted to do more at this moment than really live.

Jake wrapped his hand around mine and slipped the chopsticks between my pointer and middle fingers, keeping his hand in place as he lined up the chopsticks just so. Our hands traveled together to the plate and we plucked up a shrimp.

Our fingers and palms remained twined as we brought the bite to my lips. I chewed and swallowed before my traitorous tongue ran a lap over my lips, making certain there was nothing left behind. Jake's eyes fixed on my mouth, darkening to midnight blue this time. With our hands still joined on the table and my heart beating so loudly in my chest, no amount of Taylor Swift was going to cover up my reaction to him.

Once again we were rescued by an overzealous server, who popped over to our table to ask what else we wanted to order.

Jake turned to me. "How adventurous do you want to be?"

With his eyebrow raised in the air, practically daring me, I couldn't resist. "I'm along for the ride. I'll go where you take me," I confessed.

Problem was, I didn't think I was only talking about sushi.

Jake ordered all kinds of things I'd never heard of before, and one after the other, a myriad of food made up of bright colors and a variety of shapes and sizes appeared at the table like the circus was coming to town.

We dipped pieces of tuna into soy sauce, and I desperately tried to pick up the tiny rolls of seaweed in my chopsticks. Jake would reach over to my side of the table and take my hand, trying to help, but his touch only made my fingers tremble more. A few times, he snatched a piece of something, popping it in my mouth as he said, "You have to try this!" Our gazes would linger on the chopsticks until they were inevitably drawn to each other, where they would simmer and pop with electricity.

"So, this one time during school," he told me, "the whole team went down to the stadium when the Pirates were practicing and begged security to let us in. We sneaked back to the locker room and waited for them to be finished and stormed inside, asking for pictures and inviting them to our party." Jake's his face bright with excitement as he recounted the story from college. "Turned out they were damn impressed with our determination, and they came. *That* was a wild night."

"Certainly sounds like it." I smiled, but I could tell my mouth wasn't going as wide as I wanted it to.

"So, what was school like for you? Sororities? Where did you live?" He leaned forward on the table, his enormous forearms looking out of place on the pink tablecloth.

"Mostly just schoolwork, studying, working—I was a waitress at Billy's—and that's about it. I had a few good friends. We would run or catch a movie together. Of course, we went to a few parties, but it wasn't really my scene."

"Like Lane," Jake mumbled. "He was the determined brother, the responsible one, the one who accomplished lots of shit. Not me, I was the fuckup."

I nudged his big boot with my ballet flat. "No way. Looks to me like you're both successful, you just got there different ways. There are so many lawyers who partied their way through undergrad and law school."

"Wild that we missed each other by a year, right? How old are you? About twenty-seven?"

I nodded. I was.

"Yeah, I figured. Four years for undergrad, three more for law school, and no way you're a newcomer to the PD office. Your balls are too big."

"You got me!" I said with a laugh. "Except I went to Community for a year before transferring to Pitt, so we missed each other by two years." I waved my hand in the air as if I were reporting for class, answering roll call, or something else ridiculous because I wasn't used to dates, let alone fancy ones with demanding, gorgeous, body-building men.

"Maybe I would have tamed my partying ways if I'd met you back then." He brought my hand to his lips and kept his eyes on mine as he dropped a few kisses along my knuckles.

I had no idea hand-kissing could be erotic, but this was the most sensual sensation I'd ever felt. Tingles rushed from my hand to my toes, and then settled in other places.

I was in deep, deep trouble.

CHAPTER NINE

jake

Aly and I strolled out of the restaurant side by side, and I didn't want the night to end. It couldn't end yet . . . I still had some fixing to do.

"Want to grab a cocktail in the lounge?" I asked her, still amazed that the beautiful woman was here with me. She was more than long legs, red hair, and creamy skin, much more than I'd expected. She was a whole woman. A good person, a sexy woman, a well-educated lawyer, soft and sensuous on the inside and so damn smart and tough on the outside—like an alley cat.

"I really can't. We're working this big case at the office, and we have an early debriefing meeting. I need to be on top of my game."

She turned to face me and stood up on tiptoe to place a small kiss on my cheek. Her lips lingered for a few heartbeats along my face. They felt like a piece of silk floating over my stubble and with each breath, my coarse five o'clock shadow was snagging her perfection—a warning if there ever was one. But I was a rule-breaker.

"Thank you," she whispered, pulling away. "This was surprisingly nice."

I took her hand and led her to the other side of the lobby, next to the waterfall for some privacy, where the lapping of the water would drown out our words. Turning her to face me, I took her face in my hands and bent down to place a gentle kiss on her lips. It was nothing like I wanted to do. It was more of a caress when I wanted to devour her whole, but this wasn't the time. I feared if I took one small nibble, I'd eat her alive right in the middle of the hotel for everyone to see.

"Aly, remember when I said everything was going to change?"

"Uh-huh."

I took her hand in mine and gave it a gentle squeeze. "And you asked about my other car, and I said I'd made a different investment?"

"Jake, I don't know where you're going with any of this." Confusion swirled in her green eyes, and a line formed between her brows.

"I sold the car and used the money as a down payment on a small duplex. I now own two rental units in Highland Park. On the bus line. And I want you to live in one of them."

"What?" she shrieked, but contained her volume to an urgent whisper between clenched teeth. She snatched her hand away from me with a force I didn't know she had in her. "Jake! What in the world? I'm not a charity case!"

If I'd been looking for a way to bring out her fire, I had apparently found it.

"I know," I said in a soothing voice, trying to calm her down. "I felt indebted to you, Aly, that's all. And you and I both know, your place is awful. And dangerous. I hated dropping you off there, and now you can live at my new building. As a favor, I'll match what you pay now in rent." I might be stupid, but not dumb enough to admit I'd intended to let her live there rent-free.

"That's the most preposterous thing I ever heard!" she said before she turned and stalked toward the revolving front door of the hotel.

"Aly!" I chased after her, my heavy boots clunking on the marble floor, echoing throughout the quiet lobby.

She held up a hand to warn me off, and I skidded to a stop. Yes, I could have caught her, but I didn't. There was no way I'd make a scene—or more of one—in front of the front desk staff and valets. So I stood like an asshole on the other side of the glass door and watched the valet open a cab door for Aly. She slid into the backseat without even a glance back.

I knew it was rash and insane, selling my car and buying a rental property, asking her to move in. All of it was fucking nuts, but my brother went all crazy when he met Bess, inviting her to visit him in Florida. It had worked for him, so why not for me? We were identical twins, together since birth, so was it so bad that I wanted what he had? I didn't know how he did it, but I was going to find the fuck out. Fast.

At least Aly took a cab and not the bus this late at night, I thought as I settled into my Hummer a few minutes later and drove away.

Then I had another irrational idea. Maybe I should swing by her place and at least make sure she got home safely. Isn't that what men who liked women did? Looked out for them and shit. Or would that just scare her off?

My mind whirled, trying to come up with a way to fix this. Maybe I should have started smaller than an apartment? Like with flowers, or a puppy?

Nah.

It had been nearly forty-eight hours since Aly ran out of the hotel on me, and I couldn't stand to be around all weekend without charging into her apartment and packing up all her shit. So I opted for a weekend with my brother's family. Saturday morning, I let myself into his country house, ready for some of that domestic chaos to wash over me.

"Jaaaake-yyy!" I heard my name radiating from the kitchen, but it wasn't who I wanted to be yelling it.

"Hey, James," I said, greeting my sister-in-law's best friend. He seemed to be spending more time at Bess and Lane's country home than his own apartment in South Florida. "You're back? Don't you even work anymore?"

"I quit!" he exclaimed, then did a bad imitation of a hula dance, which I supposed was his idea of a "happy" dance.

I shook my head with a grin and let him rattle on since Lane had insisted James was good for Bess. He was part of the AA program, so he and Bess always went to meetings together when he visited them. Bess said that with James's lifestyle, he'd likely never have a family of his own, so he was always welcome to be a part of theirs.

"I'm working for Lane now," James explained. "He said he doesn't want to have to think about wining and dining clients anymore when he travels, so I'm his new lead travel person. I do all the research on where he's going, finding the best places and making his arrangements, which is a perfect job for me. I'm his own personal concierge." He flashed me a big grin before he headed back to the coffeemaker, some huge fancy Italian or French deal that probably cost a small fortune.

"Great, I guess. Where is everyone? I told them I was coming down today." There wasn't the usual noise and commotion I expected whenever I showed up here. No shrieking baby or hyper dog anywhere.

James put a mischievous smirk on his face before landing the blow. "Oh, Maddy-girl is napping, which means the dog is spread-eagle underneath the crib, and let's say, Bess and Lane are *laying down*."

"Stop! Stop right now, James. Talk to the hand," I said, raising my palm in the air. "That. Is. My. Sister-in-law."

James cackled like the mother hen he was, and I headed for the back door to find my own brand of therapy.

Spring was in the air, the sky heavy with moisture and the ground wet as I made my way to the shed out back. It wasn't Lane's space, he rarely got his hands dirty with manual labor, but he kept it well stocked for his groundskeeper—and me. It seemed like the only time I visited was when I was in search of some sort of escape from my own damn head.

Sweat dripped down my brow and lined the seam between my jeans and my waist when Lane found me chopping wood a while later. I lifted the heavy ax and brought it down with force, splitting the log in half before I tossed it into the stack I'd already chopped. My breaths came in stilted puffs, shallow inhales and long exhales as I beat the shit out of the wood.

"Bro?" Lane called from a safe distance.

Ignoring him, I brought the ax down again and the snapping sound of the log splitting rang in the air, punctuating the silence. I grabbed another and made quick work of it.

"Bro!"

This time it came louder, and I sank the ax into the wood block with more force than necessary. "What?" I spat out.

"You're the one who's here at my house mutilating wood." My twin approached with caution, his hands lifted in mock surrender as his ridiculous designer boots crunched the thawing ground.

"Right."

My head hung in shame as I told him what had happened over the last few months, starting with landing my ass in jail over Christmas and everything since, all the way up to my offer to Aly and her running away.

Lane paced the narrow patch of grass as I spoke, shaking his head. "Christ, Jake! You were in jail and didn't call? And why is it that you feel you have to fight everyone with your fists?"

We stood face-to-face in his backyard during our tense conversation, and I was pretty sure Bess was watching from the kitchen window.

"And you did what?" he said incredulously. "Sold your car, asked a woman to move for you?"

"So the fuck what!" I spit back.

"Pardon me for being confused, but you've done nothing but bed hop for years. I mean, I get it. I did it too."

His said the last part in a low voice, almost a whisper, but I wasn't sure why. Bess knew he was a man-whore before he met her.

"Yeah, I know that too, but isn't this what men do when they fall for someone? Don't they want to protect them? Look what you did for Bess."

He grabbed his forehead and leaned against a tree. "Jake, I get where your head's at, but you can't boss women around in the real world like you do in bed."

Frustrated, I turned and jerked the ax off the stump to split another log before I responded.

"Lane, I'm not you. Not everything I touch turns to gold. I've barely been hanging on for years. Now I've finally got my business going and I'm done messing around with Camper, and then I meet this woman. She's the best thing I've ever seen, she's got it all, and there's this immediate need deep in my belly. I don't want to *hit it and quit it* anymore. I don't want to be that guy, but I have no fucking clue what I'm doing."

"You could've talked to me," he said with a smirk, "when you didn't have an ax in your hand." He leaned against the tree, grinning with his arms crossed over his chest as I split another piece of wood.

"Don't be Mr. Funny right now, Lane."

"I just never thought I'd see the day with you all strung out over a woman."

"You can't keep fixing shit for me, Lane! I may not have an MBA from a fancy school, but even I'm not dumb enough to believe I can continue living life as I've been living it. I've not taken any responsibility for myself, and I have to do something about it. The first step wasn't calling you when I landed my pathetic ass in jail. As for the fight, I pretty much remember you beating AJ within an inch of his life when he went after Bess. And fucking sue me for wanting to get the girl all by myself."

Tossing the ax down, I started pacing the yard, kicking up clumps of mud with my worn-in boots. The first time I came up here, I'd worn brand-new athletic shoes. Now I came prepared for mucking around in the woods. *See, a man can learn.*

Lane sighed. "I was in love with Bess, and that fucker almost hurt her. That's different. You went to jail for Camper and her antics. Who the hell was this guy you went after?"

"That doesn't matter anymore. What matters is now I'm trying to do right, and this woman is not listening to me." I glared at my brother, our identical blue eyes staring each other down.

Lane grabbed my jacket by the lapels and pulled me tight toward him. "Jake, you're whole life women have fallen at your feet, letting you lead them on just to have a chance to fuck you. You've never had to try to get a woman to like you for more than your body."

He released my jacket and moved his hands to my shoulders, gripping them tightly. "Looks like you met your match. Listen to me good, brother. No lawyer—a public defender, no less—is going to fall into line if you boss her around. So put on your goddamn big-boy pants and deal with it. And it's not because she's smarter than you, you're just going to have to work for it."

Shrugging off his grip, I went back at it with the ax while Lane watched, my muscles flexing and straining with each lift. Sweat dripped down my back again beneath my shirt as I considered what he had said. Stopping suddenly, ax in mid-air, I confessed, "Maybe I don't deserve to be loved after what I did. If Shirley were behind bars, maybe, but not with blood on my hands."

Lane shook his head. "I'm not listening to this, Jake. We've been through this, hashed it all out. I went to therapy; you're in therapy. Shirley is beyond the statute of limitations, and you were a little kid who did nothing wrong. There's no blood on your hands. It's all on her conscience, and she has to live with that."

"Go!" I demanded as I turned my back on him. "I need a little more time out here, and then I'll come inside and behave."

Just as Lane was about to argue with me, Bess called through the open back door. "Here's Brooks. Maddy is up, and he needs to run around and lift his leg."

Her soft voice carried through the air as the dog bounded toward us, and from the looks of it, Bess may as well have announced she was naked and ready for round two. My brother perked up and headed for the house without another word.

"Hey, big guy." I ran my hand along the shiny black Lab's flank before giving him a little noogie on the head. With his tail wagging, he ran off toward a tree and did exactly what his mistress wanted him to do, lifted his leg like a good boy.

Did I want to be someone's good guy? Lose myself in someone's sweet voice? Sneak in a little afternoon delight while our baby napped?

Am I actually worth it?

Watching Brooks bound around the yard, looking for another spot to mark, I wasn't so sure, but I did come up with yet another insane idea, Plan C. Lucky for me, I was in the rural back roads of Pennsylvania where I could set it all in motion.

With that in mind, I trudged back up to the house and spent the rest of the day cooing over my brother's baby girl, counting the minutes until morning.

CHAPTER
TEN

aly

SATURDAY was downright miserable since I went to visit my mom like I did every weekend. It broke my heart to see her so frail and gray, her hands twisted with arthritis. Although I knew those years of scrubbing floors couldn't have given her arthritis, all that hard work surely didn't help.

The worst part was that she had no clue who I was until about five minutes before I had to leave. Just as my mother's memory kicked in and her face lit up at the sight of me, I needed to rush off to meet Barry for a cup of coffee so we could go over case notes. Which, of course, made me feel like the worst daughter in the world, knowing she thought I'd just gotten there and left, when I'd really been there for hours.

The group behind me jostled me a little as I shifted my bag strap on my shoulder while I waited for the bus. When my phone rang, I startled, then patted each of my pockets in search of the source of the intrusion.

A glance at the screen confirmed that the caller was exactly who

I didn't want to hear from, but I answered anyway.

At my whispered hello, Drew said, "Hey, Aly? How are you?"

What the heck was with this guy? We had a nice time, but that was it. Never mind that he didn't make my pulse race and my heart beat at full speed like Jake.

"I'm well," I said, trying to be polite. "Just getting ready to do some work." If I sounded harried, I thought, maybe we could cut this conversation short.

"You public-service people bring work home on the weekends too?"

"Looks like we do bring it home with us. I guess working on the weekends isn't all bad if it keeps you out of trouble."

Shit. Why did I have to go there and call attention to my boring lifestyle? Pissed at myself, I stomped my foot and shoved my hair behind my ear.

"So, you want to grab some dinner?" he asked.

Clearly, he wasn't taking the hint. "Oh, Drew. Thanks for asking, but I can't."

"You mean you don't want to."

His question was aggressive, coming out more as a statement, and put me on the defensive. I was starting to see why he was so successful in the courtroom. The man definitely wasn't short on tenacity.

"It's just a hectic time for me," I started, then realized it was time to be blunt. "And I can't really get involved with you right now. That's it."

All of a sudden, I was Little Miss Bold. Where did that come from?

Because I like a guy who spent Christmas in jail, and I would rather be with him. When he's not bossing me around, anyway.

"That's too bad, Al. It's just dinner. Are you sure?"

"Mm-hmm," I mumbled as I lodged the phone between my neck and shoulder, eager to hang up and confused about my own traitorous thoughts. "It's not you. It's bad timing, that's all."

"Can I try again another time?"

Tenacious. Ugh.

"Sure. I gotta go now, Drew. Talk soon?"

"Of course."

After disconnecting the call, I moved my strained neck from side to side and looked down the street for my bus. Of course it started to pour down rain while I stood there, and despite putting up the little umbrella I always carried in my messenger bag, I still managed to get completely soaked.

I wiped the excess moisture off my sleeves when I finally sat down on the bus. Leaning my head on the window, I watched the city blur by, unable to stop myself from thinking of the other night with Jake, and how mad I'd been when I rushed out of the hotel.

Who did he think he was, trying to control where I lived? He didn't know the first thing about my circumstances. Did he think this was going to get him laid? It most certainly wasn't.

I couldn't afford to be distracted right now, not with this important case on my desk. I'd met with Cameron again the other day and he was still being evasive, but not as much so. Maybe it was being overly optimistic, but I had to believe I was close to cracking him open.

I'd tried leveling with him. "If you want me to defend you, I have to know what you know, what you're hiding. So let's start over."

Cameron had paced the small room, his hands bound, shaking his head. "Just know I didn't do anything. If I could post bail, I could show you."

"That doesn't help. You can go on some mission if you get out of here, but that's only going to land you in more trouble. Plus, it's not your job; it's mine. Tell me what I need to know to help you," I pleaded.

Without another word, he'd ended the meeting, banging on the door for the guard.

Still, I had hope that I was nearing the truth with Cameron, and Jake Wrigley was nothing more than a big, huge, amazingly hot distraction.

Except . . . I couldn't stop thinking about him. Certainly not when

I was awake, and even when I was asleep, my dreams were fair game.

I'd spent the last two nights dreaming of the rugged man sliding inside me, holding his weight up on one forearm while his other hand traced mysterious patterns up and down my rib cage and over the side of my breast. He was buried deep within me, his body pressing against every inch of me, whispering sweet promises in my ear as he stroked me where I didn't know I ever wanted to be touched. Each time, just as he delved deeper and mumbled, "Everything is going to change," I'd woken on the verge of coming undone.

After having coffee with Barry that night, I went home and went to bed. Just before I fell asleep, I willed myself not to think of Jake Wrigley and his bossy ways.

It didn't work. When my eyes popped open at six o'clock the next morning—on a Sunday, no less—I jumped out of bed furious with myself. I was so sexually frustrated and charged up, but there was no way I'd take care of the itch the usual way. Vibrator be damned—it was hardly a sufficient replacement.

So I spent most of the morning clomping around my apartment in a horrid mood, working out my frustrations by doing chores. At noon, my hair was up in a messy bun and I was still in my pajama pants and ragged sweatshirt, trying to decide what I should tackle next. I'd already taken out my frustration on the bathroom tile until it sparkled and shone like something out of a bathroom cleaner commercial, and I was currently working on the area rug with the vacuum cleaner.

There I was, standing there running the vacuum mindlessly over the same damn spot, drawing the same lines over and over again, when there was a loud knock on the door. It didn't register it was someone for me and not the neighbor telling me to stop making noise until after a few more bangs, followed by a loud, "Aly!" from the other side.

I switched off the vacuum and stood still for a moment, unable to believe my ears until he roared again. "Aly! Open the fucking door! The walls are paper thin and I can hear you vacuuming!"

That was when I padded to the door and opened it a crack to find Jake standing on the other side with a tiny chocolate-colored fur ball in his hands.

"Jake? What are you doing here?"

He pushed the door all the way open and strutted right into my apartment without a word. "Shut the door, Aly. It's bad enough these walls are crap. The neighbors are going to hear enough."

I couldn't answer; I simply stared at him openmouthed. The only sounds in the room were little whimpers coming from the puppy.

Jake frowned at me, then shrugged. "Okay, I'll do it." He crossed the room again and pushed the door closed with a muddy boot, flipping the lock while still cradling the pup.

Turning back to me, he said, "Listen, I'm sorry I pushed the issue of you moving. What I'm not sorry for is meeting you. By some cruel twist of fate, I was meant to meet you, to meet a woman who's way too good for me, but who needs me to take care of her. So if you don't want to move, I bought you a dog. He may be little now, but he'll be great protection for you." Then he grinned at me, a huge grin that clearly said he was quite proud of himself.

"A dog? Jake, I work long hours, take the bus . . . I can't take care of a dog."

I grabbed the back of my couch, needing to prop myself up since my knees suddenly felt like they might fold under me. A strange combination of nerves, excitement, and fear shot through me, coursing through my blood and making me dizzy.

There was a dog in my apartment. Being held by Jake, the man I'd been having crazy sex dreams about for the last few nights. He'd stormed into my life, larger than life and full of himself, so certain that I needed him. And maybe I did.

Everything was changing and it was all so overwhelming. He stood there staring at me, expecting some sort of reaction, but I was such an emotional mess, I found myself speechless.

Finally Jake shrugged. "We'll figure it out. I can stop by and let Maverick out when I'm traveling between gyms, but he's here to stay." He set the puppy down on the floor and the little bugger made a beeline for my bare feet, licking and sniffing every inch, his tail wagging.

"Maverick?"

"Aly, meet Maverick, your very own personal bodyguard."

When another wide grin spread across Jake's face and his eyes lit up, I felt myself relenting. How could I not?

"Maverick? Hardly seems like a bodyguard to me." I bent down to pet the little fluff ball, and he immediately rolled over on his back.

"Not yet, but he's a Lab. He'll grow fast and will bond with you. He'll be so fucking attached to you, no one will be able to get near you. Right, Maverick? He's a tough dude, you better believe it." Jake crouched on the floor next to me, wrapped his arm around me, and breathed the next part in my ear. "Except for me."

His words were warm on my skin, igniting a path straight from my ear to the area between my thighs. I shifted a little, uncomfortable at the tingle that started there. It reminded me of my dreams, and the pent-up desire they'd triggered.

"It's too much," I said. "I don't even know the first thing about taking care of a dog." I kept my gaze on the floor, running my hand in figure eights on the furry belly in front of me, fearful of looking into Jake's eyes. One glance, and I was afraid I'd sell my soul for this man.

In my whole life, no one had ever gone all-out for me, not like Jake. No one had ever tried to take care of me before, and I wasn't *that* kind of girl, someone who needed a man to take care of her. I was a strong, independent woman who put herself through law school. The whole time Jake spoke, I kept reminding myself of this—I didn't let outsiders in.

"Aly-cat, it's not too hard. I already got food for him, and a crate in the truck. We'll take him to the vet to make sure he's up on his shots, and you'll take him on walks. And don't worry about the expense, I got that covered."

His words sent my thoughts into overdrive, pinging from one

issue to the next.

Aly-cat?

I got that covered.

I'm a strong, independent woman falling for the bad guy.

"How do you know all this? That he'll bond with me and will take care of me? Or even what food to feed him?"

My knees were protesting from being crouched down so long, so I slid down to the floor even closer to Maverick. Unable to stop myself, I bent lower and I took a deep whiff of the tiny pup. He smelled heavenly. I was so in love already—with the dog, that is.

Jake reached out to tug gently on the pup's ear. "I spent the weekend with my brother, Lane, and his wife, Bess. She has the best dog, Brooks Bailey. A long time ago, she went through a dark time and she rescued Brooks from the pound. Now those two are thick as thieves, and you should see the way that dog watches every move she makes . . . well, when he's not watching their baby. He sleeps underneath the crib now. So, I know." He lay down on the floor opposite me with Maverick, my new guard dog, between us.

"He is super sweet," I admitted, taking another whiff. "But it's too much. We just met, had one date, and now you're buying me a dog and calling me Aly-cat. It's all too much for me. This doesn't happen in my world."

He brought his hand on top of mine, our entwined palms now resting on Mav's chest, absorbing his rapid heartbeat together.

Yes, I already had a nickname for the dog—Mav.

"It's not too much," he said, his voice softer than I'd heard it before. "I don't believe in all that love-at-first-sight bull or kismet nonsense, but I've been in therapy long enough to know some things are meant to be. And I was meant for you, Aly, for however long you'll let me stay. So, let me in."

He leaned in and placed a chaste kiss on my forehead, its heat practically singing my fair skin before he continued. "Plus, I adopted him from the shelter where Bess found Brooks. We're doing a good deed, you and me, giving this guy a home. Up there in the country, dogs have litters all the time, and usually they're dropped off at the rescue place. Not all of them can be adopted, so some of them have to be put down. It seemed like a good thing to make sure that this little guy didn't go that way."

At that info I looked up at Jake, making full eye contact for the first time since he showed up at the door, and dutifully nodded.

Jake didn't waste any more time on words or glances. He just leaned in again, this time kissing me on the lips, a soft, tender, closed-mouth kiss. It was obvious he hadn't shaved in a few days because he had the beginnings of a scruffy beard, and I lost myself in the dual sensations of the sweetness of his lips and the coarseness of the little hairs rubbing my chin.

My eyes drifted shut and all I could feel was Jake. His mouth on mine, taking his time exploring my lips, all while three hearts beat in tandem, creating their own symphony. He ran his tongue along my lower lip, seeking permission to enter, and I opened for him. For the first time in my life, I felt lucky, certain that I was the girl everyone envied because Jake Wrigley was kissing me.

This thing between us—whatever it was—was odd, and definitely moving fast. Jake and I just met; I hardly knew anything about him, and he barely knew anything about me and my poor upbringing. My dad's memory was always with me, and my mom's dementia and the weight of my school loans loomed over me, but a beautiful, sensitive man was kissing me as if I were the most special girl in the world.

Yes, I was the lucky one.

He tasted minty and salty—all man—and I wanted more. I gave my own tongue permission to seek his, exploring his mouth the way he'd just explored mine. Jake slipped his hand around my back and pulled me closer, dropping his thumb and stroking the side of my breast through my sweatshirt. I felt myself get wet below, a pool of desire dripping into my pajama bottoms from one innocent twitch of his thumb. A small whimper escaped me, and he brought his hand underneath my sweatshirt, slowly sliding up to my breast.

Just as I was arching my back, asking for more, I heard the puppy yip and the moment was over.

Pulling away from me, his eyelids still at half-mast, Jake

whispered, "I think Mav has to take a piss. He's already stealing your attention away from me, and I'm jealous."

He grabbed my hand in his and pulled us up together with one tug, then ran a soft kiss along my jawline before scooping Maverick into his arms and clipping the leash on him.

And that was how we left on our first dog walk—hand in hand, with the cutest puppy ever tucked into the most gorgeous man's arm.

CHAPTER ELEVEN

jake

WELL, the damn dog went and ruined my moment, but I had to give it to the little guy—he got me in the door.

I'd spent the night before chatting with Bess, watching her coo over Maddy while Lane worked next door in his study, and a deep pit of loneliness had lodged in my throat. So I mentioned to Bess the idea about getting Aly a puppy.

She'd stood up with the baby in her arms and spun around. "What a great idea!" she'd declared with certainty. "You know, Lane wormed his way into my heart with all those silly gifts. Not the jewelry, but don't tell him that," she said with a wink. The giant yellow diamond on her hand cast sparkles all over the room, but she'd said that the little gifts meant the most, so I went with it.

So this morning after Lane had headed for the airport, Bess left Maddy with James, and she and I went to pick up Maverick.

Fast forward a few hours, and I'd kissed the girl I wanted and was now strolling outside her shitty apartment with her and Maverick, who was scampering ahead of us on the burgundy leash Bess had picked for him.

Life was pretty damn good.

"Here, why don't you take him," I said.

Aly grabbed the leash with reckless abandon and allowed the dog as much time as he wanted sniffing every single blade of grass. Finally, he squatted and peed—on the sidewalk of all places.

"Give him some praise," I told her. "Name what going to the bathroom is, like *good potty*."

"Really?" she asked. When I nodded, she leaned forward and told the pup in a gentle voice, "Good boy! Go potty, baby. Go potty."

I was immediately jealous. My cock hardened at the sounds floating from her mouth, combined with the sight of her hair still in a messy bun and her ass in the yoga pants she'd thrown on. *Down, boy*, I told my dick.

"What?" she asked me, and I smirked at the realization that I must have spoken out loud.

Tossing my arm around her, I said, "Aly-cat, I'm sure this isn't the right place or time, but you got me worked up, if you know what I mean."

She stopped walking and stared up at me, doubt putting a little crease between her brows.

I winked. "What can I say? You look good all messy like that, walking our dog."

"Our dog? We've been on one date, and now we share a pet?"

"Yep."

I didn't let her say anything more before I wound my hand around her neck and pulled her in for a kiss. Like a good puppy, Maverick plopped down at our feet as I took her mouth while we stood in the middle of her grimy neighborhood. She wouldn't be living in this shithole of a neighborhood for much longer if I had anything to do with it.

Aly pulled away first and took my hand as if it was the most natural thing to do—like we did it every Sunday morning—and continued to stroll for a while. Then she invited me back to her place for brunch. We made a stop at my Hummer and carried the dog supplies upstairs, and she pampered me with small talk and eggs and bacon before I reluctantly got the hell out.

I told her I needed to check on the gym, but what I really needed was a cold shower.

My phone buzzed at eleven o'clock on Monday with a text. I was in the middle of walking the construction site at the new gym when a picture of Maverick lit up my screen and the words "Aly-cat" ran across the bottom.

"Excuse me for one sec," I told Jax, my new foreman. Standing off to the side, I slid open the screen.

> *Aly: Took the bus to Oakland to let Mav out and eat lunch at home. I'm going to work from here for a few hours, so you're off duty. :)*

I texted back one of those mad faces. Then I found my man card and texted back actual words.

> *Me: Okay, good! You need to bond. In the middle of meeting. Talk later?*

> *Aly: Sure.*

Almost immediately, a cluster of nerves swept through my tightened muscles. I was busy with work and slightly relieved I didn't need to go let the dog out. But all of a sudden, I wanted to see Aly. Touch her. Smell her. And I realized that those nerves I thought were sweeping through me were actually disappointment.

Was this normal when two people liked each other? And for that matter, did she actually like me? She was home bonding with the dog I bought for her, which meant something. Right?

Pulling myself out of my thoughts, I shoved my phone back in my pocket. "Okay, Jax, let's move on."

We wound our way through the rest of the floor, inspecting the locker rooms that were almost finished. As we were checking out the aerobics studio, an idea came to me.

"Hey, Jax, one last thing. I bought this duplex over on the east side of the city. I want to clean it up, touch it up a little, and rent the units. You think you have a guy or two to spare on the weekend, someone who wants to make time-and-a-half? I want to get it done."

Jax leaned against the wall that would eventually be the back of the weight room, his feet kicked out in front of him. "I got a few guys who like to earn a little extra beer money. You got the keys? I can go take a look tonight and make a list of what I think needs to be done quick and dirty."

I fished through my pocket and tossed him the key ring before reaching to shake his hand. "Thanks, man. I'll text you the address."

Then I was back out the door and headed to the Oakland location, my first baby. I'd worked out early this morning in the burbs, putting a new trainer through his paces, but I felt like a quick workout. My gut had hardened with an unknown pang, some type of longing I'd never known, and I wanted to sweat that shit out.

I barreled my way through several sets of pull-ups alternated with bench presses before I worked my legs hard. Wall squats with dumbbells and weighted leg extensions left my thighs trembling. I opted for my private shower in the back of my office since the lunch rush was hitting the gym and crowding the locker rooms.

Leaning up against the tiles in my private shower, I rested my forehead on them and let my hand stroke myself. Yes, it was fucking disgusting that I was doing this in the middle of the work day, but I was locked away in the back of my office so I shrugged off any guilt. My workout had barely scratched the surface of my tension, and I needed to let some of it bleed out of my system. I was strung out, both sexually and emotionally, and didn't know how the fuck else to ease it. I just knew I was a wreck and had to go see my therapist this afternoon.

Visions of red hair flowing around my cock took over my imagination. In my mind, Aly dipped her mouth and took me deep, running her tongue along my tip, lapping up the drops of pre-come from the seam. She hummed and moaned while I was seated inside her mouth, the sound reverberating on my shaft, ratcheting me higher.

My hand worked overtime, pulling on my dick, tugging roughly up and down while my brain pictured Aly on her knees in front of me. I imagined pulling her hair back at the nape of her neck and fucking her rosy red lips, and I pumped faster. The calluses on my hand were a weak replacement for what should be Aly's tender mouth.

I went rougher, thought for a moment about tying her to my bed when she was done sucking me off, and dreamed of her looking up at me. Her eyes sought mine, telling a magic story, begging me to do exactly what I wanted—to tie her up and bury myself in her ginger pussy.

I came on a long exhale, shooting jizz all over the tile as I silently mouthed, *Fuck, Aly-cat, that was incredible.*

And just like that, I was hard again. My shower fantasy and jerk-off session had done little to squelch my desire. I turned the water all the way cold and stood under the spray, allowing it to cool me down. I couldn't miss my appointment with my shrink. Not today.

I slumped onto the god-awful sofa at the shrink's joint and stuck my feet up on the coffee table.

"How have you been?" Dr. Wells asked.

"I'm so messed up, even I can't believe it."

"Why do you say that?"

I looked down at my running shoes propped up on the mahogany table, their bright blue a stark contrast to the rich brown. "See these shoes?"

"Yes," she said, frowning a little in confusion.

"See how bright and amazing the blue is, vibrant and full of life?" Doc nodded.

"Now take a look at the table. It's dark and morose. There's no life in that ugly brown. It looks like shit, feels like crap, and deserves nothing more. That's me. And I'm falling for a girl who's like my shoes. Which is so messed up, Doc."

I rubbed my thumb along the callous on my palm, closing my eyes and willing myself not to fall apart.

"We're back to the same place, Jake. You feeling as if you don't deserve anything good in your life."

"I don't, but I'm going to take it this time because I can't resist this woman. That's why I'm even more of a mess." I sighed.

Dr. Wells took a deep breath. "Jake, I think it's time we invite your brother to a session. I'm afraid you're not going to ever see yourself as the innocent little boy you were, and I feel as if a little discussion between the three of us would help."

"Yeah, if that ass agreed to go after Shirley and force her to move far away . . . like Alaska where she would freeze to death."

My shrink leaned forward in her favorite chair, the straight-backed pink upholstered one that fit her so well. "I don't believe for a second that you wish ill on anyone, so don't say that again. Let's deal with what we can control, like how you think and your growing interest in this woman."

"Alyson. Aly." I felt a smile break out on my face, a genuine full-on wide grin.

As though I was looking in the mirror, Dr. Wells broke out in a matching one.

"She's perfect," I told the doc. "So beautiful, I want to devour her. Physically, emotionally, all of her, every last inch. She needs to be handled gently, but I'm all rough and dominant with her. I tried to get her to move, and that didn't go so well, so I bought her a guard dog. I'm fucking everything up, and she just kind of rolls with it. I want to stay away, not be excited when I think about her, but I can't."

"Uh-huh," she murmured as she scribbled notes.

"Here's the thing. She knows about jail and the other time, but she doesn't know this." I waved my hand in front of me, illustrating the enormity of the reason why I was sitting in this room.

"Tell her, Jake. If she's as wonderful as you say, she'll care for you no matter what."

I shook my head; Dr. Wells was wrong. Aly would run if she knew what I did.

And that was when the craziest plan yet entered my head. I decided to tell Aly the truth so she would run far way from me. Before it was too late.

But first, I just wanted one little taste of her.

CHAPTER TWELVE

aly

O~ Wednesday, I'd just come in from letting Maverick pee and was changing into lounge pants and a tank when there was a heavy knock on the door.

"Who's there?" I called through the shabby wood. No one ever popped over to see me, and I feared the worst. I wasn't even sure what that was or meant, but all these creepy movie scenes where a stranger shows up at the door and slits some lonely woman's throat came to mind.

"Jake."

Now in a panic of a completely different kind, I looked down at my tank, at my braless nipples poking through the sheer fabric, and yelled, "One sec!"

I ran back into my room and pulled off the tank, shoved my boobs in a black lace bra, and threw on a navy long-sleeved T-shirt. Stepping out of the gauzy fat-girl pants, I wiggled them off my ankles and stuffed my legs into a pair of skinny jeans.

By the time I opened `the door, I was breathless and certain my mascara was running from all the sweating.

"Hey, what's up?" I asked casually, as if Jake stopped by all the time. After all, we owned a pet together.

Jake stood in the doorway, his arm propped on the doorjamb. "I was in the neighborhood. I work right by here, and I missed Mav-man." He stepped inside and bent down to scoop up the chocolate-brown ball of fur yipping at his feet, then kicked the door closed with his boot.

I was finally able to take in the sight in front of me. There was Jake, obviously freshly showered with his hair still wet and smelling of eucalyptus, wearing a pair of faded jeans and a T-shirt that read Team Fizzle over his right pec with a muscle man curling two bowling balls.

"You like it?" he asked with a wink, noticing me eyeing his shirt.

"It's interesting. Cute, I guess."

"Good! Because I got one for you." He whipped a T-shirt from his back pocket, a women's version in lime green.

"Oh, thanks. It's like Christmas come early with you. First a puppy, now a T-shirt."

"I'm full of surprises, isn't that right, Mav-man?" He rubbed his knuckles over the dog's forehead, and the puppy's tail went ballistic.

Hey, if I were a dog, my tail would be wagging too.

"The gym plays in this cosmic bowling league. It was all part of Camper's plan . . . oh shit, I didn't mean to bring her up. Anyway, she was in charge of marketing up until recently, and she had this big idea to boost company morale. In reality, it was probably another way to get her claws in me another two nights a month."

"And this has to do with you being in the neighborhood how?"

"Because you're on the team now. Camper's gone and we need an extra player, so you're it!"

I shook my head, worrying my bottom lip with my teeth. "I don't bowl. I've never even done it, Jake." We didn't have time for entertainment like that when I was growing up, and I was never invited to the bowling parties of the kids whose houses my mom cleaned.

"It's easy," he said, dismissing my concerns. "Come on, I'll show you."

He set Maverick down on the floor and tucked the shirt back into his pocket. Then he came behind me, wrapped his left arm around my waist and brought his right under mine, pulling it back. He simulated me swinging back a ball and then swung our right arms in the air, making a whooshing sound as we pretended to let the ball go.

"You're in good hands," he said softly. His breath lingered at the back of my neck, and I felt his lips lightly brush below my ear.

"I was literally in comfy clothes when you came to the door," I said over my shoulder, "ready for a night in with my dog and the TV. I haven't watched anything in weeks, and now you want me to go bowling?"

More murmuring tickled my neck. He was still standing behind me with his arms around me, his erection touching my lower back ever so gently. I bit my lip, trying not to push back into his hard-on.

"I'm taking you bowling," he said firmly. "You can watch TV tomorrow."

I swiveled in his arms and faced him, wanting to taste his lips all of a sudden. I'd never felt more alive. My senses were running on V8 engines like his Hummer, churning out hormones and desires I didn't even know I had.

"Bowling?"

"Bowling."

"Okay," I said, giving in all too soon.

"Let's go!" He ran his lips over Maverick's fur, sending a surge of jealousy through me, and placed him in the crate. "Put this on," he said as he tossed the T-shirt my way.

Without a second thought, I walked into my bedroom and swapped shirts, then threw my hair up into a ponytail.

When we stepped outside, I was surprised to see Jake's hulk of a truck double-parked in the middle of the street with the blinkers on, waiting on us. "You could've been towed!" I told him as I climbed into the passenger seat.

"Nah, I knew I was only going to be a few minutes." He slammed the door shut on my side and ran around the front, hopping into the driver's seat.

I cut a sideways glance his way. "A little sure of yourself, wouldn't you say, Jake?"

"Everyone loves to bowl. I knew you'd come." As we rattled down my street, pockmarked with potholes, he teased, "Should I play our song?"

"Don't."

"Don't you roll your eyes. That song is growing on me. After all, it was written about you."

He pressed his finger against the radio screen and the Gin Blossoms filled the truck. Bravely, I reached out to push his hand aside and started pushing buttons, looking for something else. This vehicle was worth more than everything I owned, and I had no right to touch anything. What if I broke it?

"Oh, leave it!" Jake shouted, covering the display with his hand, blocking my way. He pushed the screen again, then snagged the volume knob and turned it up, sending some seventies funk vibrating through the truck.

"Oh yeah, now we can get ready to bowl. It's seventies cosmic bowling, did I tell you? Strobe lights and a disco ball, and a few John Travolta lookalikes."

"Oh God." I groaned. I was so in over my head.

"I mean John Travolta from his *Saturday Night Fever* days, not recent."

"Well, that makes me feel better."

"What's wrong?" He turned down the volume and glanced my way.

"I'm fine, just a bit out of my element."

"You're wringing your hands like you're going to your death." He said it with a pained look on his face, the small crinkles next to his eyes not happy this time, but sad.

"No . . . no . . . nothing like that. I just don't get out much, and I feel like you're showing me the world just with sushi and bowling."

"Good! Well there's more to show you, babe. Sushi and bowling are just the beginning."

My heart melted, turning to liquid butter with those few words. *Just the beginning.*

Once we'd parked in the lot for the bowling lanes, Jake opened my door and took my hand, spinning me under his arm before dipping me. "Ready to bowl seventies-style?"

Nodding, I put on my game face. "Ready as I'll ever be."

I wasn't at all prepared for what I'd find inside the bowling alley. A disco ball did, in fact, hang from the ceiling, shooting prisms of color everywhere. A DJ was set up in the corner with oversized headphones covering his ears, spinning vintage Donna Summer into the air.

I closed my eyes and let the familiar music wash over me. Suddenly, I was a young girl at home, my mom playing this album on our old record player, dancing as she dusted her way around our small dining room. "Someone left my cake out in the rain . . . "

A big, warm hand ran down my back and wandered up again, then tugged on my ponytail, knocking me out of my trance. "Still good?" Jake asked.

"Yep. This music reminds me so much of my mom. She loved everything from back then. The men in their polyester leisure suits, Diana Ross and Donna Summer, and the Bee Gees. Oh God, the Bee Gees. How could I forget we used to dance to this music while cleaning?" I felt a bittersweet smile tugging at my face.

"You okay?" Jake caressed my arm, grabbing my attention.

"Yeah." I swallowed, then met his eyes. "My mom has dementia. She doesn't remember much, and I only hope I don't forget any of it."

"Well, listening to music is a good way to do that. Sounds to me like you're gonna love tonight."

He grabbed my hand and led me to the shoe rental. After procuring the correct sizes and swapping them for our street shoes, we made our way to the Team Fizzle lanes, where Jake introduced me to everyone.

His team was split into two groups of four, eight people in total. There were five guys and three women, including me. Two of the men were trainers and even bigger than Jake. The other women were front-desk greeters, and the last two men were sales staff. Fizzle was clearly a bigger operation than I imagined, and the people here obviously adored Jake.

But there was something slightly off. Jake seemed to give so affectionately to his staff, but whenever they complimented him, he silently shrugged it off, seeming uncomfortable. We were having too much fun for me to slip into analyze mode, so I tucked the impression away to pull out later. Not willing to be pulled completely outside my comfort zone, I drank beer while the others drank something called Moscow Mules in iced copper mugs, and we all danced between rounds of bowling.

When the Bee Gees came on, Jake grabbed me in his arms, literally tossing me up in the air and then catching me. "How'd you like that, Legs?" he teased, swinging me from side to side, then dipping me like earlier. But this time, he placed a quick kiss on my earlobe afterward.

Sadly, my balls were drawn to the gutters, but Jake kept knocking all his pins down, making up for his sorry excuse of a partner. My cheeks hurt from grinning so much when we finally said good night to everyone.

I leaned my head back into the plush leather as Jake drove me home. "It was a good night, thanks," I murmured.

Half of me was asleep, but the other half buzzed with some unidentifiable lust. Thanks to two beers, I was looser than usual, less stressed and not as OCD. When I met Jake in jail, I'd never imagined him to have this fun side. Of course, he was all flirty and seductive despite being behind bars, but there was something pensive, almost sullen, about his mood, and it seemed to follow him everywhere.

Even when I ran into him at the bar at Roman's with Camper, there was a touch of melancholy I couldn't put my finger on. But tonight was different. He was looser, happier, more easygoing, and I loved it.

Yet as we neared my place, some of the tension seeped back in. His face was pulled a slight bit taut, and I watched his hand white-knuckle the steering wheel. We made our way toward my neighborhood, the streets littered with college kids swaying and laughing, but when we reached my building, Jake drove right past it.

"What are you doing?" I asked.

"I'm looking for a parking spot."

"Oh."

"I thought I'd help you take Maverick out. It's late, after midnight, and I don't want you wandering the streets."

"Oh." What the heck was wrong with me? Why couldn't I form a simple sentence? "Um, I go out at night here all the time. Really, I'm fine."

"Not when I'm here, you don't," he murmured as he navigated the truck into a spot a block away from my place.

I opened my door before he could get there, but as soon as I stepped out, he wrapped his hand around my elbow and guided me to the sidewalk.

A group of rowdy guys wearing matching fraternity sweatshirts stumbled out of a building. "Hey! You two havin' fun?" they called out, obviously drunk, barely able to put one foot in front of the other.

"Take it easy, guys," Jake warned.

"Okay, big guy, we're jus' asking," one of them slurred.

"Well, ask someone else," Jake said firmly, and hurried me up the steps to my building. At my door, he took my key and the lead with opening it up, then turned to me. "Why don't you stay up here and I can let the little guy do his thing?"

"Jake, this is my home, remember? We had this talk. I'm going." I tossed my purse on the table and opened the crate, picking up Maverick and nuzzling him to my face as I whispered sweet nothings in his floppy ear.

"Come on." Clearly Jake was back to Mr. I'm-In-Charge. He leashed up the dog and held the door open, locking it behind us. We strolled the other direction this time, away from where the drunken dudes were, and let Maverick do his business.

"I can take it from here," I announced when we made it back to my steps.

"No such luck," Jake whispered into my ear, then tucked a loose piece of hair back into my ponytail.

We walked in silence back to my door, Jake's hand burning an imprint on my back, even though he was barely touching me. For the second time, he took my key and opened the door, letting the puppy loose to scurry to the corner and flop down on the rug.

"Aly." He seized the back of my neck and pulled my lips close, almost touching his but not quite. "You don't have to be so tough." With each word, his lips brushed along mine, his voice a low mumble, yet reverberating throughout the room.

"I am that way," I murmured back. "Tough."

"You don't have to be with me."

I didn't have a chance to respond as Jake's lips landed directly on me this time. We were kissing as we walked backward until my back landed against the far wall. Jake grasped my ponytail and tugged my head back just a little, adding a tiny bit of exquisite pressure.

If you'd asked me a week ago if I thought pain could be pleasurable, I would have been adamant the answer was no. But not now, because this tiny bit of pain was delicious. Pulling back my head exposed my neck, and Jake tore his mouth away and ran his tongue all the way down my face, over my jaw and straight to my clavicle. He sucked on a spot I hadn't realized was so sensitive as he moaned, "Aly-cat."

My hands seemed to have a mind of their own as they slipped under his T-shirt. Up the wide expanse of his back they went, fingering each of his well-defined muscles that rippled like waves under my touch. When his thumb ran along the bottom seam of the lime-green Team Fizzle T-shirt, tickling my abdomen, I tried to suck in my belly, to make it feel more muscular like the bodies he was probably used to groping.

"Stop, I like it," he told me as his thumb continued to map my stomach. "Stop doing that."

"Jake, wait," I said breathlessly, and he froze. "It's too much. I'm not ready for this. You being here, your hand up my shirt after just showing up."

He cleared his throat and reached down to adjust himself in his pants. "I know. I've got to stop. I don't want to, but I will."

"If it makes you feel any better," I said with a sad smile, "I don't want to either. But this just isn't me."

He planted a kiss on my cheek before granting me a sneaky, gorgeous smirk. "Me either. I usually don't stop, but with you I think waiting is going to be worth it."

No longer melted butter, I was now full-on *dripping off the plate and onto the floor* butter.

"Good night. Thanks for a great time," I told him with a smile.

"It was fun, but next time, I'm keeping you to myself. Good night, Legs." Another kiss on the cheek, a wink and one more smirk, and he was out the door.

CHAPTER THIRTEEN

aly

THURSDAY and Friday were quiet. I'd spent most of the time working on my caseload, running the stairs after work on Thursday. Drew showed up to run with me, and afterward, he asked if we could go eat.

"I'm sorry, Drew. I can't. It's not you, it's me," I'd said, embarrassing myself by actually using that horrible line.

Last night, I'd come home to do laundry. Leaning into the vibrating dryer in a Jake-induced fog, I almost came from the combination of the memories and the motion.

Today Jake showed up at my door with a bottle of wine and promises of takeout if I let him take Maverick and me back to his place. I'd tried not to admit it, but I'd missed him. Seeing his muscular frame looming at my threshold, wearing a pair of dark jeans and a black T-shirt, had me instantly sexually charged. I was like a dog in heat, and Jake was the stud sent to service me.

"Let me get my stuff," was all I said. I was still wearing my green blouse and a pair of black leggings I'd thrown on this morning to work some overtime in the law library. Without a peep, I just slipped on my lined moccasins and grabbed the dog leash. I should have been annoyed at how Jake just showed up with no notice, but there was some closeness between us, a familiarity I couldn't put my finger on. It just felt right that he stopped by. Maybe it was the dog?

Maverick jumped around the luxury truck, leaving drool and paw prints all over the backseat while I sat on my hands in the passenger seat, trying not to grab the driver and shove my tongue in his mouth.

"You good?" Jake asked.

"Yeah, I just have a lot on my mind. I'm carrying a crazy caseload to begin with, plus the whole department is working on this big case. I was working on it today."

"Oh yeah?" Jake gave me a sideways glance.

"Actually, I shouldn't say this, but it's the guy you beat up. You may have seen it in the papers already. Apparently he's being charged with several hate crimes, and my team was assigned to represent him. He maintains his innocence and his right to freedom of speech, posted some sort of outrageous bail even though he refused to pay for his own defense, and now we're figuring out what to do with it all. My thoughts are obviously all mixed up on this one."

"Guy's an ass. He should fry."

"Well, I'm somewhat responsible for his fate. I really wish he had someone else defending him. He's making it impossible to do my job. He keeps clamming up and offers me nothing to go on when it comes to a defense. My partner, Barry, thinks he's covering up for a woman, but I think that's plain ludicrous. A woman? Please. He'd been dying to get out on bail, and now he finally has, but I'm afraid he's going to go all renegade or something. Anyway, that's probably more than I should say, and definitely more than you're interested in. " I let out a slow breath. "And honestly, I don't feel like talking about him anymore. How was your day?"

"I'm here if you need me, although I'll admit I may not be a huge help." He shrugged. "When it comes to rules and laws, they're not really my specialty." This time he winked and his grin was devilish.

Geez, he's such a bad boy. I'm in so over my head.

"As for my day, the usual. Work out, then work, even though it's the weekend, then work out and work some more. Saturdays are usually packed, and I like to pop in and make sure everyone knows I'm around. Not all the time, but most of the time. Being with you is the cherry on top of my day." He turned my way and finished with a broad smile.

"Really?" I asked, not sure why I needed affirmation.

"Yeah."

"So, I don't really do the whole gym workout thing," I said, desperately needing a change of subject.

"Well, you do something."

"Both eyes on the road," I instructed, unable to take the heat of his gaze traveling the length of my body. "I run, usually the stairs at the cathedral."

"That's a good workout, but do you go with a partner? Doesn't seem like you should be traipsing around there alone. Maybe I should come along? I'm big and scary."

"I've been doing it for years, and lately, Drew meets me. Occasionally."

"What the fuck?" He shot another glance my way. "The guy you were at Roman's with?"

"He's just a friend." I crossed my arms in front of me like a defensive high school girl caught cheating with the football captain. Or whatever those cool girls did.

"Hey! Sorry. What can I say? I don't want to share those legs with anyone. So, if you ever want to hit the gym, I know of one. I can get you a few day passes." He smiled, the corner of his mouth turning up in profile.

"I'll keep that in mind, but, seriously, you're okay with the fact that I'm not into all that pumping iron and stuff?"

"That's my job and my hobby. It doesn't have to be yours, Aly."

For some reason, my eyes filled, the tears threatening to drip down my face, but I kept them at bay. "You always surprise me, Jake. Why do you put on the whole hard-body, tough-guy thing so heavy? When inside you're a softie?"

"I don't know what the hell you're talking about," he said with a snort. "I'm a hard-body muscle builder. Isn't that what I just said, that I'm scary and big?"

He laughed loud and hard, and it was contagious. I grinned along with him.

"Don't worry about what you do, Aly. Like I said, working out is my hobby, not yours. Just be safe, okay?"

Day was shifting to dusk as we traveled over one of Pittsburgh's many bridges to the North Side. A pair of gargoyles stared us down from the ever-present scaffolding.

"Honestly, I just meant that you're this big tough guy to everyone else, barreling your way through arguments or fights, but in private, you have a sweet side. The way you let me be me. I'm uptight, I don't work out on one of those fancy machines. I meant it as a compliment."

Jake chuckled. "Well, I don't think I've ever been *sweet* with anyone but you. It's new for me, so thank you. But you should know, no one has ever made me want to be sweet before. Which is meant to be a compliment to you, but also a warning that I don't know what the hell I'm doing."

His hand sought mine between the seats, grabbing my fingers and setting our entwined hands down on the center console. As we drove underneath an overpass, the fluorescent lighting illuminating our expressions, I imagined mine to be wistful when it should have been concerned.

Turning into a row of modern townhouses lined up along the river, Jake announced, "Here we are!"

Apparently detecting the excitement in Jake's voice, Maverick stuck his blocky little head over the center console, dripping slobber all over our hands, his tiny tail thwacking against the seat, signaling he was ready to go on an adventure.

Jake parked inside a garage and hopped out of the driver's seat, hitting the button to close the door behind us. The sight of the garage door coming down made me feel closed in, as if I were being forced into this new stage of my life whether I was ready for it or not. Needing comfort, I gathered Mav into my arms and carried him out of the vehicle, snuggled against my chest. He was my shield, my protector, my guardian angel in a situation that was suddenly scaring the living shit out of me.

"Let's give the little guy a chance to piss before we go in. I shouldn't have shut the garage door." He raised the door again, and we walked out into the night. Begrudgingly, I hooked Mav's leash on and set him down. He immediately found a bush he liked and squatted low.

Jake snorted. "Hope the little dude lifts his leg soon. All this pissing like a chick is starting to concern me."

"Cut it out!" I said, smacking his arm playfully. "He's fine. Actually, I read online today that it's perfectly normal for male dogs to squat until even a year old."

Enveloping me in his embrace and running his palm down my arm, he whispered against my hair, "Don't always believe everything you read online, but I love that you're reading up on our puppy."

He guided me back into the garage and closed the door again, then ushered me through the smaller entry door to the house. "After you, madam," he said with a mock bow, and I just laughed.

Maverick plopped down at the bottom of the steps. He hadn't mastered stairs yet because he hadn't needed to. Every time we left my apartment, I carried him outside.

"Come on, tough guy." Jake scooped up the pup in one hand and took him up to the first floor, keeping him on his leash so he stayed close to us.

"How about we order and then we can have a drink out on the balcony?"

"Sure."

"Middle Eastern good for you? Grilled chicken and salad and rice?"

I raised my eyebrow. "Do I get dessert?"

He chuckled. "I don't think I have anything for dessert here, but how about this. I'll get something for the next time you're over?"

My cheeks warmed at the mention of next time, and I couldn't form the words. So I nodded.

Jake pulled his phone out of his back pocket and ordered the food. By the way the person on the other end of the phone greeted him, and Jake barely muttered his order before they hung up, he obviously called there often.

"What would you like? Wine? Beer? Or something stronger?" he asked as he opened a cabinet of glassware in the kitchen.

It was an open floor plan, the first floor one giant great room with a gourmet kitchen in the far corner. An enormous flat-screen TV was mounted to the back wall, a dark brown suede sectional sofa opposite it, and what looked like a hand-carved coffee table sat in between.

"White's good." I watched Jake reach up and grab a wineglass, the back of his shirt riding up to reveal a chiseled back sloping into the waistband of his jeans. I prayed I wasn't drooling like Maverick.

He swung open the stainless fridge and retrieved a chilled bottle of chardonnay. Once he'd filled my glass and handed it to me, he poured himself a Scotch, then wrapped his other arm around me and led me outside. Mav came along, his leash now tied to Jake's belt loop.

The balcony faced the stadiums, both dark at the moment, but majestic nonetheless. Jake guided me toward the railing and I leaned up against it, pressing my hips against the wrought iron as I rested my forearms on the railing, holding my glass over the edge. He stepped up behind me and leaned his hardness into my back, his warmth seeping into my veins, heating me, curing me of a longing I didn't know I had.

An elevated cable car traveled up and down the hillside in the distance, stars were beginning to twinkle in the sky, and my body was ablaze. I was afraid someone would see and call the fire department.

"Gorgeous," I said softly.

"Not as gorgeous as you."

Jake's words carried in the night air as he pulled my hair back behind one ear and placed a line of kisses along my jawline. His breath smelled oaky, laced with the same mint as the other day. A fine layer of goose bumps lined my arms and thighs, and a chill rippled down my spine.

"You good?"

"Yep."

I turned toward him, resting my back against the railing as I asked, "What about you? You good? Because sometimes when I look at you, I swear I see something that's not all right."

CHAPTER FOURTEEN

jake

I WANTED to move, run, perhaps explode, but I did none of those things. Instead I stared holes into the floor, Aly's question ringing in my head. *"What about you? You good? Because sometimes when I look at you, I swear I see something that's not all right."*

In all the years I'd been fucking women, not one had ever taken the time to ask me this or admit they'd seen the sadness that plagued me. In only a week, this woman had begun to dissect me, pulling out the most important parts of me to study and tossing out anything not worth saving. She didn't want me to give up my obsessive exercising, only to forgive her for not wanting to do the same. She accepted my dog, even dove headfirst into taking care of him.

And now she wanted to know if I was really okay. Not just okay, but *really* okay, and that was when I fell apart and lost all semblance of self-control.

Taking her hand in mine, I guided her to the small outdoor couch and set our drinks on the table. For a moment, we simply sat quietly, watching Maverick bounce around our feet while I pulled my thoughts together.

Lifting my gaze to the skyline, I said, "Aly, I'm good. Better than I've ever been, but you have to know something. I'm not a good person, and you may want to leave after I tell you what I'm about to say."

I wanted her to stay more than anything, more than I wanted my parents to still be alive, and definitely more than I wanted to toss Shirley's ass in jail. But I'd made a plan in my head, and it was to run Aly off . . . for her own good. Of course, I'd wanted to wait until after I had the chance to be with her, but the moment seized me.

"Stop!"

I turned to face her, expecting to be met with a look of disgust. "What?"

"Stop putting yourself down. I can't take it." Aly glared at me with a mixture of irritation and compassion in her eyes. Tears formed in them as I watched.

I couldn't look at her anymore; my eyes returned to being laser-focused on the view without really seeing it. "You saw my brother that night? We're twins, obviously. Our whole lives, we did mostly everything together. Especially since our parents died."

A small gasp escaped Aly's mouth, making me want to stop and kiss her instead of telling her the truth.

"It's okay now," I said with a small shrug. "Not really, but I'm used to it. What you need to know is I'm responsible for their deaths, and for years Lane covered it up."

I faced my one-woman jury as I spoke the last part. Her green blouse billowed in the breeze as her eyes closed, and I had no clue what she was thinking.

"Aly, talk to me, I'll tell you more. I'll tell you everything . . . everything I've never told anyone before, but you got to give me something." *I'll say it all and you'll run the hell away from me and find someone deserving of you.*

When her hand reached over and squeezed mine, I took that as a sign to continue.

"We had this sitter, Shirley, and she was tired and lay down on the couch, so we were left to do our own thing. Lane played with his Legos, but I went outside and started messing around with the car, pretending I was my dad. He had a classic Chevy Nova that he loved to work on. So I loosened the lug nuts like I'd seen him do, pretending to rotate the tires, and then I didn't tighten them back up enough, I guess. The next day, my parents took my dad's car for a ride and the wheels spun out. The authorities blamed the wet roads and the leaves."

Aly squeezed my hand tighter, her thumb dipping into my palm and rubbing soft strokes, her silence both encouraging and scaring the ever-loving shit out of me. When Lane and I talked, we screamed and punched. I'd never experienced this quiet attention before, except maybe from Doc Wells, but this was a different kind of listening.

"Shirley told us not to tell anyone about the car after it happened. That we could go to jail."

"That's not true!" she blurted.

"We know that now, but it doesn't matter."

Like the tough girl I knew her to be, Aly tucked her finger under my chin and brought my eyes to meet hers. "It wasn't your fault, Jake."

"That's what everyone says. My shrink, and Lane and his wife, Bess. I don't know. I was nine. Maybe I should've known better?"

"No, you shouldn't have. You were a kid! Not someone who would know better."

I didn't know how it happened, but I felt my head drop to her shoulder, seeking comfort in her even breathing and calm gentleness.

"We were doing mostly fine until last year when Shirley appeared out of fucking nowhere and wormed her way back into our lives through Bess. Now she's gone, but it's too late for us to do anything about her. The statute of limitations in Ohio, where we lived with our parents, is twenty years. So I'm fucked up, and will be for the rest of my life. There's no absolving what I did, Aly."

The longer we talked, the more wound up I had become until my every muscle felt strung taut to the breaking point. I was practically vibrating with tension when her hand came to my thigh and rubbed long, soothing strokes up and down my corded muscles.

"Jake, you're absolved. You have been since the moment it happened because you were *nine* and this adult Shirley was in charge—not you or Lane, but Shirley. And yeah, it sucks that it's too late for her to answer for it, but you need to move on."

What happened next, I couldn't help. I grabbed my tumbler and tossed back some liquid courage, and then I leaned in and ravaged her mouth, pushing her hard into the back of the sofa. My lips, hard and firm, pressed into hers, stealing from her what I coveted: innocence, truth, power from intelligence. They took all of it, drinking the best out of Aly.

It started as needing a taste, just one small sip from her, but I couldn't stop. I pushed myself over her as I kissed her, letting my hands and imagination roam, thinking of more. More Aly. All of Aly. In the wake of all my madness, my cock was rock hard and jutting into her soft stomach, seeking what I was afraid to request out loud.

A moan made its way up from my chest and I tore my lips away for a second, allowing it to make its way out. "I just needed a taste, a little of your goodness," I whispered into her cheek before grabbing her mouth with mine again.

My mind was barreling through what my body wanted to do to the woman in front of me, all legs and hair and heart, when she pulled away.

"Jake, stop for a moment," her lips mumbled along mine.

"I'm sorry, I didn't mean to push that fast." My forehead naturally fell onto hers by some type of magnetic pull.

"That's not it. Why did you say *one taste*? Is that what this is about? A fling? A one-night thing?"

I shifted and my hand found its way to her lower back, pulling her tight, almost on top of me. "Don't you want to leave after what I said? I'm a monster. That's why I work out, because that's all there is to me—strength. If I didn't exhaust myself in the gym several times a day, what other types of damage would I do?"

Her lips settled on mine as she gave me a soft, lingering kiss full of meaning, but not lust or passion or the need to fuck. Pulling back, she said, "Jake, you're not a monster. You were a child. Not even a teenager."

My fingers found their way up and down her back, drifting from the nape of her neck to the waistline of her pants, itching to dip inside.

"Jake," she whispered, "my dad was the victim of a terrible crime. A hit and run. He wrapped his car around a pole when my mom was pregnant with me. He'd gone out to meet a buddy for a drink and never made it there. For years, she didn't know what happened. I grew up with my mom telling me it was a random accident. That's what she thought."

Aly inhaled and let out a deep sigh, her breaths hitching with emotion. "Then years later, we found out he was into some mob guy for money, and the accident was supposed to be a warning. They thought my mom knew and would cough up the money, but she never came forward. They didn't come see her until the statute of limitations on his murder was up. Those thugs sat in our living room and waved a gun at both my mom and me."

Tears streamed down her face and I placed a finger over her lips. "Aly, you don't have to do this now if you don't want to."

She shook her head. "There's a point. That statute was up and there was nothing we could do. I wanted to blame my dad, but my mom told me, 'Aly-girl, he made a mistake and borrowed money from the wrong people, but that doesn't mean he deserved death.'"

Turning to me, she grasped my chin and looked deep into my eyes, demanding my attention. "He was absolved of his part, Jake, just like you. You were doing something wrong, but it wasn't right for Shirley to tell you to lie. You're *already* absolved."

aly

ALTHOUGH the night shrouded our bodies in darkness, the faint moonlight illuminated our faces, making it impossible to hide our true emotions. Jake looked like I felt—rocked to the core. Now he knew why I was relentless at pursuing justice, insisting that the truly guilty be punished, but most people didn't know my motives. And likewise, now I understood the sadness and conflict that lurked deep within his blue eyes.

Why did it all feel so right, and yet so dirty? I should despise who he was, what he'd done and who he'd become, but I didn't dare. Somewhere inside me a switch had been flicked on with this man, and I didn't want to power it down. Not yet.

Still, I wasn't sure why I felt like baring my soul while grinding myself all over him was the answer. I was a vixen in his arms, a powerful, sensual woman when I was in his grasp.

"Aly." Jake brought me out of my fog, his deep voice penetrating my rattled brain. "I'm so sorry you had to go through that, but you survived it. And now you're saddled with me. But I want to do right by you, protect you. These muscles aren't just for show. I need to use them for something."

My sneaky hand found its way to his heart, pressing against his chest to feel the easy constant heartbeat of someone who practiced breathing steadily for a living. I wanted to reach inside and keep that constancy, that calmness, but decided to borrow it for however long Jake wanted to share what he called my goodness. He might want to protect me, but I needed him to set me free. With him, I wanted to soar, to actually live not just survive, and I wanted to love.

Our heavy conversation was cut short by the doorbell and our food. Before opening the door, I saw Jake put Mav in a small crate in the corner I hadn't noticed earlier.

He bought a crate for his place?

I didn't ask about the crate because with a big bag of takeout in his hand, I couldn't help but notice how his forearm flexed while setting it on the breakfast bar. My tongue sneaked out to lick the tiny bit of drool spilling from the corner of my mouth. Yes, that's what happens when a sex-starved lawyer who graduated with high honors sees a sexy-as-fuck forearm. We drool.

"Sit," Jake instructed me, and I did. Settled on the tall bar stool, he laid out the food in front of me and two dinner plates. "Shit, one second," he muttered, and took two strides to the other side of the kitchen to grab forks and serving spoons.

"More wine?"

"Just a little."

He grabbed a bottle of water for himself and topped off my goblet before sitting next to me.

I watched Jake load his plate full of protein and salad, slightly embarrassed to dip a small piece of pita into the hummus in front of me. Sheepishly, I tore a tiny corner of the delectable carb and plunged it into the dip.

"Hey, take this." Jake ripped a large hunk of pita and passed it. "Remember what I said? All that exercise stuff is for me. Not you."

And just like that, we ate Middle-Eastern food at Jake's bar, chatting and laughing, the seriousness of our talk on the balcony forgotten.

We were finished eating when Jake snagged the back of my stool, dragging the entire chair with me in it toward him. "All good, Legs?"

My skin prickled and heated at the nickname. I nodded and stood up to clear the plates when Maverick whimpered in the crate.

"Leave it," Jake said. "Let's take the little guy out."

He snatched my hand in his and dragged me back outside, hand in hand. We strolled the north side of Pittsburgh, quiet but for the sound of the river streaming past in the background, the hum of traffic in the distance, and my heart beating as loud as a gavel in the courtroom.

"Jake, I'm so confused. This isn't me. Meeting—"

"A perp," he offered.

I laughed. "No, meeting anyone. I don't really do this. Dating. But here we are walking this puppy and sharing secrets, and it feels so good. But I don't do this."

"Neither do I, so let's try." He changed the subject, not giving me a chance to respond. "Let's talk about something positive. See that?"

He pointed at the baseball stadium, and I nodded.

"The team hired me. They want the team to use my gyms when

they're not working out in-house. Since I played in college, they want me to make a plan specifically for some of them at the gym. So, that's good. Since I can't play anymore, at least I get to be a part of an organization."

"That's great!"

"Yep, but I've got to keep my fighting ways in the past. Because they would definitely frown on that."

My stomach roiled with chicken and hummus. Why did we have to keep coming back to that night, to the reason why I shouldn't be here?

"And they're going to appear in my print advertising, so it's a win-win."

"You should be proud."

"Well, this time I really am because this was all me. Usually, Lane is the idea man and I'm the brawn. But this I came up with on my own."

I squeezed his hand, and we slowed to allow Maverick to squat before heading back.

"I think I should go now," I said when we made it back to the garage.

"Sadly, me too. If you stay, I'll have my way with you, and we need to wait until it's absolutely perfect, Alyson Road."

I gave him a forced smile. Actually, I wanted to stay, but he agreed I should leave. I was a twisted, messed-up girl who was finally in like with a guy after years of denying myself. And I had absolutely no idea how to act.

"Come on, I'll take you."

Jake flung open the door to the Hummer and I climbed in. He set Mav in my lap, and we sped off into the night. At my apartment, he double-parked the SUV and walked me with the puppy in tow to the front door.

"I'm going to go on my own from here," I said with all the authority I could muster. Jake semi-growled and began to protest when I stood on tiptoe and kissed his rough lips as I slid my hands through his thick hair.

"I'm good," I told him as I broke away from his mouth. "I need some time to digest all that's happening here. On my own. Give me that."

Wrapping my long hair around his fist, he pulled me in for one last closed-mouth kiss. Then he turned and trotted down the steps, but stopped at the bottom to look back up at me, his eyes radiating a deep need that tugged at my heart.

Then he frowned and called out, "Go!" as he pointed to the door.

I nodded and picked up Maverick, then pulled open the heavy door and headed inside.

CHAPTER FIFTEEN

aly

As I unlocked the door with Mav squirming in my arms, I heard the Hummer rumble away. I was drained and tired, but even if I'd been wide awake, there was no way I would have ever been prepared for what lay before me.

My place was wrecked. The furniture was all tossed about, garbage tipped over, the fridge wide open, the blanket from my bedroom dragged through the living area, and paper was scattered everywhere. My briefcase sat empty in the epicenter of the mess, a note tacked into the top of it by a knife.

A lump the size of Mount Washington formed in my throat, and my stomach clenched painfully. Someone had been in my place and gone through everything of mine, leaving a knife stuck in my briefcase. *A threat?*

I need to run, leave, go to the authorities, call Jake. Something!

My mind raced with everything I should have been doing, but my feet were glued to the floor. I couldn't move a muscle. Standing there like an idiot, I squeezed my eyes shut and prayed for it to all have been a bad dream when I opened them.

But my place was still a violent mess when my eyes opened again. Concentrating on breathing, I realized I was squeezing the dog to my chest when he yipped. "Sorry, little buddy," I whispered against his small head and rubbed his ear, not daring to put him down.

I walked with false bravado toward the note. My hand trembled violently as I reached for the piece of stark white paper folded under the knife—and just before I pulled it out, common sense overtook me. I needed to call the police. If I removed the knife or tampered with anything, it might ruin the chances of figuring out who did this to me.

I stood up on legs almost as shaky as my hands and reached into the purse still hanging from my shoulder to pull out my cell phone. It took me three tries to dial 911 successfully. My finger kept bouncing and catching the two or the eight.

A woman's brisk voice answered. "Hello, 911, how may I help you?"

"I've been robbed or I don't know. Someone's been in my apartment. My name is Alyson Road in Oakland." I backed up toward the threshold where the door met the hall, putting some much-needed space between the scene and myself.

"Ma'am, are you okay?" she asked quickly, her businesslike tone turning concerned. "Are you inside your apartment? Is anyone inside with you?"

"No. Yes. N-no, I don't know."

"You may be in shock. You need to leave and go outside in case the intruder is still hiding somewhere inside. I'm dispatching police and an ambulance to 1121 South Hughes Street. Is that where you are, ma'am?"

"Yes. Apartment 3B."

As I hurried down the steps to the vestibule of the building, a party buzzed loudly on the floor below me. They were having a great time while I was being robbed or assaulted, I wasn't sure which, and for some irrational reason it made me angry. I, on the other hand, was doing my best to juggle the phone and the puppy and not fall down the steps and break my neck.

"I'll stay on the phone with you until help arrives," the dispatcher said in a soothing voice.

I whispered okay into the phone; it was all I could muster. The anger had been fleeting; tears were building. Screams were crawling up my throat, and my heart was at war inside my chest.

I slipped around the side of the apartment building and leaned against the cold stone. "I'm here," I said for my own benefit as I cuddled Mav closer.

"Me too," the operator assured me.

Sirens ripped through the night, blue and red lights swirling on the street like a laser show. A moment later, two uniformed cops approached me with caution.

"Miss, are you Alyson Road?"

I nodded.

"Dispatch said you've had a break-in. We're here to help," the dark-haired one said. The guy with blond hair trailed a few paces behind, surveying the area with his hand on the gun at his hip.

I nodded again.

"Are you okay?"

Another nod.

"Can you tell us what happened?"

I nodded again, and the ridiculous notion that I must look like a bobble-head doll came to me. Stifling a manic laugh that tried to bubble up my throat, I pressed my lips together, unable to respond.

"We're here now," the policeman said. "It's safe to talk. My partner, Officer Simms, is going to go upstairs and take a look at your place."

"It's apartment 3B," I finally said. "There's a note. On my briefcase. S-s-stuck there with a knife."

"Yes, ma'am. I'm going to go look," Simms assured me.

"I'm Officer Petrisky," the first one said. "Can you tell me when you arrived here tonight?"

"Just about fifteen minutes ago."

"And you were out?"

I went back to nodding.

"Was your dog home?"

This time I shook my head. "He was with me. We were having dinner at a friend's place." I didn't have time to consider what or who Jake was to me.

"Who would that be?"

"Um," I said, then hesitated. "Jake Wrigley."

"Is that your boyfriend?"

The question unsettled me, so I said, "I'm with the public defender's office."

"Do you want us to call someone?"

One more head shake.

"So is this Jake a boyfriend?"

"No, sir."

"Did you have plans in advance? When did you know you would be out tonight?"

"I'm not sure why that's important."

But I did; I knew how this worked. They were going to question Jake. In their eyes he was either my alibi, a suspect, or both.

"Petrisky?" Simms called from the doorway.

"Yeah?"

"Look at this." The blond cop walked outside, waving something in his gloved hand.

Petrisky turned to me. "The note. Did you read it, ma'am?"

"It's Alyson, not ma'am."

"Did you see it?"

Shaking my head for the millionth time, I said, "I know better than to tamper with evidence."

Simms held it out for me to see.

FiX thE CaSe.

The note was handwritten in black marker in uneven block letters, some capitals, others lowercase, apparently in an attempt to disguise their handwriting.

Simms barked into some walkie-talkie like cell phone. "Yeah, I need you to run a guy over to a Jake Wrigley's place for me. Apparently he had dinner with the victim tonight at his place. She took her dog too."

"Jake had nothing to do with this." I tried not to beg, but I knew what they would find if they dug deeply enough.

"Just doing my job, Ms. Road."

"You got the knife? You're going to run prints?" I asked.

"Yes, and a guy's coming to photograph the scene. You won't be able to clean up your place until we dust for fingerprints and finish our investigation. Do you have somewhere to stay?"

I looked at the ground. Of course I didn't have anywhere to stay. After paying for my mom's nursing home and the extra care for her, I had no savings I could dip into for a hotel. And I had a dog. Panic rose in my throat as I mentally sorted through my options, which were nil.

"I'll figure something out," I said with as much confidence as I could.

I'd set Maverick down on the ground when the police arrived, and he was now pulling me toward the grass, his nose to the ground. I let him lead me a bit, and he stopped to pee. Distracted, I didn't even tell him he was a good boy. I was staring at the outside of my building, wondering why the hell no one came out to check out what was going on, and then I remembered I lived in a college building. Everyone was more than likely drinking and doing drugs; no one was about to come out and chat with the cops.

"May I go up and get some fresh clothes?"

Simms offered to escort me back to my own home and watched while I sifted through my bras and panties, filling a small bag with everything I needed.

With tears burning my eyes, I called a cab and told the officers I was going to the Holiday Inn for a few nights. Instead, I went to the nursing home and curled up in the chair next to my mom's bed. I'd sneaked Mav inside the building in the duffel bag, and held him tightly in my arms as I cried myself to sleep.

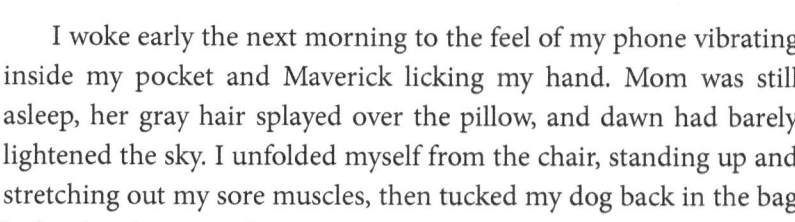

I woke early the next morning to the feel of my phone vibrating inside my pocket and Maverick licking my hand. Mom was still asleep, her gray hair splayed over the pillow, and dawn had barely lightened the sky. I unfolded myself from the chair, standing up and stretching out my sore muscles, then tucked my dog back in the bag before heading outside.

"Go potty, little guy," I said as I placed the puppy on the ground, then checked my phone.

Three missed calls and sixteen unread texts, most of the messages from Jake. The calls were from the police.

The texts pretty much all read the same except for the last one.

> *Unknown Number: Work your magic on the big dogs or I'll snatch your dog.*

My chest tightened and my head throbbed at the prospect of being threatened further. The message could refer to any number of cases, but in my heart, I knew which one it was. It was something to do with Cameron.

Was someone protecting him or out to get him? Or was it Cameron himself threatening me? I was supposed to be defending the man, and I was doing my best despite not wanting to take the case. It didn't make any sense.

I tapped the icon for the office and dialed Barry's extension. It was Sunday, and he always went in to review notes for the week.

"Barry Bruno," he answered.

"Barry, it's Aly."

"Shit! Are you okay? Where are you?"

"I'm fine. You heard?"

"Yes. You need to come in so we can talk?"

"I will," I said, letting Maverick pull me around as he sniffed everything in his path. "Do you know anything? Did you hear any chatter?"

"Can't say for sure who did it. I have some thoughts."

"I figured. I have to go. I'll see you in an hour or so, and we can discuss it."

Hanging up on Barry, I reached down to pet and rain praise on the puppy for doing his business before I called Jake. Despite the pit of regret lodged in my belly, I knew I couldn't make him wait any longer.

"Aly! Are you all right? Why didn't you call?"

"I'm sorry, I didn't want to drag you into this."

"A little late for that. For a moment, I was the cops' number-one suspect. They swung by here last night with all kinds of questions. After all, I showed up last minute and took you back to my place with your dog, leaving your place wide open to a break-in. Plus there's the little issue of you letting me out of jail scot-free."

"Oh God." I held the phone tightly to my ear, pacing the same patch of grass outside the nursing home, the pollen lingering in the dew clogging my throat. Or was that my own stupidity?

"I'm sorry this happened to you, Aly. I didn't do it, though. You believe me? The guy didn't press charges; you were free to let me go that night. Plus you know Cameron hit a trigger with me, a nasty one. I wouldn't have fucked him up if he hadn't. Aly?"

"No, I don't think it was you, but they're not going to buy it unless I find them a suspect. We need to stay away from each other while I do."

"Goddamn it! Don't do this," he pleaded. "Don't make me the bad guy. I'm not in this situation. I'm the good one, trying to help." He paused for a moment, then said, "Move to my place."

"I can't move into your place!" I shrieked, then composed myself as I glanced around, hoping no one was around yet this early in the morning.

"Calm down, Legs. I meant the duplex unit I offered you."

My breathing kicked into high gear. How did he manage to be so infuriating and sexy at the same time? And how did I end up being the desperate damsel in distress? I was perfectly capable of taking care of myself—usually—but my options were so limited at this point, I didn't know what to do.

"It's really not up for discussion," he said, trying to reason with me. "I know your place is all tied up in the investigation, and the only other place you can go with a dog—quickly—is my rental. I'll be by at four today to help you take some stuff over to your new digs."

"Jake." I sighed, my resolve dissipating. "I have to run into the office and discuss this with my coworkers."

"County building at four?"

I nodded. I was back to that again until I heard Jake growl my name into the receiver, thinking I hadn't responded.

"Okay."

CHAPTER SIXTEEN

aly

AFTER showering quickly in my mom's bathroom, I hurriedly headed to my office. Maverick was a good boy, curled up in my duffel bag on the bus until we hit town, and when I got off the bus, I leashed him and set him on the ground. We walked toward the county building, me with my work face on, and him squatting every chance he could. When I got to the county building, I picked him up and placed him inside the bag again for the elevator ride up to my office, giving the security guy a quick flash of my ID and a bright smile.

Once inside my safe place, surrounded by law books and legal documents, I relaxed for the first time in twenty-four hours, including my impromptu date with Jake.

I'd barely settled in when Barry stuck his head inside my door. He was wearing khakis and a button-down shirt and sweater, like he usually did when he came into the office on a weekend. On someone else it might look preppy, but his slacks were wrinkled and his sweater had a stain that looked suspiciously like tomato sauce.

"Aly, we have to talk. What the . . ." His eyes grew wide. "What the heck is that?"

"Come in. It's my dog, my new puppy. We were displaced last night. Don't worry, I'm making new living arrangements tonight." I waved a dismissive hand in the air as if I faced crises like this regularly.

Frowning, he tore his gaze away from the puppy and focused on me. "Whatever. Listen, you know who did this? You know what he wants?"

"He wants us to get rid of the charges."

Barry dropped into my guest chair with a huff. "He's in the wind, our guy, jumped bail. No one knows where the fuck he is, but he's either lurking around you or having someone else do his dirty work is my guess." He rested his elbows on the chair's arms, drilling his eyes into mine over his entwined fingers. "I found out last night that he went MIA. They're going over traffic cam footage looking for him. The freaking ankle monitor they put on him isn't working, but I don't know why. It's anyone's best guess as to where or when he'll turn up. You need to watch your back, Aly."

Frustrated, I blew out a long breath. Knowing Cameron had found a way to ditch his ankle monitor changed everything. "Why didn't you call me?"

"I thought maybe he'd turn up by morning, but then this happened with you. Shit!" he exclaimed, then gave me a questioning look. "Maybe you should come stay with me? I'd feel a hell of a lot better knowing you're safe."

What the hell is going on? I have more offers than ever before to stay with men?

"Barry, don't be ridiculous. I'm moving to a new apartment. A secure building," I lied. "I'll be fine. Let's find our client. We work together; we can't live together."

"I worry about you, Aly. You try to be so tough, but we all need a little help."

Uncomfortable, I steered the subject back to our client. "I just don't get him—Cameron. He says he didn't do any of it, claims the photos were planted in his apartment, yet he makes a big deal about his belief in free speech. So why run like this? What point is he trying to prove?" I ran my hand across my brow in frustration and squeezed my forehead, attempting to keep the headache looming at bay. "I should've known better. His actions were right there, niggling in the back of my brain. This is on me. I've been distracted."

"Don't do this to yourself. He's acting insane, but it feels like too much of a put-on," he said, focusing his gaze over my shoulder like he always did when he was pondering something. "Does he want an insanity plea? Why would he want that if he claims he didn't do any of it?"

"There were pictures of the crime scenes in his apartment, taped all over the walls. Like bragging rights."

"This guy is zigzagging all over the place. Did you ever get him to mention any names of close friends or girlfriends?" He ran his hand through his greasy hair; obviously he'd skipped a shower this morning.

"No, although it certainly felt like he was protecting someone. Just go!" I told him. "Get out of here and find Cameron. I have to meet with the cops from last night again and get some work done. When we find him, we'll demand some answers."

Focusing back on me, Barry reached over my desk and squeezed my hand, something he'd never done in the two-plus years we'd worked together. It was meant to be brotherly, I was sure, but somehow it didn't feel like it.

Either way, I couldn't dwell on that right now. I needed to figure out how I was going to deal with my new landlord.

At five minutes after four, I walked outside to find Jake's Hummer waiting for me in front of the county building, pulled up next to the curb with its flashers on. As soon as Maverick was released from my bag, he started going nuts in the same way I wanted to. Jake got out of the truck wearing ragged dark jeans, a tight-fitting black T-shirt, and some type of athletic shoes, looking formidable and delectable as he walked toward us.

Afraid my own tail was wagging, I simply said, "Hey."

"Hey, you." He opened the truck door for me, then picked up Maverick from the ground and settled him into my lap. "He's not going to be able to do that much longer, you know, sit on your lap. He's going to be eighty or ninety pounds when he's done growing."

"I guess I'd better enjoy it while it lasts," I said with a grin, not willing to let the little guy go at the moment.

Jake jumped into the driver's seat and we sped off toward my apartment. When we got to my building, I climbed the stairs reluctantly, and my hand trembled a little as I unlocked the apartment door, ignoring the caution tape run across it.

Jake waited outside with the dog while I tiptoed around the scene. I wouldn't admit it to him, but I wanted to be in there as little as possible. I felt so violated and vulnerable; whoever had done this had rifled through everything I owned. And if it was Cameron, how could I defend him effectively now? Between my fear and my anger, I couldn't possibly give him the best defense.

I stuffed some clothes and toiletries in another duffel bag, grabbed my chargers, Maverick's food and bowls, the crate, and a sleeve of cookies, then locked up behind me. As I ran down the front steps, Jake threw open the Hummer's passenger door as if he sensed my urgency to get the heck out of there.

The truck was quiet as we set off for another side of town. Highland Park once was the "in" neighborhood with its tree-lined streets and gorgeous parks. For a while it suffered a small decline, but now it was hot again. Large maples surrounded mansions, row houses, and smaller freestanding brick houses—all which Pittsburgh was known for. Kids played out on the sidewalks, and young couples enjoyed their Sunday, walking their dogs to the independent coffee shop in the center of the neighborhood.

When we pulled up in front of a dark red brownstone, Jake announced, "Here we are," and threw the truck into Park.

I turned slightly in my seat to face him. "Are we going to discuss anything?"

"If you're asking if I raided your apartment, the answer is no. Because that's fucking ludicrous. I was with you the whole time, remember?"

"That's not what I was asking." I reached over the center console and ran my fingers over his muscular forearm.

"If you mean rent, I won't accept anything more than what you were paying for the shithole in Oakland."

"That's not what I meant either, although I plan to pay you rent. What I meant was . . . this is going so fast, and now I'm dragging you into all my work stuff and this break-in. Geez, I must look so needy."

"Just stop. Come on, we're going in." He set his free hand on top of mine and squeezed it. "Let's go."

He threw open his door and hopped out to come help me, then he snatched the pup.

"The unit on the right needs a little more work," he explained, "so let's get you set up in the left. Everything's been inspected and is working right. My guys may need to do a little work while you're here, but they'll be neat."

The left side of the brownstone had obviously been maintained. The door opened to an exposed brick entry. To the left when we walked in was a living area with a huge stained-glass window looking out onto the yard at the side of the house. In the back was a fairly updated kitchen, but with those old-fashioned knobs on the sink, the white porcelain ones I'd always loved that read Hot and Cold. A staircase led upstairs.

While I explored my new digs, Jake propped open the back door and let Maverick run out and squat. Overwhelmed, I spun in a circle, taking it all in, and realized the place was full of furniture.

"Um, Jake. Why is there so much furniture here?"

He shrugged. "I bought it to go with the unit. I was going to rent it furnished, so now it's yours."

I stopped dead in my tracks and leaned on the banister, newly sanded and painted. "Jake? I can't."

"You can. Come on, I'll show you upstairs and then you can get settled."

Since Maverick still hadn't gotten the hang of stairs yet, Jake picked him up and carried him with us. Once on the second floor, he tied the leash to his belt loop again, and Maverick bounced around his feet, excited to explore the two bedrooms and bathroom upstairs. The master bedroom was dominated by a king-sized sleigh bed.

Frowning, I turned to Jake. "Seriously, I can't accept this."

"You can. Gotta have room to sleep with those long legs."

My vision blurred and I blinked furiously, but the tears made it hard to see.

"I have to go," Jake said quickly, as if sensing I needed time to compose myself. "I need to get out to the suburbs and check on a few things in my other location, and then swing by the construction site on the other side of town before the week starts. Can I bring dinner later?"

"Why don't I go to the store and cook?"

"Another time." He leaned in and pressed a soft closed-mouth kiss to my lips, then handed me the puppy's leash and walked away.

"Wait, Jake!" I called out, and he stopped in the doorway. "Thank you."

He gave me a big smile. "I'm going to run in your bags and the dog crate, and leave the keys on the hall table. Make yourself at home."

Unfamiliar emotions swirled inside me as I listened to Jake run down the staircase, his heavy boots thudding on the hardwood stairs. In other circumstances, they might seem threatening, but not now, not with Jake.

Funny how we met and where we ended up—so far.

CHAPTER SEVENTEEN

jake

"LANE, I need a favor," I yelled into my dash Bluetooth.
"What's up?"

"I hate asking. I'm trying to do shit on my own, but I'm seeing that girl—woman—the one I told you about. Someone broke into her place and tore the shit out of it, and now she's living in my rental like I wanted, but—"

"Say no more," Lane said, cutting in. "I got a guy to look after her."

"Look, I don't want you fixing this, bro. I just want the intro. I'm paying for it and dealing with him, but you're right. She needs eyes on her."

"I have a guy whose team keeps an eye on AJ, makes sure he keeps his distance from Bess. They're good. Not cheap, but worth it."

"Text me their number. Let them know I'll be calling."

"Okay. And Jason?"

I huffed out an exasperated sigh. "You must be about to get all serious. No one has called me Jason since Mom died."

"You deserve to be happy, Jason. Jake. It doesn't matter what I call you; you're my brother."

"Text me the number, Lane. Leave all the mush to Bess."

I hurried to the South Hills to Fizzle Squared, checked in with the manager on a few issues, then headed over to Cubed, north of the city. Pleased with the progress Jax and his team had made, I sped back to Oakland and ran on the treadmill for a half hour. I needed to blow off some aggression.

As my feet pounded the belt, sweat poured down my back, soaking my tank, and music pounded in my ears. Heavy, dark lyrics rained into my brain, which probably wasn't smart. I was wound up, more than tense. I should probably be listening to Enya or some New Age junk. At the moment, I was so keyed up, the only thing keeping me calm was the call I'd made to the private investigator. He was going to put someone right on it. They'd keep an eye on my rental, tail Aly, and keep a lookout.

When the thirty minutes were up, I hopped off, even though I could have stayed on for hours. After quickly showering and changing, I called the pizza shop I liked to splurge on and ordered a large pie. On my way to pick it up, I stopped for a bottle of wine. I was about to head straight to the rental at that point, but then realized there were no wineglasses or plates there, so I stopped to pick up some of those too.

Finally at the door, I debated letting myself in, but then decided against it. This was Aly's place now. I knocked once, twice, before I rang the bell.

"Who's there?" she called.

"Me with food."

I sounded like an idiot. I didn't know how to do this. Up until a few months ago, I was a fuck-and-run kind of guy. Now I was rescuing girls, hiring private detectives, baring my soul, and picking up pizza for dinner.

The lock unclicked and when the door opened wide, Aly stood there wearing a big T-shirt and leggings.

"Pizza?" She looked at me with an eyebrow raised.

"Hey, I can still have a good time."

"Oh, good, you remembered plates. There's nothing in the kitchen, obviously. Tomorrow, I'm going to stop at the store."

Carrying the pizza in one hand and a bag with the wine and dishware in the other, I made my way into the kitchen. "Want me to drive you?"

"No. No thanks. I've got to resume my life, and like you said when you first told me about this place, it's on the bus line."

"Oh, Aly-cat, what am I going to do with you?"

"Feed me!"

We sat on the stools at the narrow breakfast bar, eating pizza and sipping wine. Aly seemed calm and relaxed, yet I was anything but. Concerned about her safety, I was on high alert, listening for every sound. Maverick slept in the corner in his crate, and I wanted to take him outside and pretend to let him pee so I could check out the yard. But Aly was telling me a story about her one failed attempt at visiting a sorority. It must have been funny because she was tied up in fits of giggles.

"All those girls sat there staring at me in my worn-in faded jeans, white T-shirt, and ankle boots. I wasn't sure why they were staring, but then I realized they were all in black. Black slinky tops and dark jeans and knee-high boots and covered in jewelry. Get it? They all looked the same, and they wanted me to do that?"

A tear escaped her eye. "I'm sorry," she said, swiping at the tear and swiveling her stool to face me. "I didn't mean to get all weird and laughing at the same time. It's been an emotional twenty-four hours."

I turned and brought my hand to her face, smoothing my thumb under her eye before bringing her in for a kiss. "You're not getting weird, and yes, it has been a lot in the last twenty-four hours." *Christ, where's this coming from?*

"But you got to know this, Legs. I had those girls. If you had one, you had 'em all, because you're right, they're all the same. And you're different, which is why I really want to stay and take off your clothes right now."

She didn't let me finish. Instead, she took my mouth with hers and kissed the fuck out of me. I grabbed hold of her hair and pulled her head to the side, releasing her lips and taking control. My tongue slid up her neck to her earlobe and I sucked—hard. After I let it go, I whispered in her ear, "You're not in control when it comes to this. I am."

Aly moaned and gasped at the same time. She was probably wet as fuck. I'd be willing to bet she'd never been dominated before, and I couldn't wait to get the chance. I didn't get all freaky with the dominance thing, just needed to be in command. I liked to go a little rough when I wanted, and soft when I needed something different. It was a control thing for me. I knew this from my shrink—because who doesn't talk about their sexcapades when they're on the couch?

Dr. Wells would tell me, "Jake, you lost all control when your parents died and Shirley took away your ability to make it right. You crave control, but you also need distance. It's a recipe for loneliness."

Well, maybe I didn't want to be distant anymore considering all the romantic shit I was spewing, but I sure as hell wanted to be in charge. Women usually went all for it, but I suspected Aly might have trouble with it. She was such a take-charge kind of person that she'd need to let go; I'd known this somewhere deep in my gut. Maybe that was why I'd taken it slow.

Shit! What the hell did I know?

aly

Visions of whatever they called that stuff . . . the painful stuff . . . BDSM, I think it was called, floated through my mind when Jake said he needed to be in control.

I bit on my lip. I wasn't a virgin, but I wasn't a dirty girl. Or was I? Because here I was incredibly turned on just hours after my home was broken into, and I was living in some guy's place. A guy who needed to be in charge. My teeth continued to worry my lower lip.

"Hey, you there?" Jake ran his knuckles over my cheek. "Aly? Don't let your mind run away. I don't want to hurt you. I would never make you do anything you didn't want to."

I nodded, swallowing any doubts or regrets. "I know."

"Do you?" His eyes were filled with doubt, now more gray than blue, and his brow furrowed.

"Yes." My response came out almost muted. It was a whisper of a whisper, a hoarse concession to what was happening. I was telling the man I'd met in jail after he was arrested that I trusted him to be in charge—in bed—and not to hurt me.

"I don't like to hurt women," Jake said in a low voice. "I just need to control the pace, the mood, maybe be a little rougher than gentle, but never when it means pain. Never."

He almost seemed to be explaining it to himself, but I didn't want to challenge him right this moment. His need for acceptance was so plain on his face.

"I believe you," I said softly, letting my eyes tell him I was sincere. "I don't think you'd hurt me."

I reached out and ran my hand up and down his arm, smoothing the soft hair sprinkled there. He'd shrugged off his leather jacket when he first came in, and now he sat before me in a navy T-shirt and jeans. I kept my eyes on his as my fingertips cruised his forearms, stopping at his elbow and waiting for permission to travel onward.

Somehow, I knew he'd want this. So I waited.

"Go on," he said, his voice hoarse, needy.

My fingertips trailed under his shirtsleeve, pushing it up to reveal a well-defined bicep covered with a tattoo of a tree, its leaves falling through the air. The tattoo sat high on his shoulder and I wondered at his choice. Why a tree, and not a skull and crossbones or a smoking gun?

"For my parents," he said softly before he brought a hand to his face and covered his pained expression. "Shit. I've never really told anyone that," he said from beneath his hand.

"It's okay." I let my hand continue to wander, then brought my lips to his shoulder and placed a soft kiss on the tree. "Is that all right?"

His palm quickly found its way to the nape of my neck and pulled me tight and close. "It's more than all right. I want more. I want those lips all over my skin, everywhere, kissing and sucking. But I can't start because I won't stop until I'm deep inside you and you're screaming my name, your voice hoarse with pleasure."

I swallowed the lump in my throat and kissed his Adam's apple—it was as far as I could reach with his hand gripping my neck. Although I wasn't in pain, I felt secure for the first time in a long time. Safe in his rough touch.

"I'm not a virgin." My lips grazed his neck as I spoke. I couldn't look at him. "But I'm innocent . . . at least, more than you."

"I got you, Aly-cat. I want to take care of you. Never wanted to do that with anyone. I'm not going to hurt you, but let's not start what we can't finish."

"I want to start."

He swept me up in his arms and encouraged me to wrap my legs around his waist before he carried me upstairs. As soon as we hit the master bedroom, Jake shoved me against the wall and pressed his body weight into me. I felt his erection hard against my stomach.

"Dig your heels into my ass," he demanded, and I did. I should have felt crushed, but it felt more like I was wrapped up in a cocoon.

I was turning into someone I barely recognized. A sex addict, and Jake had never even been inside me. Yet.

We kissed, a deep, open-mouthed kiss so very different from the way he normally kissed me. His tongue swept along the roof of my mouth before he pulled it out and sucked on my lower lip. A moan rumbled from his chest, and I felt it wander through my whole body. A slight shiver ran up my spine.

Jake stopped and leaned his forehead into mine. "Okay?" he muttered.

"Yes."

"Feel good?"

His fingers traced down my side—over my shirt—and trailed back up underneath the cotton fabric. I felt his calluses scratch against the surface of my skin, and small goose pimples broke out along the way.

"Feels really good," I said in return.

Jake tore my shirt off in the next moment and my hands flew up on their own, allowing him to lift it over my head. He tossed it on the floor and brought both my hands over my head, holding them high with one of his, supporting my weight with his body as he went back to kissing.

We kissed and ground against each other, pelvis to pelvis, then kissed and ground some more. At every turn, Jake let me know how far to go or when to back off.

I was excited, more so than I'd ever been. I'd had three lovers—one in college, one in law school, and one since. College and law school had been all about experimenting. Of course, my sex partners had been introverted geeks like me. None of them were like the raw hunk of man who was now carrying me to the bed and spreading me out in front of him.

Jake shimmied off my leggings, revealing my cotton thong. He swiped his finger up the seam, putting pressure of my most sensitive spot through the fabric.

"Soaked," he murmured. "For me?" He raised an eyebrow and looked at me expectantly, which was ridiculous. It wasn't possible for me to be this wet for someone else.

But since he'd stopped and apparently expected an answer, I gave him one. "For you."

His index finger slipped under the small strap and ripped the thong away, revealing me completely. Jake sucked in a breath, then ran his finger up my slit and down again. He entered me with one finger and then two, before he brought his lips down to mine and fucked my mouth.

The most erotic thoughts I'd ever had filled my head. Five minutes with this man fingering me, and I wanted it all. All of him. Everything life had to offer. *With him.*

"Jake," I mumbled into his mouth, and he stilled.

"You okay?"

My nails traced up and down his back. "Yeah, more. It feels good."

His thumb landed where I needed it as his fingers continued to pump in and out of me. A small climax grew into something epic inside me. I came on his name—it came floating out of my mouth in a whisper before it whipped out on a scream a second time. He placed his free hand on my chest to still me while the fireworks racked my body. All the while his fingers continued to slide slowly in and out of me, draining me. It was the most epic orgasm ever.

He kissed me again, his tongue lapping my lips in concert with the motions of his fingers before sweeping through my mouth. "You could dig your nails deeper next time," he murmured against my lips, his breath tickling my mouth as he spoke. "Leave me with evidence that you liked that as much as I think you did."

Next time? I wasn't sure anything could top this time.

"You still have all your clothes on and I'm totally naked," I said with a pout. "And you're the one with the hot body."

"First things first."

He sat up and straddled me, careful not to let all his weight cover me as he licked his two fingers that had been inside me, taking time to run his tongue up and down each one. Tiny sparks flitted up my core at the carnal display, embers of desire I didn't know I was capable of.

Watching my reaction, he tugged off his shirt and tossed it aside. Then he took my hand and brought it to the top of his fly and said, "You do it."

With shaking fingers, I undid the button and unzipped the zipper. He stood and kicked off his shoes, then shoved his jeans off. His muscles rippled on every inch of his torso, his six-pack—no, eight-pack—on full display. I gave myself permission to drink him in fully, taking in his decadent quads, so huge and firm. Just like his erection.

He came back and spread out on top of me, keeping his weight on one arm as he reached his other hand to stroked his shaft. After just a few strokes, he released himself to take my hand and guide it under his, showing me how to do what he'd been doing moments before on his own. His eyes closed at my touch, and he moaned.

"Feels so good, Aly. I know you're nervous, and so am I. This is new for me too. Trusting someone."

I squeezed him a tiny bit tighter and pumped my hand a little faster, causing him to groan.

"Do you want me?" he asked, his eyes still sealed shut, hiding any reservations or fear he might have had.

"Yes."

When he opened his blue eyes, I saw myself, my reflection needy and wanton swimming in him. He got up, leaving me drowning in a sea of Jake without a life preserver. I wasn't a strong swimmer, but something about this man made me want to cross the Atlantic.

I watched him pull a foil wrapper from his jeans, tear it open, and slide it over his shaft. Need filled my throat, blocking my airway. If he didn't slip inside me soon, I was going to expire, combust, or go stark raving mad, but I waited because he was in charge.

Then he did what I so desperately wanted. He held himself over me while he guided himself slowly inside me, inch by delicious inch, until his length hit the deepest part of me, touching me where none of my previous lovers had.

Oh my God. I'd heard of the G-spot, and now I knew what all the raving was about on the pages of *Cosmo* and *Marie Claire*. I always considered those magazines to be for other women—gorgeous, sensual woman who were nothing like me—but I would definitely have to hit the newsstand this week.

Jake's breathing hitched as he started sliding in and out of me at a leisurely pace, hitting that spot over and over, each time dragging a louder moan from my throat.

"You feel so fucking good," he said in a hushed voice. "So tight and wet. Like heaven but better, because you're Aly."

His hand brought both of mine back over my head like when we were against the wall, and he picked up the pace. Just when I thought it couldn't get any more wonderful, his free hand reached for my clit. I never knew I adored my clit so much, but when his finger flicked over the nub, my back came off the bed.

This time it wasn't fireworks, more an explosion like a bomb or a nuclear weapon. Something out of this world rocketed through me, draining me completely.

Sated, I lay on the pillows, the sheet drawn up over my chest while Jake went to dispose of the condom.

"I don't have any towels," I called out as the reality of my situation hit me.

I'd been forced from my home and was living in a rental property owned by the man I'd just made love with—or slept with, whatever it was. The same man who was walking toward me, holding a wet washcloth and wearing nothing but a wide grin.

"It's okay," he said. "I had some stocked in the bathroom from the gym."

Jake gently cleaned me up, tossed the towel on the floor, and gathered me in his arms and held me until I fell asleep, this wonderful man who must have let Maverick out to pee while I slept.

And he was the same man who was snoring softly next to me when I woke up Monday morning.

CHAPTER EIGHTEEN

jake

I was late. Wearing the same rumpled clothes I'd worn yesterday, I threw the truck in Drive and hit the road. In all my years of mindless fucking, I'd never slept in, missed a workout or bailed on my routine. I felt strange. Not like myself.

With Camper, we never spent the night together. She'd wanted to, but I wouldn't allow it. Before her, there'd been Courtney. I'd been semi-serious with her, taking Christmas ski trips and having sleepovers, but I never fucking missed my morning gym time.

I'd woken up in the bed with Aly, the sleigh bed or whatever the fuck they'd called it. The one I'd bought for the rental, bought for her, denying it every step of the freaking way. The spot next to me had been warm and soft as I'd reached my arm around. I'd been sated and content, my mind neither running nor tense, and my cock hard as a fucking sledgehammer.

My heart was beating like I was pumping iron as I turned onto the main drag toward the gym. What the fuck?

Aly had been lying there quietly when I turned to face her, and her eyes met mine. I'd brought my hand to meet her cheek and she'd whispered, "Good morning."

Aly. With her big smile and soft expression as she looked at me, Aly's green eyes had said what I feared most in life. *I like you. Want more from you.*

People shouldn't like me or want more from me because I wasn't whole. I couldn't give more. Tainted and impure, I was nothing but a shell of a man, good looking on the outside, but that was it.

That was when it hit me. My hand banged the dash as I turned into my parking lot. That was why I didn't feel like me.

I felt whole.

But I wasn't whole. I had a past. A bad one.

Aly saw through that. But why?

She saw me as good, and wasn't that what I wanted? To protect her?

Apparently some of her goodness was rubbing off on me, but it shouldn't stick. It couldn't. Not on someone like me.

When I swung open the front door to Fizzle, Chloe gave me a concerned look from the front desk.

"Everything okay, Jake?" she asked, pushing her chest out toward me. Somewhere along the way, she'd gotten the wrong idea about her and me.

"Yeah, why?" I stopped and leaned my elbows on the counter, averting my gaze.

"You missed your workout. And you weren't here when I opened up." She made a silly pouty face that a few months ago, I would have considered sticking my cock into just to make it go away.

"Changing it up, Chlo. A guy can change it up." No way I was going to put my anxiety, fear, or fucking feelings on display where I worked. "Anything happening?" I asked.

"No. I got all the guest passes ready for the baseball guys like you wanted and put them on your desk in the back."

She sat up high on her stool, her blond hair twisted in a braid and her tits spilling out of a Fizzle tank. It didn't do much for me anymore. It was like the standard uniform for a gym worker. These days, I jerked off to tight black slacks and blouses, unbuttoned and revealing cleavage.

"Cool! Thanks. I'm going to hit the weights and then head straight to my office."

After I changed into workout gear, I went straight for the free weights section of my gym and racked weighted plates onto a bar. Then I bench-pressed until I couldn't feel my pecs anymore.

The gym was still quiet, mostly college girls on the treadmills and a few grad students pretending to be tough on the elliptical. The early-morning hours, lunch, and evenings were our busiest times, but I suspected when word got out the professional ball players were dropping by mid-morning at both our locations, traffic would increase.

With the tension mostly bled from my body, I showered and went to work. I threw on a pair of track pants and a Fizzle T-shirt I kept in my locker, then strode back to my office. I made calls, checked invoices, and ordered some more equipment for the new gym. The bank had granted me a sizable line of credit due to my current success, not to mention my clean financial record thanks to Lane bailing me out a few times.

Lane was in for a third on the new place. Actually, Bess was. He'd put it in her name so she would have some equity.

Mid-morning, Chloe popped her head in and reported that a few members of the baseball team and their trainers were here and ready to work out. She couldn't hide how smitten she was with the men. I gave them a quick tour and set them up in the free-weight station with a new brand of weighted balls I was carrying.

Back in my office, I pulled out my phone and sent a text.

Me: How did it work with the bus?

I returned a few e-mails, mostly to vendors, while I waited for a reply.

Aly: Good. Came on time and took me right where I needed to go.

Me: Still wish you would've let me drive you.

Christ, what the hell was going on with me? I had no control over my fingers and their typing.

Aly: I wanted to see how to get the bus from there. Anyway, taking a half day. Going to run the steps and grocery shop. Thank you for everything.

Me: When are you stair running?

Aly: Why?

Me: I want to check out your legs.

Because I'm a sick, twisted man who wants you, I thought, but can't keep you.

Aly: Huh-uh. Not working out with you.

Me: How about dinner?

Aly: I'll cook.

Me: At my place.

Aly: Which one?

Me: Mine. Where I live. The rental is yours.

Aly: Okay.

Me: Okay? Just like that? No arguing?

Aly: Okay. Can I bring Mav?

Me: Pick you both up at 6:30.

Aly: Okay.

I needed to check on my baseball players, but first I made one more important call. To my shrink. I was going to need to see her soon. Like yesterday.

I felt like I was standing there in my body, but it wasn't me inside anymore . . . or some shit like that.

It was still light out when I pulled up in front of my rental and jumped out to get Aly and the puppy. They were waiting on the front stoop, Aly's legs in painted-on jeans, and Mav's tail wagging.

Pushing back any doubts, I approached the pair. "Hey!"

"Hey!"

"Are you settled? Feeling okay?" I surveyed the neighborhood and spotted a dark blue Ford Explorer down the street. Aly didn't notice it, but it must be my guy.

"I'm good. We need to discuss rent." She unfolded her long legs and stood up from the steps, her hair falling to one side of her face.

Leaning close, I kissed her closed mouth gently. Then I grabbed the leash and pushed her up against the brick wall and kissed her not so gently, fucking her mouth with my tongue.

Once we were both out of breath, I said, "Come on, let's go before I fuck you up against this wall for the whole neighborhood to see."

Her eyes grew wide and she opened her mouth, but nothing came out.

"Let's roll, Aly-cat." I grabbed her hand and guided her to the sidewalk.

We hustled into the truck and after we'd been on the road a few minutes, she asked, "So, what is this?"

I glanced at her, but her eyes remained transfixed on the road in front of us. "What? Dinner?"

She turned toward me. "Jake, listen, I know I'm not experienced like you. But I am independent. I've been in charge of my fate since day one, and I also may not be well traveled or indulged, but I need to ask. What is this? Us. A one-night thing? A one-month deal? You testing the waters in a different place?"

I kept my eyes in front of me as I said, "A good place. Not testing, but seeing. Seeing what can be or could be. I don't know, Al, but when I saw you in the jail, I was inspired."

"By my legs?" A smile turned up in the corner of her red lips.

"Yes." I faced her and winked. "I wanted you in the worst way, but then the idea of you stayed with me. We kept running into each other, and I don't know. For the first time in my life, I didn't feel one hundred percent bad."

"Jake," she said, her voice full of warning.

"Aly, I'm bad." I gripped the steering wheel fiercely. "What I did. Even if I was young and didn't know, I should've done something about Shirley sometime in all these years."

"You didn't know, couldn't know what to do. Like my mom. How could she have known my dad's accident wasn't an accident?"

I turned to cross the bridge over to the North Side as dusk fell, coloring the sky purple and dark blue. "That's different. You two didn't know. I'm not a decent person, but I'm trying. Lane is making a life, and I want to also. I just don't know what that life looks like."

"And us?"

"I don't know what that looks like either, but with me, you'll be safe."

My mind churned. Physically, she'd be safe; I'd protect her against anything or anyone. As for her heart, I wasn't so sure about how safe that was. But I liked how I was feeling too much to consider the other options.

Parked inside my garage, we got out of the truck and she followed me into my home. All of a sudden, I wondered if she'd stay the night. I desperately wanted her to sleep next to me, to wake up next to her and slip deep inside her as morning broke the sky. I clenched my palm at my side, punishing myself for turning into such a pussy-whipped, lovesick idiot.

At the top of the stairs, I placed my hand on her lower back and guided her toward the kitchen. "Want a drink?"

"Just some water. So, what should we make?"

"We could grill. I have chicken and vegetables. And angel food cake with berries for dessert."

Her eyes lit up like the dashboard of my Hummer. "Dessert?"

"I promised."

"Good thing I ran a few extra flights today."

I meant to get the chicken out of the fridge but cornered her against the counter, my hand roaming down her thigh. "I'm going to have to go out of business because that whole running stairs is apparently way better than working out in a gym."

She laughed.

"I'm not kidding, those stairs are going to put me out of business."

My nose grazed the tip of hers as my hand continued its descent down her thigh before climbing back up again. Her quad muscle flexed under my fingers, and a moan escaped my mouth. We stayed like that a beat or two, our breaths in sync, and my hand fell once again—this time not stopping until behind her knee. I lifted her right leg and pulled it around my waist, leaning her ass into the granite counter, and pressed my cock into her heat. Need seeped through her jeans, permeating the kitchen with lust.

I moved my lips to hers and kissed her.

CHAPTER NINETEEN

aly

My tailbone rested on the counter as Jake held me in place, his erection making itself well known against my seated thigh. I tried to lift my pelvis for more pressure, hunting down the release I experienced the other night, but he wouldn't allow it. Jake's hand remained firm on my hip, keeping me exactly where he wanted me until he released my lips and was on the move.

On his way down there, down below.

Oh. My. God.

"It's Jake. Maybe even Jason if you're good."

"I said that out loud?"

"Yeah."

His mouth grazed my belly button as he spoke. His left hand had my shirt lifted slightly and he was causing a forest of goose pimples to grow all over my stomach. He licked his way down to the top of my jeans, and with one flick of his fingers, they were unbuttoned. Sadly, he pulled his tongue away from my skin, but only for the ten seconds it took him to pull off my boots and tug down my jeans. I lifted my hips and shimmied my butt off the counter to help.

This, he allowed. Then he pried my thighs as wide as they would go and brought his face where only one man had ever done so before. At first, it was a light caress, a tender teasing with his tongue. A touch here, a swipe there, looking for the spot, but there wasn't a particular spot that was more sensitive than any other. I was a goner the second the tip of his tongue grazed the edge of my vagina. Or was it my pussy? How was I supposed to refer to myself down there when Jake was clearly getting down and dirty and making me wild?

Jake tilted me back on the counter and dove in harder. He attacked my core with a skillful vengeance, a sense of purpose I'd never experienced from a man. The back of my head rested on the cabinet, my eyes squeezed shut as I took in every nip, lick, and taste. My pelvis reached and my hips strained for every movement. My lower body certainly didn't want to miss out on anything related to Jake's tongue.

"Stop squirming," he demanded.

"Jake?"

He kept his hands where they were, but looked up at me. My green eyes and his blue ones were like two differently charged magnets. "I don't have much experience with this," I admitted.

"Even better. Ready for me to rock your world?"

He didn't wait for an answer. He dipped back in, his tongue sliding down my fold and up the other. Finally, he made his way to slip his tongue deep inside me and sucked me to the brink of orgasm. His thumb drummed my clit—that damn clit, I barely knew it existed a month ago.

My pussy pulsed with need as I felt his tongue driving in and out of me, my clit swollen, my libido awakened and doing a happy dance. Tiny moans and whimpers and pleas and begs for more continued to spill from me.

I was on the precipice, on the verge of something even more unknown than the night before, when Jake pulled away his tongue and blew a warm breath on my clit before stroking it with his even warmer tongue. My orgasm ripped through me, my muscles tensing, blood surging through my veins, and my head swam with visions of Jake's tongue tasting me.

Sweat lined the back of my neck underneath my hair, my hands shook from the climax channeling through every one of my limbs, and Jake didn't let up. He lapped up every last shiver as his tongue eased up on its pace, slowing and cooling me.

"Wish I could eat you every night for dinner." He winked as he stood up, adjusting his pants.

In response, I opened my eyes and reached for the top of his jeans.

"Huh-uh, ladies only tonight. Now we eat. Get dressed."

"No, that's not fair."

"Remember? I'm in control. I'm in charge, and I say it's dinnertime. Tonight's all about you, Aly-cat."

On shaky legs, I stood and reluctantly slipped back into my pants so we could make chicken and grilled vegetables together. We saved the angel food cake for later, but we never ate it.

I got a chance to return Jake the favor from earlier, and it was much sweeter.

Tuesday I woke up in Jake's bed. Alone. Next to me on the pillow was a note. It was a ripped page from a 2010 calendar, and Jake's very messy handwriting was scrawled across the lines in red marker.

Hey, Aly-cat! Good morning. I left to work out. Took Mav to the gym with me. Don't be mad. Make yourself at home. I left my iPad on the counter with the bus schedule pulled up. I know how you insist on taking it. I'll swing by YOUR place and drop Mav later.

—JW
THANKS for a great night.

What the heck did that mean? Thanks for a great night? He took my dog to work? Our dog? I ran my hand over my face, rubbing my eyes, certainly smearing yesterday's mascara everywhere. What time was it?

I rolled over in bed and found the clock. It wasn't even six thirty in the morning. What time did this guy work out? Luscious memories of his body hovering over me, his biceps flexing, sweat running down his chest as he made love to—or slept with—me ran through my mind. Okay, so I had a one-night stand, or maybe a few-nights stand. Was there such a thing?

Get over yourself, Aly. People do it all the time. It's the twenty-first century, and women can have sex whenever and with whoever they want.

I tossed my legs out of bed and stumbled on sore limbs to the bathroom. There was a folded towel on the counter, and I took that as an invitation to shower. Afterward, I put back my jeans back on from the day before—without underwear—and smoothed the creases out of my white blouse.

As I hunted through my purse for earrings and a necklace, I hit the jackpot. Thanks to being reliant on the bus, my bag had eventually turned into a home on the go. After all, I couldn't just jump in my car and run back home if I'd forgotten something. I snatched out my makeup bag and discovered a pair of clean underwear hidden beneath it. Quickly, I shed the jeans, donned the panties, and pulled the jeans back on. *Much better.*

When I hit the kitchen, I wasn't looking my professional best but it would do for a day in the office. Luckily, I didn't have to be in court all week. I scanned the bus schedule for the North Side and realized I was doing well on time.

I stopped at the small coffee shop near Jake's place and grabbed a muffin and a black coffee, and made it to the bus stop just as my bus was pulling up. After scoring a good seat by myself, I tucked my bag under my feet and rested my shoulder against the window as I watched the North Shore breeze by as we headed to town.

Anxiety tightened my belly as I thought back to our conversation last night. I'd asked Jake what we were and he didn't know, but it didn't seem like he felt we were a one-and-done thing. So, what were we?

I yanked the cord for the bus to stop a few stops before the county building, needing the walk and the fresh air to regain my lawyerly confidence. There was no way I could ever show weakness in my job. The prosecutors would eat me alive, and my clients would run for the hills.

Wait! Isn't that exactly what my current client has done?

As soon as I arrived at my office, I trekked to Barry's and walked in without knocking.

"Maybe it's my fault," I blurted without a hello. "You know I never wanted to be a part of this team. Maybe Cameron sensed that? And I should've listened when he demanded he didn't do it."

"Aly, don't be ridiculous. Sit down." Barry pointed to the chair.

I plopped down and rested my head in my hands. "Barry, you remember the guy who beat up Cameron? The one I let out of jail?"

Barry leaned back in his chair, frowning. "Cameron wasn't going to press charges. You had no choice."

I looked away, unable to meet his gaze. "I know, but he and I have become involved."

"What?" His eyes widened.

"Yes."

"That's so unlike you, Aly."

"Yes, I know, but I can't second-guess my decision right now. He must've seen us together because who ever sent me a text mentioned the dog. Someone's watching me."

"Who? Cameron?" Barry leaned forward.

"Maybe? It seems like the only logical choice."

Just then, my phone buzzed with a text.

> *Unknown Number: I didn't do it. I'm an ass but it wasn't me, so fix this.*

My hand shook as I read the message for a second time and passed my phone to Barry.

His expression hardened as he scanned the text, then he returned the phone to me. "We've got to find him. Text him back and tell him to turn himself in and tell us his story in person. While you're doing that, I'll contact the police and have them ping his phone to see if we can get a location."

My heart raced as the ramification of all the lines I'd crossed became clear. I'd willfully broken the rules with my relationship with Jake, and that bad decision was coming back to haunt me with a vengeance.

"It's going to be okay," Barry assured me. "I'm on this. We're going to bring him back in and hear—really hear—what he has to say about all the pictures in his apartment. If he didn't do the crimes, only hung the pics of them on his walls like some sort of sick tribute, someone close to him did. And maybe he knows who that is."

In a daze, I shook my head and stood, then walked back to my office. In the dark comfort of my tiny workspace, I messaged the unidentified caller back, hoping it was Cameron, and then left for police headquarters to file a report.

My phone buzzed almost right away, and a shiver ran down my spine. Was it him? I realized I wasn't thinking of Cameron, and an even colder shudder rocked through me as I pulled out my phone.

How could I get so man-crazy when my career was in shambles and my life was threatened? Was I nuts?

> *Jake: Did you make it to work okay? Is it okay for Mav and I to pick you up in town?*

I didn't answer, just shoved my phone back in my bag and went about my business.

CHAPTER
TWENTY

jake

A LY didn't respond to my text. Was she mad at me? Maybe I shouldn't have left this morning before she woke up, but I needed to work out. It was part of my survival routine. Without it, I felt too exposed and raw; I was a ticking time bomb without the release.

Fuck! I slammed my hand into my desk. I'd never done this relationship thing before, and now I knew why. Because it sucked. Sucked big hairy balls.

My phone rang and I snatched it off the desk, hoping it was Aly. *No such luck.*

"Hey," I said after swiping my finger over the screen.

"What's happening in the North Hills?" Lane asked.

"All good. On track now and set to open in the fall. I'm looking at an October grand opening."

"Good. Glad Jax is working out. What's new with you?"

"The big dogs from the baseball team are working out at my place. After two sessions, they love it. Want to put in some of my equipment recs in the stadium and find them some shit to travel with."

"Good, that's all good. And the girl?"

I sighed. "I'm pretty sure I messed it up. How 'bout Bess? By the way, why the fuck do you keep fading in and out?" I stood and paced, kicking at the foot of my desk in frustration.

"I'm in France with shit service. Bess is good; she stayed back home. May from the hotel is helping her with Maddy. James went back to Florida for a few weeks, thank fuck. God, I love the little gay Napoleon, but he needs to know he doesn't run my house."

"He does, Lane. Bess lives and breathes for him."

"Yeah, I fucking know. I got all these frou-frou decorations everywhere. Now, how the hell did you screw up with this girl?"

I sat back down and propped my feet up on my desk, holding the phone between my neck and ear. I'd just started to tell him what happened when a very unwelcome visitor burst into my office.

"You know what, Lane? I gotta go. I'll talk to you later." Not waiting for a response, I slammed my phone facedown on the desk and stood, thoroughly pissed off. "Camper? What the hell do you want?"

"Jake." She doubled over in front of my desk, red-faced and gasping as tears slid down her cheeks.

"What's wrong?" This was totally unlike her. Camper might be a lot of things, but she wasn't a crier. I came around the desk and ran my hand down her back in smooth strokes. "Camper, why the hell are you crying?"

I gathered her in my arms, hoping like hell this wasn't a ploy to get me back in bed. More drama from her was the last thing I needed.

Camper clung to me, her cries coming out in raspy gasps, but she didn't respond.

"Camper?" I shook her. "Snap out of it. Talk to me!"

Finally she looked up at me, hiccupping her words through her tears. "I came out of my apartment this morning and there was this chick waiting by my car. Tall, skinny, blond, and blue-eyed with some weird accent. She kept muttering something about how I slept with her man."

"Did you call the police?"

She shook her head. "No, she had this huge knife and was waving it all over the place. She kept saying in broken English, 'You tainted him, diseased him.' I don't even know what she was talking about. Then she took the knife and stabbed all my tires and used it to scratch all over my car door. I couldn't run or do anything because she had this young guy, maybe only eighteen, holding me back."

"What the hell? Who've you got yourself mixed up with, Camp?"

She collapsed in my arms, and I leaned on the desk to brace the both of us. "No one. I've been sitting at home, upset about losing you."

I rolled my eyes while I automatically patted her back. Jesus Fucking Christ. Why couldn't I just fuck complete strangers? Now I had this crybaby ex-lover/ex-employee stuck to me like goddamn glue, and my heart and head were all twisted up over Aly.

"Sit down," I told her, leading her to a chair. "Tell me this again. What exactly happened?" The whole thing sounded so insane, I had to hear it a second time.

Camper reiterated the same story and burst into another round of tears.

Of course, my phone was buzzing every minute while I sat and consoled Camper, and there wasn't a fucking thing I could do about it. I was probably missing Aly's text or call, but it was clear this was serious.

Together, we called the authorities and Camper repeated her story for the third time, the stupid suburban detective scribbling down all the details and promising to call as soon as they found anything out.

Finally, the police decided to escort Camper back to her apartment so they could have a look at the crime scene, and I was free to check my phone.

I had one text from her. One stupid text.

Aly: Something came up today at work and it's going to mean an all-nighter here at the office. Can you keep Maverick until tomorrow?

Shit! She was mad!

I texted her back, scrambling for a way to fix it.

> *Jake: Of course. But how about I run some dinner to*
> *you? I can bring dessert too.*

It wasn't until after I made it back to Fizzle's city location that I heard from her again.

> *Aly: Thank you but not necessary. We're going to call*
> *out for pizzas. Why don't I cook tomorrow as a way to*
> *say thanks? You can bring Mav then. Six thirty?*

Well, maybe she wasn't as mad as I believed. I kicked the drawer to my desk closed, causing the entire piece of furniture to move, the pens and shit on top scattering everywhere.

What the hell did I know about all of this? Nothing, but I still texted back that I'd be there. Then, being the ass I truly was, I sweet-talked Chloe into watching Maverick while I did an extra-long workout.

At a quarter to seven the next night, fifteen minutes late, I threw my Hummer into Park in front of the rental unit. The one I bought for a female do-gooder lawyer with green crystals for eyes, red hair, and legs for days. A woman who had no business being with the likes of me, yet she'd spread her legs for me, moaned my name, and came on my face.

I'm going to hell.

I stood on my—*her*—porch after ringing the bell, the dog jumping around my feet as I wiped my sweaty palms on my jeans. I wasn't standing there waiting for just a fuck. A woman was about to cook me dinner, after shutting me out for a day. I was nervous as hell.

Eating with Camper was easy; we worked together. What I was about to do now was completely different, no comparison at all. I'd just squeezed my eyes shut, trying to shove out any thoughts of Camper, when Aly answered the door. I definitely wasn't going to tell her about Camper showing up at my office the day before.

"Jake? You okay?" She stood there wearing tight jeans and some loose white shirt, blouse, or whatever you call it, along with those knee-high boots that drove me wild.

I blinked. "Yeah, yeah. Fine. It's been a long two days and you're . . . I don't know. Seeing you has seemed to wipe it all away," I stammered. Scary part was, I meant it.

"Well, thanks. Come in." She picked Maverick up and gave him ten too many kisses before setting him down.

"What about me?" I asked, kicking the door shut with my foot and turning the lock. The click separated us from the rest of the world, which was the best news I'd had in twenty-four hours.

"Saving the best for last," she said in a whisper, as if she'd embarrassed herself with her forthrightness. On tiptoes, she wrapped her arm around my waist and asked, "May I?"

I didn't answer. My mouth took hers in a hard kiss. Biting her lower lip when I was done with her, I said, "That was punishment for yesterday. Making me wait."

I'm definitely going to hell. I shrugged off my jacket and tossed it on the banister.

"I couldn't avoid that," she said as she walked toward the kitchen with both Maverick and after her. "We had some stuff come up at work."

"Oh yeah?" I raised an eyebrow. "Something with your break-in?" Unsure of where to go or what to do, I stood uncomfortably in the middle of the kitchen, itching to take Aly upstairs.

"Sort of. I really can't say. So, can I get you a beer? Water?"

Why couldn't she tell me? I wanted to tell her everything, explain what happened with Camper, but was unsure if it was appropriate.

"Water's good. You having wine? I'll open it."

"Sure. That would be great."

She scooted behind me, her tits brushing against my back as she made her way to the fridge. I grabbed her by the wrist and leaned her against the fridge as I kissed her. It was like muscle memory. I didn't even realize I was doing it until I did it.

The icemaker hummed behind Aly, the vibration a steady beat in the background as my tongue assaulted her mouth. "Put your hands on my back, under my shirt," I demanded into her mouth. "I want to feel your nails scratch me."

She hesitated a beat before I felt the soft pads of her fingers lift my shirt and her nails scratch up toward my shoulders. My tongue dove deeper into her hot mouth. The kiss was messy, hurried, and desperate on my part. Desperate for the woman, eager for her virtue to wash over me and erase my sins—but nothing could really do that.

"Jake," she whispered, pulling back. "Dinner's going to burn."

"Hmm?"

"Dinner?"

"Fuck it," I said, sweeping her off her feet. I lifted my knee to hit the Off button on the oven before I carried her out of the kitchen.

As soon as we hit the bedroom, I started talking, spewing my feelings and shit. "I didn't like not seeing you yesterday. I know you were upset I wasn't there when you woke up." Still talking, I yanked her shirt off and grabbed a handful of her tit. "But I got to work out. It keeps me sane, and you seemed comfortable."

I bent down and wrapped my mouth around her pretty pink nipple and sucked hard. She grabbed my hair in the back, pulling it and drawing its length through her fingers. I'd been thinking of shaving it again, until now.

"I want you to trust me, Aly-cat. I want to be tough for you, but I can't do that if my head isn't right. Do you get that?"

My hand worked her other tit, kneading it, flicking her tight, hard nipple as I plundered her mouth. Her creamy skin was pinking up everywhere I touched, and my cock kept getting harder.

Her lips broke from mine. "I get it, Jake. I do. I wasn't mad." She moved her hand out from my hair to my cheek, her soft palm grazing my stubble. "I wasn't mad. You don't always have to think you did something wrong. I had work stuff going on. That's all."

My cheek prickled under her touch and my heart tumbled with emotion. Yes, my bad-ass black heart tumbled.

CHAPTER TWENTY-ONE

aly

J AKE was a little boy stuck in a grown man's body—except when it came to sex. When it came to feelings and emotions, he was stunted. Even though I'd felt like a jilted schoolgirl that morning when I woke up and he wasn't there, he was obviously pained over leaving me to do something he so obviously had to do.

My shielded heart broke for the man in front of me. I'd always envisioned falling in love, but never imagined doing it with a needy bad boy. In my dreams, the man I fell for was stable, predictable, and soft. Not rough and brisk.

"You know what? Let's go have that drink and dinner." Jake released me, then efficiently tucked my boobs back into my bra and slipped my shirt back over my head.

"Okay," I said hesitantly, thoroughly confused. What was happening? Hilary had texted me that morning about coming to visit, and the prospect of it was feeling more necessary. I needed advice, and not the kind I could ask about at work. The questions I had were way too personal to ask someone I worked with.

Jake gathered my hands in his and gave a light squeeze. "It's a good thing, Al. I want you, don't you worry, but just realized I wanted to slow shit down. I don't want to pressure you. I want to, I don't know . . . hear about your day. I'm going soft." He winked and led me back downstairs, where he opened the oven and peeked in.

"Lasagna?" His eyes lit up and a huge grin transformed his face.

"You eat that?" I asked.

"Of course. Not often, but my mom used to make it. It was one of the things my grandma would cook when I'd be sad . . . after they died."

Reaching past him, I set the oven back to 350 and wrapped my arms around Jake's waist. He's lost so much, I thought as I leaned my cheek against his chest.

He kissed the top of my head, his lips lingering and tickling my hair. "I tried not to be sad, really hard. Mostly, I didn't show my feelings. If I was having a shitty day, I'd either beat the crap out of Lane or one of my buddies, but every so often, shit would rain down on me. I'd get so overwhelmed or sad, and my grandma would make lasagna. It always helped."

"This is my mom's recipe," I murmured against his chest. "I hope you like it. Before she lost her memory, she'd always show me how to make something new on Sunday. Even when I was little, we'd cook on Sunday for the week, and she'd let me do little things to help. It was just her and me against the world, and letting others in was hard. No one really got it other than my college roommate, Hilary."

He squeezed me tighter to him, his heart beating like a wild drum inside his chest, mine playing in rhythm with his. Even our breathing was in sync. It had only been a few weeks, months if you went all the way back to Christmas Eve, but it felt so right.

"How about that wine?" he asked.

I'd gone to the grocery store and liquor store on Monday, and I had to admit it was much easier taking the bus from Highland Park there than from Oakland. I also felt like an adult and not a student when I went. Thanks to Jake.

"Sounds good." When I placed a small kiss over his heart, he tipped my head, touching our foreheads.

"Good," he whispered. Releasing me, Jake looked through the cabinets until he found the glasses we'd used the other night. I'd put them in the cabinet next to the plates he'd brought and bowls I'd discovered. When I raised an eyebrow, he said, "What?"

"Tell me the truth. Did you do all this for me?" After handing him a bottle of wine, I gestured around me at all the furnishings. When he didn't respond, I asked, "Well?"

I wasn't going to let it go, even though he was acting like opening up the bottle of wine was the hardest thing he'd ever done. "Jake?"

"Yeah, I did," he said in a low voice, avoiding my eyes as he pulled the cork from the bottle.

"Why?"

"I don't know. I just felt I had to. Let it go, Legs." He brought me a glass filled with dark red cabernet and held it to my lips, tipping it so some of the liquid slid down my throat.

"Mmm."

"More?" he asked.

I nodded, but took the stem of the glass from his hand. "I'm a big girl. I can drink all on my own."

He tickled my rib cage. "Oh yeah?"

Laughter came spilling from me, and Jake chuckled along. Maverick started yipping at our feet, so Jake tossed him up in his arms, and that was how we spent our time until the lasagna was ready. Wine in hand, tickling each other, and laughing at the puppy's antics.

Over dinner, he gave me a pointed look. "Bowling tomorrow, you know."

"Oh no! Not again?" I said, feigning shock. We were sitting side by side at the buffet, and he had turned to face me, drawing my legs between his.

"Again." He reached over and took my hand, turning it over in his before he leaned closer, as if he were going to share a secret. "I'm going to help you so we don't lose," he whispered against my hair.

"Oh yeah?" I flipped my hand in his and ran my finger over his palm.

"Yep. When it's your turn, I'm going to come up behind you and position you just right, then help you swing your ball exactly how you need to. You're going to have to be still, though, because if you shake your ass too much, my cock is going to get hard."

"Jake." I smacked playfully at his arm as heat crawled up my neck to my cheeks.

"Oh, I'll definitely have a chubby to begin with, but if you move that tight ass just an inch, my big guy will be ready to play."

"I'll be sure to remember that," I said seriously with my face on fire. "Maybe I'll wear baggy bell-bottoms to go with the seventies theme? This way my butt and legs are adequately covered."

He shook his head and ran his free fingers down my boots, which I just realized I still had on. "No, I like your sexy lawyer look very much."

Tilting my head, I let my hair cover my growing embarrassment. "It's called chic on a budget."

"I don't give a crap what it's called. I like it."

His hand wound under my hair, gathering me close, and he kissed me. We sat like that for a while, his hand massaging the back of my neck, his lips touching mine, saying without words what we didn't voice out loud.

This wasn't casual; it was something more, something unexpected but real. I wasn't sure if it was lasting, but it felt right. And almost too good to be true.

The calluses of his fingers scratched my skin just right, his lips and stubble tickled my face, and the unspoken message caressed my heart.

I was a poor girl in a rich person's world. Did I really think I'd end up with the stand-up, conservative lawyer type? No, they only wanted me for a quick lay. Like the guy back at the lawyer meet-and-greet. But Jake was different.

He was a tough guy, rough around the edges, but he wasn't the bad guy he believed himself to be. He was gentle and kind, especially when no one was looking. He was like the quarter you found lying on the ground. Dirty, but the best-found money after you shined it all up, the state you'd been missing in your coin collection. Maybe Wisconsin? Or Kansas? The one damn quarter you'd been looking for everywhere, but had no idea it would turn up in the puddle next to your boot on a rainy day.

Jake tugged at the zipper on my boot, sliding the left one off and then the right. I slipped off my stool into his arms and soon found myself spread out on the couch, Jake shimmying my jeans off. He kicked off his shoes, throwing them in the corner, and slid my underwear to the side.

When he brought his mouth to the edge of my thong and breathed in, I whimpered. "Jake," came tumbling out of my mouth in a hoarse whisper.

"I got you, Aly-cat," he said, and then brought the tip of his tongue to my spot. *The* spot. With a firm grip on my hips, holding me in place, his mouth assaulted my folds, his tongue dug deeply and he paid special attention to my clit. When I tried to lift my hips, he wouldn't allow it. "Take all of it, Al. Come hard," he mumbled, his mouth barely leaving me.

I brought my hand to his hair and tugged. He kept threatening to buzz it like I'd seen in old photos of him, but he didn't.

"Harder," he demanded, and I pulled his hair with more force. Locks of his hair were tickling my hip bone, and I gathered those and yanked. He never let up, the soft cotton of his shirt rubbing my inner thigh, his tongue on an all-out assault of my clit—a good kind—and his fingers digging into my hip.

When I came apart, his name ripped from my throat and reverberated around the room. In that moment, my whole world was this man, a diamond in the rough who taught me how to bowl and . . . how to live life.

"Good, baby?"

He sat me up and kissed me, his mouth tasting like me down there. I'd thought I would mind the first time it happened, but there was something strangely erotic and intimate about it. He pulled away to rip his shirt off, exposing his broad chest, mostly smooth and hard with a small smattering of hair.

"Suck me a little before I get inside you."

It wasn't a question but more of a gentle demand. His tone was rough, but his blue eyes were full of something more passionate—warmth, caring, a touch of tenderness. It was such a weird dichotomy. To be aggressive in bed—or on the couch—but the motivation behind it all sensitive or something touchy-feely. I couldn't exactly make sense of it, but I liked it.

Getting on my knees, I undid his jeans and quickly pulled them off. He turned to the couch and sat down, his erection reaching for me. *Straining for me.* I stayed on my knees and dipped my mouth to his length. I licked him from tip to base and back up, stopping to suck on the tip and taste his pre-come before taking the same path again.

"Suck it, Aly."

I brought my mouth around the top and took in as much as I could. He bunched my hair in his hand and guided my head. The pace was slow at first, and I dragged my tongue along with my mouth up and down.

"Scrape me with your teeth. Lightly," he said, his voice almost hurting with want.

I allowed my teeth to softly graze him, and a loud rumble made its way from his chest. We stayed like that for a while, me teasing him with a delicate lick or nip, and softly sucking his dick, until he nabbed my hair a touch harder.

"Suck me harder. Hard." He led the faster pace and knew exactly where to halt me before I gagged. "Jesus, fuck, does this feel good. I don't want to blow, though."

I rested my mouth at his tip, swirling my tongue at the hole, a tiny bit of salty substance seeping out.

"Come here." He guided me to his lap, holding me above him as desire coursed through my body. When I hesitated, he whispered, "I'm clean."

"I'm on the pill . . . to regulate—"

I didn't have time to finish. Jake brought me down on him quickly, filling me up and making me whole in a way I'd never dreamed about. Even when I'd sat daydreaming in the corner while my mom cleaned the mansions, or when I stayed up late studying in graduate school, I never dreamed of needing a man in the way I'd come to need Jake.

With him, I wanted to live.

He guided my hips faster, lifting my pelvis and pulling me back down on him, his quads doing all the work as his mouth sucked on my breasts, one after the other. A second orgasm built inside me and I panted as I tried to move with him. When he circled his hips, hitting me in the G-spot he'd found so easily, I shouted. I didn't even know what came out of my mouth, but it didn't matter. I was floating, soaring, flying . . .

Living.

We fell into a tangled heap together on the couch until Maverick whimpered. Jake got up to let him pee and said, "Stay there. Don't move. I'm going to clean you up as soon as I get back."

I must have dozed off because the next thing I remember was being half-asleep when Jake got out of bed early the next morning to go work out.

Sadly, I didn't get a chance to see Jake for the next few days. I even missed bowling night. My mom had taken a turn for the worse and between running to check on her and keeping up with work, I was spent. Jake was so sweet, texting every few hours to check in on me, sending Mom a matching hydrangea to the one he'd sent me, even offering to visit her with me.

I didn't want him to see my mom like she was or my face when I was visiting. Most of the time, it was tearstained from staring at my mom with a feeding tube. The thin piece of plastic tubing now wound over her face and disappeared into her nose, tan-colored liquid pumping through it to keep her body alive. Over the past weekend when I'd been busy falling for the guy, she'd given up eating.

Guilt took up residence in my heart and lungs. Right next to love—or lust?—whatever it was that I felt for Jake.

Barry kept giving me weird glances at work, as if he was worried about me. I'd kept the whole thing about my mom to myself. I couldn't afford to have him think I'd dropped the ball on the case, so I plowed forward.

Like now, I sat in my mom's dreary room studying my case notes as she rested, her eyes closed. I was going over holes in the case when Jake texted.

Jake: I'm outside, let's go! Time to eat and relax.

I didn't answer. Instead, I tossed all my crap in my bag and ran out the front doors, reveling in the fresh air and fading sunlight of late afternoon. And Jake.

Seeing him in his usual ragged jeans with a white dress shirt made my blood pulse and my heart beat harder. The sleeves were rolled up, revealing his corded forearms and tanned skin. His hair was slicked back, still wet from the shower, and I knew it would fall all around his face when it dried, and I'd want to push it away from his blue eyes. He was stunning, handsome, rugged, tough, and oh so sweet.

"Hey! You didn't have to do this," I said, feeling totally out of place in my black leggings and oversized sweater next to this Greek god.

"Yeah, I did."

He opened the truck door for me and helped me up, his hand riding up my leg and pulling away my sweater, then pinching my rear. I smiled to myself.

"Hungry?" he asked.

I didn't get why he saw himself as so evil. He'd been a young kid, and I wasn't sure who had convinced him of his guilt. The babysitter? Although I could never imagine someone doing that to a kid. Jake had explained when we'd talked over the weekend that Shirley had been an alcoholic back then and drinking heavily. Still, it didn't make sense.

"Yeah, I'm starving," I said, turning toward him as he pulled out of his illegal parking spot.

"Where to?"

"Can we do something easy, casual? The diner?"

"Sounds perfect." When he directed his smile toward me, my heart thawed and started to beat normally again, something it couldn't seem to do when I was in the nursing home. Then something struck me hard.

"Wait!"

Startled, he braked and turned to me, leaving the Hummer stopped in the road.

"Don't be mad," I said quickly, "but I just need to say that even though my mom is lying in there dying, when I see her face, I see peace. Somehow over the years, she learned to forgive herself and my dad, and I guess the guys involved with his death. I know it's messed up, but I think she figured she needed to live her life and move on."

Jake frowned at me and said, "Aly," in that warning tone of his, the one he used when I pushed him too far.

"No, listen. I didn't think I wanted to live my life until I met you, and now I do. I want you to want to live too, Jake."

He pressed his lips together as he tightened his grip on the steering wheel, his knuckles whitening as he stared at them. "I'm trying, Al. But this is no quick-fix thing. I've been carrying this for a long time, and sometimes I wonder if I'll ever be able to get past it. You got to understand that."

I love you. Do it for me. You can let go. Those words were all there ready to roll off my tongue, but they didn't. Jake was still hurting, and I didn't want him to do anything out of guilt.

After all, he'd already found me a new apartment and given me a dog. It was enough. I couldn't beg him to love me.

Still concerned, I decided to drop it for the night. Time would make it easier to share my true feelings.

"I do. I do, Jake." I squeezed his rock-hard thigh and he nodded.

Someone had finally pulled up behind us and tooted their horn, so Jake glanced in the rearview mirror and gave an apologetic wave as he stepped on the gas. "I let Mav out," he told me, a smile brightening his face.

"Thanks. The poor guy probably misses me. Maybe we should go home?"

"Can't. I promised Roman I'd bring you by."

"Roman? Ha!"

"I was in for lunch yesterday, and I may have mentioned you."

"Really?" I smiled as I perked up.

"Yep. Asked him if he remembered that tight piece of ass who was in with the stiff lawyer a few months back." The corners of his mouth turned up in a smirk.

"Jake!" I yelled and punched his arm, not really making any difference. The guy was a brick wall. *Except inside.*

We rode in comfortable silence, listening to music as we crossed the bridge and headed through the tunnel to the southern suburbs. I was a regular world traveler these days.

As the Hummer sailed along on the parkway, Jake gave me a mischievous grin and put on *the* song.

"Ugh, stop it with that!" I shouted as I hit the Stop button.

He chuckled loudly, his laughter radiating through the vehicle and my heart.

I took over the radio, and this time Journey blared through the speakers. Jake hummed and I sang most of the way to Roman's. When we got out, the sky was beginning to fill with clouds.

"Let's go, before you get all wet. I hear cats don't like that." He gave me a quick wink and slipped his arm around me, guiding me to the door. Tucked under his chin, I felt safer than ever.

When we ran into the restaurant, Rome saw us and rushed out of the kitchen area, grabbing me and squeezing me tight. "I didn't believe it! This guy here snagged you up!"

His voice bellowed around the small dining room, but everyone was too busy eating and drinking to notice. Embarrassment swept over me nonetheless, but Rome ignored it.

"I like my lawyer and all," he said with a wicked grin, "but I'd rather hire you! Although it's a good thing for me that I don't need one," he added with a wink.

Rome tossed his arm around me and led me to a corner table near the window where we could see the tiny lights twinkling along the lampposts along the sidewalk outside. This was a neighborhood where everyone looked out for each other, kissed their spouses hello at night and good-bye in the morning. It was a place where kids grew up without worries. The type of community I'd never seen myself a part of, let alone going on a date in, yet here I was.

The server ran out all kinds of protein for Jake—his regular order, obviously—and a special dish for me, compliments of the chef.

Over dinner, we made small talk. Jake asked a little about my mom, but the subject depressed me and I didn't feel like saying much. Chatter and the scent of garlic and herbs swirled through the room. Once our entrées were done, we shared a dessert. Well, Jake had a bite, and I ate the rest.

"You're fattening me up so I have to join your gym!" I protested.

"Never," Jake said, spooning some tiramisu into my mouth. As I chewed, trying not to moan at its goodness, he swiped a little whipped cream from the corner of my mouth with his thumb.

We stared into each other's eyes, our emotions on the rise, but my words caught in my throat. Jake also looked like he wanted to say something, but nothing came out. The awkward moment stretched out as I sat there, my feet sweating in my boots, my hands tingling under the table, my heart galloping at an unsteady pace.

Say something, Jake.

But he didn't.

After he paid our tab, we kissed and hugged Rome, then headed for the exit. As we swung open the restaurant's front door, the clouds broke, letting loose a heavy downpour.

Jake grabbed my hand and we made a run for it, but as we got close to the truck, he stopped and picked me up in his arms and kissed me, allowing us to get soaked.

It didn't matter; I was already drenched with unspoken feelings. I cared for this guy. I was letting him in—one meal, one kiss, one act of kindness at a time.

Easing me down his tight body, he whispered in my ear, "Be my

Aly-Cat."

"I am. I am, Jake."

My feelings for him had grown so strong in the last few weeks. Jake wanted so badly to be good to me, to take care of me, but strangely I felt I needed to strap on my cape for him, be his protector.

For him, I would be strong, like I was at work. And for a few minutes every day, I dreamed of enjoying a lifetime with Jake, of *having* a life with him. I deserved that, I thought. Or at least to imagine it.

CHAPTER TWENTY-TWO

jake

I was speeding to therapy. It had been two weeks since I'd last seen Dr. Wells, and I knew we would have to discuss Aly. Part of me didn't want to. I liked having her all to myself.

We were going on three weeks seeing each other and had slipped into an easy routine. I knew she wanted more but was letting it go my way, allowing me to call the shots, taking my temperature at every turn. *It was all too easy.*

I think that was what scared the fuck out of me, and precisely why I needed to chat with Dr. Wells. An easy routine never lasted for me; something always happened to screw it up. Shirley babysitting us had been an easy routine that went bad. Camper working for me and ending up in my bed had been another easy solution gone bad. The carnage was all on my hands. I'd been a fool in both circumstances.

I should let Aly alone, but I couldn't. Like baseball in college. I couldn't let it be and ended up injured, unable to play.

But Aly and me together felt too good. Every few nights, we'd meet up for dinner and then stay at either her place or mine. She was busy with that fucking ridiculous case—why she was protecting that fuck-face I didn't know—and she was a little more secretive than I would have preferred. She didn't say much at all. The dude had been on the lam, and now he was stuck in his apartment with an ankle bracelet. Why the fuck wasn't he back in jail? Apparently, he held some trump card and Aly—*Aly!*—had made some deal on his behalf.

I tried not to let it bother me because she continued to put up with my shit. Whenever we stayed together, she accepted being disturbed by an early-as-fuck alarm and waking later to an empty bed. She didn't try to make me stay or get all silly sad over my early-morning routine. It didn't go unnoticed.

I was trying to respect her boundaries, the way she respected mine.

This past Sunday, I took her to see my new site. You would have thought I'd taken her to the top of the Empire State Building or the Great Wall of China. She was so thrilled to see the gym floor being laid, and oohed and aahed over the locker rooms. Her genuine interest and excitement made me feel like Jay Z or Tony Soprano or some tough guy like that. I felt like a real *somebody* when I was with Aly.

"This is so spectacular! I need to join a gym," she'd said, teasing me, and I'd kissed the shit out of her right in front of the guys working overtime.

After we'd toured the whole place, we went for a ride with Maverick out to one of the state parks. We took a long walk in the woods, her hand in mine, the dog bouncing all over the place at the end of his leash. A few times, we stopped to kiss, touching our lips together gently at first, and then always ending up in a mad frenzy. About a mile and a half into the trail, silence fell around us except for the occasional bird chirping or small animal scurrying up a tree, and I pushed Aly up against a tree.

She'd been wearing these tight-as-hell dark blue yoga pants that fit to each and every curve, caressing her ass and quads. The weather was pretty chilly that day, so she'd had one of those big chunky sweaters on over a skimpy tank top, and I couldn't help it. I reached over and pushed it off her shoulder, revealing her cleavage and round tits. I kissed her hard, exploring her mouth ruthlessly before I leaned over and kissed a trail down her neck, over her collarbone until I settled on the top of her mounds. My tongue ran laps over the luscious skin, making its way to her even more delicious breasts. I took my thumb and rubbed it over her hardening nipple, and her moan filled the air.

The dog had lost interest in us and fallen asleep at our feet, so I dropped his leash and slipped my hand into her pants, thrilled to discover she wasn't wearing any underwear. My finger delved right into her already wet folds, slipping out and skimming the lips before diving back inside. One finger, then two, with my thumb on her clit. She liked that, I knew.

We'd been fooling around a lot these last few weeks. Not all the time, though; it wasn't just about sex. We'd talk, laugh, tickle, and end up fucking each other's brains out.

I had a lot to talk about with Wells regarding Aly, and wasn't sure if I should be looking forward to this appointment or dreading it.

After parking the truck, I hurried into the shrink's office. When she ushered me in, I tossed my leather jacket over the back of the uncomfortable couch, then sat down gingerly on the dainty piece of shit and kicked my feet out in front of me.

Doc looked over her glasses at me. "Good to see you, Jake. You missed an appointment."

"I know. Got caught up with work and life."

"Care to tell me about it?" She leaned forward, setting her notepad down on the table in front of us.

"Gyms are coming along. The new one is back on schedule and going to open on time. Lane's happy about that. Bess is happy, of course. She needs to see me happy."

"That's a lot of happiness." She raised an eyebrow. "Are you happy?"

"Part of me can't believe the success I'm having in business. I was always such a fuckup, and still am."

Tapping her pen on her pad, she frowned at me. "You can't think that entirely."

I shrugged my shoulders. Who knew? *Once a fuckup; always a fuckup.*

"I don't know. I know I don't deserve to have all this *happy*, especially with a woman," I said, using air quotes on the word of the day.

"Why not?"

Enraged, I stood and paced. "Because! Because of what I did, but here I am . . . happy . . . and falling for a girl."

"Maybe you're forgiving yourself?" Doc asked, not asking me to sit like she normally would.

I was so filled with tension, my muscles flexed and strained to the point I thought I'd rip my jeans. Back and forth I paced, my heavy black running shoes looking out of place on the pink carpet.

"I'm not doing that," I spat out. "This was about me helping someone, doing good, but I'm sucking out all of her greatness, all her shine. I don't deserve it."

"Jake, sit."

She used her no-bullshit voice, the one she rarely brought out, so of course, I listened.

"You need to think long and hard," she said, pinning me with a caring but firm glare. "You are good. Better than that. You don't need another person to give you goodness. Maybe you two are sharing all that's wonderful about each other? This woman and you."

I shook my head, but considered what she was saying. Aly had been through something similar, and she survived. Look how she was conquering the world and not allowing a stupid statute of limitations to ruin her life. Could I do the same?

No. I couldn't.

"I can't be happy until Shirley pays somehow. And now Camper is back; she's like a fucking fixture in my life. She had this weird attack outside her apartment and came running to me. Now she checks in every day. I don't know what she wants, but I can't keep it for much longer from Aly."

"Why don't you say anything? And why didn't you in the first place?"

Dr. Wells crossed and uncrossed her legs, and for a moment I was distracted at the thought of Aly's long limbs—wrapped around me, laid out in bed waiting for me, walking a step or two ahead of me with Maverick.

"Camper thinks I'll do something," I said with a snort. "Come to her rescue or some white-knight shit like that, but I made her call the police this time. I can't get involved, risk getting into a fight anymore. What would Aly do if I landed in jail again?"

Frustrated, I smacked my hand onto the table in front of me, sending the doo-dads scattered over it rattling all over the hard surface.

"What the fuck? Why didn't you even flinch?" I yelled at her.

"Jake, I've seen you get pretty violent and punch a hole in my wall. In the year or more that I've known you, you've never been violent with another human unless there was good reason. I'm not condoning violence, but I'm not afraid of you."

"You should be," I said savagely. "I kill people. That's what Camper wants from me. My evil is all I'm good for. And Aly thinks I'm good, but I'm not. I definitely don't deserve the peace she brings me."

"You need to think about what you're saying, Jake," Dr. Wells said in a soothing voice. "That's not you. I know you're tough, but you don't like to see others suffering."

When I said nothing but just shrugged, she continued. "Look what happened when Bess was hurt and Lane asked you to run to see her. You told me you ran. Look who made Lane come to terms with his pain? You."

"I'll think about it."

Done with this, I stood again and snagged my jacket from the back of the couch. As I headed out, more weight than I'd ever bench-pressed rode on my shoulders out the door.

CHAPTER
THREE

aly

I REALLY needed some time to think, about work, actually. Cameron was screwing with me. Even in his absence, I was starting to think he took me for a PD who was still wet behind the ears. I wasn't, yet he thought he could keep manipulating me. There was no way I could continue to allow that.

The last few weeks with Jake had been amazing, almost dream-like, but I needed to take off my Cinderella ball gown and slippers, and gather my strength. Work needed to come first, so when Jake texted around five o'clock, I was torn. I hadn't seen him since he left me in his bed before sunrise two days ago, but I had something to prove to myself. I couldn't keep giving all my energy to him. *Could I?*

Jake: Dinner? Want to go out? Sushi?

Me: I can't tonight. Got to work.

Jake: Seriously?

Me: :(

Yes, I'd turned into a silly, confused, constantly daydreaming, emoji-using girl who didn't know if she was in like or in love when it came to Jake Wrigley.

Jake: I wanted my favorite dessert. YOU.

As I sat on the bus reading his text, I blushed, wanting and needing him.

Me: Tomorrow? Rain check?

Jake: It's a date.

I got off at the stop for the Cathedral of Learning, needing to run the stairs a few hundred times to get my head right. I should have just told Jake and asked him to join me. He'd been asking to come run with me for weeks, and I wanted to see him.

I also desperately needed some perspective. On Cameron. On my mom, who was failing. But mostly on Jake.

My feelings for him were multiplying exponentially. He was so harsh and rough on the edges, but he'd flash his baby blues and I'd see a softer side. He needed to be accepted, and I wanted to do that. How long he would allow it, I wasn't sure.

I'd already changed clothes at work, so I shoved my stuff in a locker and headed to the stairwells. Campus was quiet. It must have been spring break or something because the hallways were empty.

Happy to have the place to myself, I stuffed my earbuds in and hit Play on my phone. Justin Bieber blared in my ears—absolutely, the Biebs was my secret love—and I began climbing, Jake still at the forefront of my mind.

Tension poured from my muscles as the sweat dripped down my back. I went up to the top and ran back down before beginning my ascent all over again. After a couple of rounds, for a second I missed having Drew there. He'd have been a decent distraction from the nerves and bad feelings running through me.

Maybe I could have shared some of Cameron's case with him. Jake was too close to it, and he freaked out every time I brought it up. He also didn't believe it wasn't Cameron who broke into my place; he suspected there were others involved.

Officer Petrisky had told me they had lifted half a print off the knife, not enough to make a match, but it was enough to rule out Cameron. He said he didn't know who did it, and although the cop promised he was keeping his ear to the ground, I wasn't sure I believed him.

A couple of weeks earlier, I wasn't even sure Cameron was innocent, yet I had to believe my client. He swore he knew who did it, but kept stringing us along in our investigation with false promises. He insisted there was going to be another incident and that he would help us make an arrest, but nothing had materialized yet.

In reality, I was getting nowhere with my client; he still hadn't come through with the miracle he'd promised. Earlier today, I'd had to get blunt with him when he'd called me from an unlisted burner phone.

"I can't continue to defend you if you don't give me something," I'd told him. "You're hanging yourself."

At that, he'd become snippy with me. "I have my reasons. Sometimes you do shit without yourself in mind. I don't know why, but I am. So just say I'm innocent, and wait."

"But I can't do that with you on the lam and without evidence," I'd insisted.

He'd only huffed and puffed, but before he disconnected the call, I could have sworn I heard a woman in the background saying, "Tell her—" But Cameron hung up too quickly.

Well, it looked like Barry was right. Cameron was mesmerized with the "power of pussy." It didn't matter; I couldn't keep him out of jail for much longer. The department was losing patience and wanted someone to pin this on, and it was going to be Cameron if he didn't give up what he'd promised.

Not quite knocked out for the evening, I decided on one more go-round with the evil steps. A soft, tender song about love and forgiveness played in my ear. Visions of kissing Jake and him holding my arms in place, my legs wrapped tight around his hard torso, played in my mind as I ran, pounding the stairs.

It was time to tell Jake how I felt, I decided. Time to share with him what I wanted, and ask him if he could give it.

I was smiling, happy with myself for finally finding some clarity on the Jake issue, when I heard the door to the stairwell bang closed. I looked behind me and saw a tall blonde lacing her shoes and stretching her hamstrings. I'd never seen her before on the stairs, but was happy to have some company. The building was so quiet; I missed the hustling of the college kids. It reminded of a time when I thought I was so responsible, as opposed to now, when I truly *was* responsible.

She blew right by me, running up the stairs faster than I'd ever seen anyone do. Surprised, I watched her take the flights as if they were nothing; she was like the bionic woman. I was already tired, so my breathing was jagged and uneven as I tried to catch her, lifting my quads and pushing through the ball of my foot.

"Hey," I huffed out when I finally closed in on her. "Amazing job."

She nodded and smiled, then picked up her pace yet again.

"I've been doing this for years and can barely keep up with you," I admitted when we were side by side.

She stopped dead in her tracks and looked straight at me. "Really?" she asked, her left eyebrow raised.

I pulled an earbud out and smiled. "Really!"

"Interesting," she said in some strange accent. "Lucky for me."

Those were the last words I heard before everything went black.

Chapter Twenty-Four

Jake

The next morning, Aly still wasn't returning my calls or texts. She'd promised we would see each other last night, but she was MIA.

What I feared most had come true—she finally saw me for the dark asshole I was. Which was good for her, exactly what I'd thought was best for her, but shit for me.

I cranked the bar over my head, rattling the weights, and slammed it back down again. I swore I could taste her on my tongue, feel her mouth taking my cock deep.

"Take it easy, boss," Tony yelled.

"Keep your suggestions to yourself, Tony."

This was my second workout of the morning. The baseball guys were coming in, and I needed my head right.

Where was she? Should I run by the rental to check on her? Her office?

But I hadn't stop by unannounced in weeks. We had a routine.

Getting my head on right seemed more and more like a distant fantasy.

I stood and slapped more weight on the bar, testing my limits to the maximum. I watched the veins bulge in my biceps as I raised the bar. Sweat trickled over the ridges of veins and muscle. I put the weight back up again, hauling it higher in the air every time, grunting through clenched teeth.

Nine Inch Nails radiated through the gym, doing little to ease my temper. The song was raging, the lyrics "I want to fuck you like an animal" assaulting my eardrums. Out of breath, I fumed, needing Aly more than I'd ever needed anyone, and hating myself for it.

Once I was done, I tore my bar apart and racked the weight plates, then finished with a round of curls before hitting the showers. I decided after the baseball players left, I'd surprise Aly at work. It was almost opening day, and I had to make sure those dudes were happy. We were set to shoot the billboard ads the following week. So far, it had been a sweet arrangement.

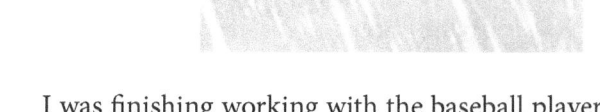

I was finishing working with the baseball players, doing a series of stretches on yet another new roller ball I was trying out, when Chloe walked out on the floor.

"Jake?"

"Busy, Chlo," I huffed out.

"Someone here for you."

"Is it Camper?"

"No, it's some guy who reeks of smoke. Says he knows your girlfriend?"

"My what?"

"Your girlfriend."

"Hey, guys." I turned to the guys I was working with, trying to laugh it off. "I'm going to see who this is. Probably some nut," I said with a forced grin. Then I turned to Tony. "Hey, can you stretch the guys out?"

"Yeah."

Scowling at my front-desk girl, I said, "Go, Chloe. Tell him I'm coming. No need to stand and stare."

I took a deep breath to calm myself and swiped my damp hair back as I made my way up the stairs to reception. The piped-in music faded as I closed in on the man standing there waiting for me.

"Can I help you?" I crossed my arms in front of me, flexing my biceps.

"Um, I'm Barry," he said, paling a little as he took me in. "I work with Alyson. She didn't come into work this morning. I called her phone a few times and she didn't answer. Thought maybe you'd know where she is?"

Anger flashed through me as I saw red. Bright fucking blood red. "What are you accusing me of, lawyer boy?"

"Nothing!" He held his hands up in surrender and cleared his throat, but he still sounded like he had a frog stuck in there when he spoke next, shooting his words out rapid fire. "Nothing, I promise. Aly is gone, our client's out on bail but his ankle bracelet isn't working, and I want to call the cops but I wanted to make sure she isn't sick or just taking a day off with you."

Before he'd even finished, I grabbed the schmuck by the shoulder and dragged him to my office. "Call the cops," I yelled at him once we were behind my closed door. "She's not with me or sick. You guys let that bastard out, and now he has her!"

I watched Barry pull out his phone with shaking hands and hit the button for a contact at the police department. He told them Alyson was nowhere to be found, and they already knew about the monitor going haywire.

As I waited impatiently, I was reminded of the similar scene with Camper last week. How many times was I going to call the cops from my office? Jesus Christ, I was turning into a humanitarian.

When he finished the call and shoved the phone back in his pocket, I growled, "If something happens to her, I'll kill you *and* that guy I already beat the shit out of. I don't care if I go to prison for life."

Barry just shivered, the stupid, worthless idiot.

"Go!" I shouted at him. "Go look for her. That's what I'm going to do."

I stormed out of my office, not waiting to see what Barry did. As soon as I got in my truck, I called Bess, only to learn Lane was out of the country. She demanded to know what was going on, and with the chatter of an AA meeting happening in the background, I told her.

"Did you hear me?" I asked.

"I did. You have to calm down, Jake. The police are going to help."

I hung up. I didn't have time for her positive vibes. Next, I called the detective I was paying, and found out she didn't come home last night.

"I thought she was with you," was the excuse he offered up.

Furious, I hung up on him too and sped off to the rental.

After using my key to let myself in, I found Mav in a puddle of pee and shit in his crate. Scooping the poor guy up in a towel, I carried him out crying and whimpering to the yard where he relieved himself. Then I hauled him straight to the basement sink and washed him off. After giving him some food and a small walk, I felt slightly more centered, closer to Aly, even though she was nowhere to be found.

I kept texting Barry, and he kept texting back, assuring me, "We're on it."

Bullshit.

I had to find her, but needed someone to take care of Maverick. I pulled out my phone and called Bess back, this time asking nicely if I could meet her halfway between here and there with the dog.

Thank God she never said no to me. An hour later, I pulled into a rest stop and waited. Bess showed up fifteen minutes later in her enormous SUV, Brooks jumping around in the back.

"Where's my niece?" I asked.

"I left her with May back at the house. She was off today and was watching Maddy while I went to a meeting and to volunteer. Don't worry about her . . . Maddy's fine. Give me the puppy, and go do what you need to."

"Thanks," I said, raking my hands through my hair and pulling on the ends, causing pain to sear through my scalp. I needed to feel something.

"Jake?" Bess called as I was hopping back into my driver's seat. "Come spend the night at our place."

"I'll see," I yelled and slammed my door closed.

I wanted to gun the engine, but waited for Bess to pull out and exit. I watched her hit the road, a small compact car right behind her, and then I peeled the fuck out of there.

CHAPTER
TWENTY-FIVE

aly

SOMEONE was dragging me by my hair, the roots pulling on my throbbing scalp. I tried to open my mouth to scream, but it was taped shut. My legs dragged along something rough and jagged, and tiny pricks—maybe splinters—tore through my yoga pants. My brain willed my eyes to open despite the droopiness settled in the lids, but they were also covered with tape.

The tender skin of my lips was already peeling off, sticking to the adhesive taping them, and salty tears gathered in pools below my eyes. I squeezed my eyes shut, even though I already couldn't see a damn thing.

Losing my sight completely forced me to listen harder so I strained my ears, trying to pick up any sounds. What was I listening for? Clues, noises, anything, my captor's breathing.

Desperation and anxiety bubbled up my throat and a scream escaped my lungs, only to be blocked by the tape.

"Mmph!" filtered through the tape covering my mouth, rather than the shrieking *Help!* I'd wanted to release.

A sharp jab made contact with my shin, and I heard a loud crack, like a snap. Quickly, it registered the snap was actually my own leg bone.

Pain screamed through my body, and I was dropped to the floor with a thud. My head hit the floor hard, thankfully making everything go black once again.

The whine of a small motor awakened me, then a grinding noise, and for a second, I wished it hadn't because the pain only intensified, blasting through my leg. I tried to move it, but it was completely lifeless.

Grunting from the effort, I kept trying to move my lower leg, but it wouldn't budge. The whine roared to life again. I shifted, trying to roll to the side, off my face, but something fell on top of me. Something sharp poked into my rib cage, and I didn't dare move.

"Where are you going, missy?" The voice that rang through the room was loud and feminine at the same time. Hoarse and seductive, foreign and familiar.

Fear froze me as I shook my head, unable to say anything.

"I'm going to take the tape from your eyes, but no sudden movements. I got my stiletto angled exactly right to puncture a lung if you do."

I sensed the warmth of a body part near my face, and let out a violent scream as the thick piece of duct tape was torn from my eyes.

Blinking against the light, I looked around to find myself on the floor, but I had no idea where I was. A woman was standing over me, smirking at me. She seemed somewhat familiar, with blond hair and heavily painted eyes, but I couldn't recall where I knew her from. I didn't hang out with models or strippers or exotic dancers. This lady was attractive, curvy but fit, with big pouty pink lips and her glossy hair that was perfectly straight.

Who was she?

"So, what do you think now, Ms. Justice?"

I went to try to rip the tape at my mouth so I could answer her with a question—*what was she talking about*—but I realized my hands were tied behind me. How did I not notice? It must have been all the splinters residing in my thigh. Wait, I wasn't feeling them anymore.

Actually, I didn't feel my leg at all.

Terrified, I lifted my head and peered down at my body. I was wearing familiar leggings and a T-shirt, as if I'd been working out.

"Hello?" Blondie asked, her accent coming out a bit thicker.

I'd been running the stairs. That was how I knew the woman! She was in the stairwell, running fast as hell. She'd spoken to me right before I apparently blacked out.

Was she the person who did this to me?

I moaned, murmuring behind my gag to get her to release the tape, and she did. Although the whole *fast like a Band-Aid* thing didn't really apply. It felt as if an entire layer of my skin was ripped from my face, and wetness—which I assumed was blood—dripped onto my chin. The coppery taste on my tongue as it reached out to wet my lips confirmed my suspicions.

Fear set up camp in my heart. I was going to die here, and I didn't even know why. All I'd ever wanted was to live my life peacefully. I wanted to do better than my parents had, perhaps not survive paycheck to paycheck. Until I met Jake. Then I'd wanted it all.

That was why this was happening. I wanted too much.

"What do you want?" My question came out scratchy, my throat raw and painful.

"A new kind of justice, Ms. Road."

I tried shaking my leg. Desperate, I needed to feel it. Pain shot up to my groin and straight to my solar plexus. Silently rejoicing, I felt my leg. It was there!

My leg. One leg. Half the pair.

The pair Jake drooled over. He called me *Legs*.

My brain floated out of the room, ignoring the woman pacing in front of me.

He also called me Aly-cat . . . and Legs.

I want Jake back.

One minute I was dreaming of Jake, and the next, the breath was knocked from my lungs. A scream ripped from my throat and I lifted my head to see the blond bombshell standing on the pieces of my leg—correct that, bone—in big-ass heels and leather pants. She ground her heel into my exposed leg, causing more blood to come from somewhere and louder snaps.

Sweat poured from me, all the moisture escaping my pores. My eyes were dry—I had no tears left—and I simply whimpered.

"I want justice, Ms. Road. For me and my people," she said, her words sounding as if they were far away as my consciousness wavered.

"From me?" I forced out through my bloody lips.

"You are defending my boyfriend, Gus Cameron, and I know that stupid limp-dick is up to no good. He wants to pin it all on me . . . and yes, most of the handiwork was mine. But I'm needed out here in the world to keep our race pure, to bring more justice for the Aryans."

I took a deep inhale and tried to pull myself together. Breathe in, breathe out. *Focus!*

My client, Gus Cameron, was her boyfriend. He was waiting to turn someone in . . . was it her? Were all those pictures on the wall of his apartment hers? Had she committed all the hate crimes, and he only covered for her?

"He should've never fucked the blond Jew," the woman spat out. "He should only dip his dick in Aryan pussy. I told him that, and he didn't listen. I know she looked pure, being blond, but the bitch wasn't. He's going to pay because you're going to fix the case and send him to prison."

Fix the case?

Wasn't that what the note said, the one left in my ransacked apartment? Did that make this woman my stalker?

"Okay, I don't want to die," I said slowly, croaking out the words. "I need medical help. Why don't you help me, and then I'll help you?"

"No! No medical help until the deal's done and Cameron's back behind bars."

I would die if I didn't get help soon; I was bleeding out. Already

I was light-headed, having a hard time concentrating, and my vision kept going in and out.

A sob escaped my throat as my mind whirled. I wasn't made to survive this type of thing. I was the daughter of a maid, a sheltered girl, poor but not necessarily tough. Praying frantically, I started making promises to God, to any higher power who would listen. A bright light flooded my face and I was sure it was Him—God—or maybe it was the light calling me.

Why did this woman have such a thick Russian accent? Hitler hated the Russians. Then I remembered reading something in my case preparation about neo-Nazi hate crimes, about some Russians declaring themselves Aryans.

The light brightened, and a booming voice rang out. "Marina! What the fuck? What the hell did you do?"

"You! You did it. You were going to turn me in and let them slaughter me like a pig, Gus. So I'm taking matters into my own hands."

"You can't fucking do that, Marina! She works for the government. You're going to fry for this. I was trying to get us a deal. Fucking Christ, now what am I going to do?"

Lightness and darkness alternated, swirling around me. Voices faded in and out, and then I heard what sounded like a gunshot. I was pretty sure my body jerked at the sound, but that was only in theory, in my rattled brain.

Sometime later I realized my lap was soaking wet; I must have peed myself. Silence took over, and darkness returned. Unable to do anything else, I continued to lie there for a time, resting my eyes as I contemplated how much I really wanted to live.

With pain jolting through me, I turned my head and looked around.

There was blood everywhere, all over my skin and clothes. At the sight of the dark red liquid spilling from me onto the dirty floor, my head spun like the Tilt-A-Whirl at the carnival. My vision blurred, turning hazy as light came and went. I wasn't sure if it was a dream or reality. The light seemed to be seeping in from somewhere, but I didn't know where.

Was this death? Would I never live? At the thought, shrieks escaped my throat, barreling up through my vocal cords.

I'd never hurt so badly in my life. My eyes kept drooping from the shock and the pain. I didn't know where I was or how the hell to get help, but I wanted it.

I wanted to live. I didn't want to just survive, but I needed to breathe his air, Jake's air, to live with him side by side. But like the blood seeping from my body, the chances of him finding me were slipping. Fading. Everything was darkening, and then the light came again.

"Help!" I screamed, but it came out more of a ragged whisper, my throat completely raw from earlier. "Help!" My voice echoed off the wooden walls that surrounded me, walls I hadn't noticed before. I was in some kind of barn, but I didn't know where.

How would anyone find me?

I'm going to die here.

Light blasted into the room and voices took up residence in my mind. This was it. It was over. I was in heaven or hell, or maybe it was purgatory. I didn't know.

"Ma'am?" a soft voice called to me. "Ma'am," the voice repeated, and a hand shook my shoulder.

I didn't want to go. I'd changed my mind; I wanted to stay dead. I was ready to die. Whatever was left of me wouldn't be enough for Jake . . . or for me.

"Miss, I'm here to help you. Can you blink or nod if you can hear me?" It was a woman's voice, and she was gently untying my hands.

A swallow tumbled down my throat, and I nodded once, or at least I thought I did. I wasn't sure if I did or not. Did the woman even see it?

"It's okay, honey, I'm here. My name is Shirley, and I'm going to have my husband lift you now. There's no way we can wait for an ambulance. We've got to get you to help."

I watched as this stranger with red hair like mine ran a hand down my arm, saying soothing words as her middle-aged husband wrapped a blanket around my shoulders and lifted me. Shivers continued to rack my body. My lifeless limb hung by a thread, and blood dripped from me as he carried me to a small compact car.

The woman named Shirley sat in the cramped backseat with me, holding my head steady in her lap with one hand and putting pressure on my leg with the other. With every jolt of the car, pain crashed through me, and I moaned.

The car ride faded in and out. Murmurs, quiet discussion floated around me. I was pretty sure I heard someone say, "We need to go to the local hospital, can't make it all the way to Pittsburgh."

Where was I?

My focus drifted to sushi, and bowling with Jake. I thought about his gym, and how he was always asking me to go there. I was thinking so hard about him, I swore I heard his name on repeat.

"Jake, Jake, Jake . . ."

The next thing I remembered, I was waking up in a hospital bed. Dazed and confused, I blinked my bleary eyes, comforted by the certainty that was the Pittsburgh skyline I saw outside the window.

But the older redhead who sat in the chair next to me, holding my hand, her I wasn't certain of.

"I'm going to get your Jake now," she whispered to me.

My eyes were blurry and I squinted, trying to make out who the woman was, and how she knew Jake. "Bess?" I murmured, wondering if I was imagining the woman being middle-aged.

Bess is young? Right?

The stranger shook her head.

I reached out and grabbed her wrist and squeezed tight. "What happened? Who are you?" My voice sounded foreign and ragged, and I was beginning to imagine the worst.

"Darlin', you were kidnapped, but I rescued you. I'll tell you the rest later. I'm sure Jake is very worried about you. I waited until you were awake to go get him. Had to make sure you were really going to be okay," she said in a hushed tone.

Everything was so fuzzy to me; her words sounded as if they were coated in a layer of static. My head throbbed and my body burned with pain, but neither were close to the odd absence I felt in my heart. Something was wrong with me—really wrong—but I couldn't put my finger on what it was.

"Wait! What happened? Jake? How do you know Jake? Why do you keep talking about him? Please don't leave me here guessing," I pleaded with the woman as she stood to leave.

"I've been looking out for him." Her expression was pained as she twisted her hands together, the knotted joints reminding me of my own mother's hands. "It's what I should've been doing years ago, but I fell short. It's how I found you. Now, let me get the nurse and tell them to call the authorities, and then I'm going to get Jake. It may be a while. I'm not sure who took you or why, but when we're all together, you'll tell the police what you remember. Until then, get some rest, Alyson."

I shifted slightly in the bed, straining to hear the woman whispering in the hall.

"I'm off to alert her other friends," she said outside my room, "but I think you should call 911. I found that woman brutalized after a violent crime."

"Ma'am, why are you just saying this now? I thought you said she had an accident?"

"It wasn't time for her to be found yet," was all I heard before her footsteps retreated down the hall.

Who was this woman playing with my destiny?

CHAPTER
TWENTY-SIX

jake

I PACED the same path I'd paced a hundred times already, my feet practically wearing grooves in the hardwood in front of my brother's fireplace. Sunlight poured through the windows, throwing golden beams in my path, and I wanted to kick them. Spring weather had fully taking over, summer on its way, but I was anything but bright.

In my head, I was back in the driving rain, lost in that alley, looking for answers to life. Graffiti God kept flashing before my eyes. Fucking God. Who the hell did he think he was raining down shit on my life?

My fucking life had sucked beyond belief because I had my parents' blood on my hands and now this. It was my job to take care of Aly—God's way of helping me absolve myself—and I'd fucked it up and she was gone. Disappeared into thin air.

As far as I knew, the police had turned up zip. Barry had gone out looking, and then apparently fell drunk on liquor and guilt. The last time I spoke with him, he was slurring so badly, his words were nothing but gibberish. I'd tried to call him a few times since then for updates, but his phone went right to voice mail. Just like I'd thought; the man was fucking useless.

As I was thinking of the nicotine-reeking devil, my phone buzzed.

"You sobered up?" I belted into the phone after slamming my finger across Answer Call.

"Yeah. Sorry 'bout that, but this is all my fault. Al didn't want this case. I pushed it."

"Get to the point, Barry." I didn't have time for his sob story.

"Police have a lead. Stay tuned."

"Where? What?"

"I can't say. Stay around and available. They just called me."

Click.

The little ass had nerve.

Against my better judgment, I'd agreed with Bess when she had begged me to come stay with her after the first night, insisting I not be alone. Aly had been gone with no news, and I knew for sure I was meant to go through life alone. I couldn't do this even when Bess kept saying I could. I wanted to slam my fist into the mantel, but I kept it together for Bess.

No more rescuing or love fantasies for me anymore. That was done. I'd be on my own forever now.

My entire body was tense to the breaking point, my muscles jumping from unused adrenaline that pumped through me. A million emotions yanked me back and forth, driving me insane—anger, frustration, uselessness, worry, confusion, and rage. The rage kept me going.

Through it all, my head whirled with disjointed thoughts.

Dr. Wells kept calling, and I kept hitting Ignore.

Lane was on an earlier flight home.

James was coming from Florida to be with Maddy, so Bess could babysit me.

I wasn't working out. All I did was pace and swear and swear and pace.

I needed to go home, crawl into bed and ride this awful nightmare out. Maybe I'd wake up on the other side of this dream and not tamper with my life or anyone else's problems.

Spent and worn out from my own mental berating, I leaned my head into the mantel. The edge dug into my forehead, and I wanted to slam my whole fucking face into the piece of shit. I wanted the pain to leave my heart, bleed from my soul. Who was I to think I deserved a bowling partner, let alone happiness?

"I'll get it," Bess yelled from the kitchen.

"What?" I lifted my head, dizzy and dazed.

"The door, Jake. Didn't you hear the bell?"

I shook my head, not caring. When I didn't move, Bess hurried past me to the front door.

"What the hell are you doing here?" she spat out in a hushed voice.

Curiosity and concern for Bess pulled me from the living room. I stepped into the foyer only to become enraged when I saw for myself who was at the door.

"Get out!" I screamed at our unwanted visitor, my voice cracking.

The woman put her hands up in the air, and her knobby fingers shook. "Jake, Bess. I know where Aly is." Her words came out fast and rushed before we could slam the door in her face.

"Shut the fuck up, Shirley." I stormed to the doorway and stood next to Bess, looming over the older woman I hated more than anyone, her red hair a reminder of who I was really missing. "Do. Not. Fuck. With. Me."

Bess looked from Shirley to me, and her eyes widened. She laid a warning hand on my arm. "Calm down, Jake. Let's hear what she has to say."

Shirley braced herself against the doorjamb, her hand visibly trembling. Her chest heaved and her eyes filled with tears as she turned her weathered face up to me.

"You're not going to be happy," she said in a wobbly voice. "I was back to keeping an eye on you and Lane. A few days ago, I was watching Bess because I knew Lane was out of town. Then I saw you come out and give her the dog. The last few weeks, I'd been so happy to see you'd moved on with the redhead, buying her a dog and everything."

Frustrated, I slammed my fist against the doorframe. "Shirley, none of this is telling me where my Aly is. Fucking get to it!"

Startled, she reared back and nearly lost her footing, but Bess braced her fall, holding her upright.

"S-she's in the hospital," Shirley stuttered, her eyes wide with fear. Of me. "Alive, but she's there because I found her."

Bess and I exchanged alarmed looks, then I glared back at Shirley. "What the hell?"

"Someone took her. Didn't you hear me? I was keeping an eye on Bess because Lane's away. When she met you at the rest stop, I followed her there. When I saw you two together, I was confused as to what was going on, so I tailed Bess."

"The compact car was you?"

She nodded. "I saw you give the dog up, and was devastated. I thought you'd broken up with the red-haired girl, and I cried all the way to work. When I was covering the late-night shift at the diner, this woman came in all disheveled and used the bathroom to change. She came back out all dolled up in leather, makeup, and heels. I couldn't help but take a look at her when she went outside, and I saw your girl—Aly—slumped in the passenger seat, her eyes closed."

"Shirley," I growled. "Spit it the fuck out."

"I told my boss I was sick and left work to follow the woman. Once we stopped in front of this abandoned barn that sits way off a state road, I called my husband, Wayne, and gave him detailed directions, so he came to help. If I didn't follow them, no one would've found the barn. It's been abandoned since I've lived in the area, and that's close to a decade. I don't even think the teens use it to party anymore, it's so hard to find."

She paused for a second, and Bess twirled her hand in a hurry-up gesture.

"Anyway, poor Wayne had been so mad at me for sneaking around after you boys and watching you, but your girl was lucky I did in this case. Of course, Wayne wanted me to call the police, but

I said no. I was going to be your hero, and I am! I stayed outside the barn, peeking in through cracks in those old wood walls. I could see Aly was hurt but alive, and I waited until the right time."

Her face brightened with hope and her eyes sparkled with pride until I glared at her. She shrank back and continued in a rushed voice. "As soon as that other woman was taken away by a strange man—a big bald guy with a gun in his hand—I went right in. It was early morning, and there was Aly. I took her to the hospital and made sure she was okay. For you, Jake. I didn't give them much to go on until I left to come here. This time, I was going to make everything right."

I snatched my keys off the foyer table, ready to hightail it to my girl. "The local hospital?" I yelled. "Why didn't you call the police? An ambulance? You're not a fucking saint, Shirley, and you're not God. You're a sick bitch. You don't get to decide when the police get involved and when they don't. Like you did in the past." My heart galloped in my chest, spit gathered in the corners of my mouth, and my head pounded with anger.

Shirley's face crumpled. "There wasn't time, Jake. I saved her. For you!"

"Stop with all the self-righteous crap. Where's Aly? Are the police with her now? For Christ's sake, Shirley, do you have to fuck with *everyone's* lives?" My fists balled at my side and I could feel the veins bulging in my neck, my heart pushing blood through my body so hard, I could hear it whooshing in my ears.

Her hands twisted together as she stepped aside from the doorway. "She's back in Pittsburgh. They Life-Flighted her there for surgery. She's in a room now, and I've been sitting with her the whole time."

Bess finally lost it. "Aly's been gone for three whole days from what we can gather, and you've known where's she's been for a day and a half and didn't think to tell anyone? We've been pulling our hair out, Jake is ready to tear my house down, and the police have turned up nothing," she whispered through clenched teeth, shaking her head, her hands trembling. "I can't believe it, Jake's been crawling out of his skin, and you held the key to stop him."

"I needed to make sure she was going to be all right," Shirley said with a pathetic shrug.

Bess pulled up to her full height, nearly vibrating with fury. Her fists were bunched in front of her as if she was prepared to fight to the death. "Shirley, you are so messed up! You're acting like this is nothing. You knew we were going frantic looking for Aly, and then you sit back and wait to come here? How dare you! And then you stand there shrugging as if it's no big deal."

"Please," Shirley begged as tears spilled over her cheeks. "You have to understand. I didn't want to cause Jake any more pain if Aly . . . died."

"Died?" I roared. "Get the fuck out of here, Shirley! Thanks for finding Aly and deciding when I should know she's alive. You're pretty damn good at deciding what I should and shouldn't say. Seems to me, it's history repeating itself." I shoved past her as I ran out the door.

"Jake, I just thought we could put that all behind us now!" Shirley called out after me.

"You've got to be fucking joking. No fucking way," I snarled as I jumped into my truck, then looked back at Bess. "Come on, Bess," I said as I started the truck.

Bess waved me off. "You go. I'll follow after I call May and get her to help."

Shirley looked between the two of us with a pathetic expression. "What about me?"

"Fuck off." I slammed my truck door and peeled out of there.

aly

Tears dripped off my chin onto my puke-green hospital gown as I lay in my hospital bed, my head spinning, confused. The doctor's words still hadn't settled.

"You've lost the lower half of your leg. Nothing we could do . . . tried everything, but too much damage . . . nerves, bones . . . clean amputation above the knee."

A jumble of random words sifted through my mind. The words *clean amputation* were on repeat, but not fully registering.

Footsteps sounded in the hall, coming closer as the machine monitoring my pulse beeped. I blinked up at the man and woman in uniform who entered my room and stopped by my bed.

"Hi, ma'am, we're . . ."

They were apparently with the police department. Their names could have been Cat and Dog or Tom and Jerry; it didn't matter. Nothing was sinking in.

Clean amputation, clean amputation, clean amputation.

"Sorry to disturb you," the female officer said, and I tried to focus on her next words, but failed. "The hospital reported you were here . . . a woman brought you in . . . and you're finally awake after they saved your life. We're here to help you."

Nodding was all I could manage, so I bobbed my head once or twice.

My life, but not my leg.

"Do you have family?" the male officer asked.

I shook my head. My mom would be of no use. These days she usually didn't even know who I was.

"Significant other?"

Shrugging, I mumbled, "Not sure what he really is."

"Do you know the woman who brought you in? She seemed very concerned about your well-being."

"No."

"Was she the person who did this to you? It appears as though your coworker reported you missing over forty-eight hours ago, but we haven't been able to reach him since."

I shook my head again.

"Do you know where you were? How this happened? Who may have been responsible? How you got there?"

I cleared my throat. Fiery embarrassment licked at my vocal

cords and I coughed. The man in uniform handed me a plastic cup of water. After I took a sip, I cleared my throat again, and this time a trickle of shame trailed up my throat. I was a strong, independent woman—how did this happen to me?

"I was in a barn of some sort. Not near here . . . I don't think. A blond woman, Russian accent, attacked me during my workout." Squeezing my eyes shut, I wheezed.

"Take your time, ma'am."

How many times was I going to be questioned? I'd just done this a few weeks ago with the officers at my apartment.

"I think her name was . . . Marina . . . that's what I overheard the guy, Gus Cameron—my client—call her. He was there, *I think*. I don't know, I could've been hallucinating. But she took me . . . Marina. I think she drugged me, and then Gus came and took her."

The female officer focused on her little notebook, apparently taking notes, and the man nodded at me to continue.

"And she broke my leg."

Understanding slammed into me, and a shriek and a defeated cry ripped through my throat. I flexed my right foot. It was there! Then I could have sworn I felt my left foot flex too, but when I looked down toward the end of the bed, the covers on that side of the bed were flat. There was nothing there.

"My leg is gone!" I shrieked as Barry ran into the room, his hair a greasy mess, his shirt wrinkled, his face twisted in pain. "Help! Help! My leg!" I kept screaming as long as my vocal cords would allow.

The officers scrambled and one raced out of the room, calling out, "Nurse? Help, nurse!"

Frantic, I grasped at Barry's arm and yelled, "My leg is gone, where is it?"

A woman dressed in scrubs rushed into the room and pushed Barry out of the way. Leaning over me, she patted my shoulder. "Honey, you have to calm down. You were in a terrible accident. Your leg was damaged, but you're alive." She ran her hand up and down my arm, trying to soothe me, before lifting a syringe to my IV.

"No!" I heard a familiar deep voice yell just as I faded out.

CHAPTER
TWENTY-SEVEN

jake

"SOMEONE tell me what the fuck is going on here?" I shouted, raising my voice over the beeping machines, practically hyperventilating as the room closed in around me.

One of two police officers standing in the room stepped up, blocking my view of Aly lying in that damn bed. "Sir, I'm sorry, you're going to have to leave if you're not immediate family."

I shrugged his hand off my shoulder. "I'm not going anywhere. That's my girl in that bed. With a stump for a leg. What the fuck happened?"

"Sir, please."

"Get your fucking paw off me."

The old Jake rumbled deep in my belly; angry-and-fighting Jake was taking over. I was mad-at-the-world Jake, the man I'd been before her, my Aly-cat.

"Legs!" Tears squeezed from my eyes as my legs weakened and I dropped to one knee.

"Sir, you're going to have to take this out to the waiting room."

"Legs," I shouted.

"Jake!"

Bess was next to me, her dark hair spilling over her face as she leaned down to hug me, her own eyes filling with tears. She ran her hand down my back. "Jake, stand up, honey. Aly's in the bed over there, she needs you. Okay?"

"Ma'am, I'm sorry, but who are you?" the female officer asked.

Bess ignored them until she helped me upright. Turning to the officers, she extended one hand in greeting as she swiped at her tears with the other. "Bess Wrigley. I'm this man's sister-in-law. This is Jake Wrigley, and that's his significant other lying in the bed."

Her expression soured as she jerked a thumb over her shoulder. "And this is Shirley, she's the woman who found Ms. Road and brought her here. She may be able to answer some of your questions."

I vaguely remember the cop saying something about being back to speak with me, not to go far—fucking-A, I wasn't going far—and Shirley following the officers out of the room.

In a haze, I stepped away from Bess and staggered to the bed, then did what came naturally. I crawled in next to Aly. The bed was narrow, so I made myself as small as possible, lying on my side next to her. Hesitant, I ran my hand down her leg closest to me, and let out a sigh of relief when it seemed fine. Then my hand hovered over the left, scared to hurt her. There was one of those air cushions vibrating life into the stump.

Frustrated that I couldn't do anything for her, I simply cupped her cheek and kissed the edge of her mouth. Trying to avoid the IVs that ran into her arm, I watched her chest rise and fall with each beep, and closed my eyes with my arm wrapped around my Aly-cat.

"Jake." The voice was ragged, but I swore I heard my name spoken in my dreams.

"Jake." There it was again.

I struggled to wake up. Prying my eyes open, I found Aly looking at me. Her nose was red and swollen; she'd been crying. Realizing we weren't alone, I glanced around. Bess was still sniffling, curled up in a chair in the corner, and a cop stood in the doorway.

"Al, you had me a fucking mess." My knuckles grazed her cheek, and she brought her hand, the one free of wires, to my rough cheek.

Her eyes squeezed shut as she whispered, "I don't have a leg."

"Shh." I gathered her close and rubbed my cheek against hers, mindful of my stubble. "Shh."

We stayed like that for a while, her cheek tucked into my neck, a river of tears falling from her eyes and sliding down my throat. Eventually Bess left the room, murmuring a few words to the cop as she left. My shirt was soaked, and my head was a fucking mess.

"Aly, what happened?" I had to ask.

She looked up at me and lay back on her pillow, closing her eyes. "I still don't know it all, but I was running on the stairs, and then I was in a barn with a Russian woman yelling about fixing the case, and going on and on about justice. Cameron showed up and took her. My leg was already crushed. I don't know how it first broke . . . I think it was broken when I came to . . . but then that woman kept stepping on it."

Inside I was screaming, but on the outside, I schooled my expression. *Stepping on it? Jesus Fucking Christ.*

"I don't have a leg," she whispered, her misery plain. "You can't call me Legs anymore."

"Doesn't matter, babe. I got you. We're gonna find that bitch and guess the fuck what? Rain justice."

She didn't say anything more, only sobbed.

Aly alternated between sobbing and sleeping for days, but refused to say anything more. The physical therapy people came and went, and she merely nodded or shook her head when necessary.

It broke my heart that she wouldn't talk to me, but I understood. She had a lot to process, so I gave her the space she needed, mentally anyway. Physically, I stuck to her like glue.

I ignored Shirley, who waited in the hall or the waiting room for a week. I slept and showered in Aly's room, despite her ignoring me. When the nurses kicked me out of the room to tend to her, I did push-ups and sit-ups and pull-ups and power jabs in the waiting room.

Bess checked on Aly's mom, and then went home to her own family and my dog. Tony brought me clothes from the gym. Reluctantly, I called Camper and asked her to check on the construction. After all, she owed me. When we spoke on the phone, I told her about Aly, and we eventually made the connection between Camper's stalker and the woman who attacked Aly. The police were able to get a pretty good sketch from Camper's description.

Afraid of his woman, who I learned was named Marina, Gus Cameron turned himself in. He spilled everything she'd been up to, including how he'd found Aly and what condition she was in when he dragged Marina away. He did call 911 to send help, but by then, Shirley had taken Aly. The cops had thought it was a prank call when they found an empty barn, so didn't bother to look close enough for blood or evidence.

Barry stopped in daily to report to Aly on the case's progress, stale smoke and coffee on his breath. Aly continued to be silent. She listened to his updates with a blank expression and nodded at what seemed like the appropriate times.

Drew Fucking Burnes sent flowers. I wanted to throw them in the trash, but instead I set them on her windowsill and read Aly the card. She didn't even smile as I hoped she would.

The police finally caught Marina. While searching her bag, they found a key to a storage locker where she kept enough evidence to lock her up without bail until she would stand trial. She had been the one setting up hate crimes all over the city. Yes, Cameron shared beliefs with her, but he was mostly the hired muscle and Marina was the mastermind.

Of course, Cameron immediately cooperated, and I didn't know what kind of plea deal they cut with him. But at the end of the day, I had to give him props—he got that bitch away from Aly with only a gun shot in the air. Who knew what his original plan was, or if he even had one. According to Barry, Cameron probably thought he could protect his girl and pin it on someone else. But he rolled over like a dead fish when given the chance, handing over Marina, unharmed and smeared in guilt.

With all of us rallied around her, fierce Aly didn't lift from the silent fog she'd cocooned herself in. She went about everything that was expected of her, doing her stretches and following the hospital staff's instructions. But all the while she stared blankly, not speaking, ignoring what happened to her, and apparently not caring.

One afternoon, a woman named Hilary showed up to visit. I assumed this was the roommate Aly had mentioned once before, and I welcomed the support, swallowing back tears. I was a mess, and not a very manly one. Everything between Aly and me had grown so deep and gone so hard, I didn't know much other than she was the one for me, and she was lying there suffering.

I didn't care whether it was irrational or not. I just knew she was my "it girl," and I needed her back.

Apparently, Aly's friends at work had called this Hilary, and she immediately hightailed it to Pittsburgh from Cleveland.

"You must be Jake!" The vivacious Asian chick pulled me in for a hug. The tiny thing must have only weighed a hundred pounds soaking wet, but when she yanked me hard into her skinny arms, I felt comforted for the first time in days.

Relief swept over me as I mumbled, "That's me," into her shiny black hair, trying to steal some of her enthusiasm.

She reached up to pat my back, telling me how sorry she was for what we were going through. "I love this girl too, you know," she whispered, then pulled away and looked up into my eyes, hers glistening with unshed tears.

All too soon, she pulled away and seemed to bury her worry deep inside before she plopped down on the bed next to Aly. Smiling brightly as she chattered about random inconsequential things, she dug through her enormous purse until she found a hairbrush, then nudged Aly until she sat up and turned her back so Hilary could brush her hair.

Aly didn't speak, but tears slipped from her eyes as Hilary rambled on.

When she noticed Aly reach up to swipe away a tear, Hilary stopped and caught Aly's chin, turning her face toward hers. "Aly, honey, I know you don't trust easy, but you trust me, and I'm telling you it's going to work out," she whispered.

Reaching her hand to brush Aly's hair away from her face, Hilary went on. "See that man? He's it for you. I knew when you told me about him a few weeks ago. I could see the twinkle in your eye. It had never been there before, and I want to see it back. So you get better and when you are, you'll see I'm right."

When she left a few hours later, Hilary squeezed my hand, sticking her business card with her cell number written on it inside my palm. "Stay strong and keep me posted, Jake. She doesn't have too many people in her corner. She needs you." With a gentle kiss on the cheek, Hilary left me to pretend to be brave again.

After ten days, my beautiful Alyson Road went to rehab a mute, and we—Bess, Lane, James, Barry, and even Camper—all continued to move forward, crossing our fingers she'd come around soon.

CHAPTER TWENTY-EIGHT

aly

DISGUSTING salty-smelling sweat trickled down my back. Even the underarms of my T-shirt were soaked through.

"Good job, Aly!" my physical therapist chirped at me.

I didn't respond; instead I repeated the task once more. Using only my arms, I transferred myself from the chair to the bed and back again. My right foot dragged on the floor, and my stupid stump hung there useless because I refused the temporary prosthetic, wanting the constant reminder of my half-a-woman status.

I went back and forth a few more times before finally falling back on the pillow. Settling my right leg and shutting my eyes, I tried to sneak in a cat nap, even though I didn't believe they would let me stay there and be comfortable.

"Aly, we have one more exercise, and then you can go back to your room," Little Miss Chipper said, and I nodded.

I didn't talk anymore. Sadness coursed through my entire body, rendering words useless.

Why did I need to speak anyway? I wasn't practicing law. I wasn't working or studying or climbing stairs. I wasn't falling in love. I was in an awful-smelling, ugly, bleached environment surrounded with other victims. Some suffered from strokes while others had been in accidents. They were a cross-section of society, both old people and young daredevils, and I despised all of them.

I was rehabbing, which was another way of saying I was broken and they were trying to fix me. There was no cure for losing half your leg, apparently.

"Crutches or chair?"

Sunny, my therapist, was so peppy and cute. She was all smiles, all the time, and I hated her.

I heaved myself back to the chair and up onto my crutches. No way was I riding in a wheelchair. They tried to do that with me a few times, and I became so combative, they had to sedate me.

We did the stupid stretches on the mat, then Sunny worked out the kinks in my neck. The neck rub was heavenly, so I actually muttered a thank-you before loping back to my room on the crutches.

Finally settled in my bed with my eyes closed, enjoying a quiet moment being left the hell alone, I heard a soft knock on my door and huffed out a sigh.

Who now?

No one ever left me alone. Jake came every day, always with goodies in hand, both for me and for the nurses. Sometimes they were smoothies, other days they were some organic vegan brownies that were supposed to be full of protein. Whatever. I wasn't interested, not in food or anything else.

Jake would murmur with the nursing staff about me, probably going over my progress with them, and then would sit with me while I didn't say shit. He'd run his hand up and down my arm, telling me all about the gym. And every day, he would say he was sorry.

He mentioned never letting anything bad happen to me again each time he visited. But what if *I* was the bad thing happening to him?

"I don't know what happened with us," he told me two days ago. "It was quick. One minute I was a bachelor, and the next minute, I wanted to take care of you every second. It was like I saw a better me in you. I know I bossed you around and made you move, but something hit me hard with you." Trying to catch my eye, he leaned closer and whispered, "Please, Aly, say something."

Yesterday it was, "Aly, I care for you, I'm not going anywhere." He'd brought dinner—grilled chicken and rice—and I refused it, pointing at my tray.

I'd been here at rehab close to a month. Each day, I banked on them giving up on my bullshit, but apparently they decided I was getting a prosthetic. It was ugly and a poor replacement for what once had resided there. Then I was going home.

Well, not home, to Jake's place. Of course, I assumed the crew would all be there, the usual bystanders always encouraging me to "do it" and "conquer this" and "achieve that."

"Aly?" my visitor called.

I swiped a hand across my face, concealing the newly fallen tears, then looked toward the door. Bess stood there, her brown hair flowing down her back, her two skinny legs tucked into dark jeans, and a broad smile on her face.

"Can I come in?" she asked, false enthusiasm filling her words and facial expression.

I nodded, although another cheerleading session was the last thing I wanted.

She sat down on the edge of the bed like she did all the other times she visited. Usually she'd rattle on about her baby or Jake, how much he cared for me, or something like the weather. Summer and the promise of new life was everywhere except in my ugly, desolate rehab room.

I was stuck inside, unable to do anything. Who cared about the weather?

Bess held my gaze and used her no-nonsense "mom" voice. "We are going to talk today, Aly. You're going to speak to me, and we're going to make plans for when you go home."

Saying nothing, I just stared at her as if she were speaking a foreign language.

Undeterred, Bess went on. "We've all given you time, but that ends now. Jake is a wreck. He's going to murder someone if you don't come around. It's time for you to be strong for yourself. You're alive and that's what counts."

When I raised an eyebrow, she sighed.

"Look, if you can't be strong for yourself, be strong for him. Jake's barely hanging on. The guilt, the sadness, everything, it's tearing him apart. He's hopeful one moment and depressed the next. Then there's Shirley. He hates her for what she did when he was a kid, but is grateful to her for saving you. It's driving him nuts."

No one had ever bothered to fill me in, but I finally put it all together about my rescuer by eavesdropping on Bess and Jake talking in the hallway. Shirley wanted back in Jake's good graces and to make amends, so she was using my severed leg as a bargaining chip. Apparently Jake wasn't buying it. Yes, he was thankful she found me and told her so, but that didn't erase all that had happened years ago.

When I learned that, I'd sat in my hospital bed and half wished she'd have let me bleed out and die. After all, my life was over. I was nothing more than half a woman, a gimp. No one would want me, and why would they? I didn't deserve happiness.

Shirley had come to see me once, back when I was still in the hospital. Bess turned her away at the door, but promised to call her and keep her posted from time to time. Although that was what Bess had said, I wasn't sure if she'd followed through with it.

As Bess sat there lecturing me, alternately giving me a pep talk and then trying to make me feel guilty, emotion spiraled up my spine. I was sick of all the sappiness and wishful thoughts. I was going to *murder someone*, forget Jake.

Practically spitting fire, I finally spoke, letting Bess have it. "He looks fine to me. Jake. All buff and hot. Girls must be climbing all over him."

Her eyebrows rose with surprise and she gaped at me. It was the most I'd spoken since the day I woke up with one and a half legs.

Giving her no time to respond, I shouted, "Look at me, I'm half a woman! I can't compete with those gym girls, and Mr. Hard-body deserves better. A real woman, one who can get down on her knees or wrap her legs around his waist while he slams her into the wall." Lowering my voice, I narrowed my eyes on her and said, "Did you know he likes to dominate, be in control? What about with a gimp?"

It was mean of me; I knew that. Bess didn't need to hear about her brother-in-law's sexual proclivities. I knew it was over the top, but I wanted her gone. A month's worth of pent-up anger and self-pity spewed from my mouth as I sat up straighter, laying into Bess whether she deserved it or not.

"He needs a woman who works, uses her degree she fought to earn. Not a woman who hobbles like an old lady afraid to go back to work, one who's scared and looks over her shoulder, worried that someone's going to kidnap her again."

Bess gave me a sad smile. "You are a whole woman, Aly. *You* are who Jake wants, not the girls at the gym. I've never seen him at peace until the few weeks you two were together and happy."

The tears turned on again, a raging flood that ran down my face. "No. I don't want to believe it."

In my heart, I knew Jake was devoted and dedicated, but my brain couldn't accept that. My emotions had reverted to the first few weeks I knew Jake, when I wanted to pretend there was nothing between us, that he wasn't a sweet and kind man, and I was only having fun.

But what we had was so much more, almost right from the beginning. It had been a strange sequence of events, but they belonged to me, to us. The truth was, I loved the man, and for Jake's sake, I couldn't allow myself to get wrapped up in his life again, or allow Jake to get attached to me.

"I can't listen to this," I mumbled.

"Yes, you will," Bess said with certainty. "Listen, you know I was an addict. I was beyond broken back then, and it took me years to get my life together. I get it; I get *you*. When I met Lane, I didn't think I deserved him. And now I think, what if I didn't have him, or our baby, or even James?"

Swiping at my wet cheeks, I let out a snotty snort. "That's different. Look at you—you're young, sexy, beautiful, making a difference in the world." I pointed at her slight frame settled next to me.

"You're all those things too," she said.

Wildly I shook my head, pressing my lips together, refusing to engage in discussion.

Bess grabbed my arm and shook me. "Aly! You are not shutting down anymore. Stop it."

I shrugged away from her hold and turned my face away from her. The goddamn tears came fierce and heavy, slanting in a hot trail down my cheek.

"You're going back to Jake's," Bess said firmly. "His home, not the rental. Did you know he renovated a room in his basement? He brought equipment from the gym for you to rehab with. You're going to get your life back, Aly. For you. For him. For me. He's too afraid to ask you to live, to fight. He's going through the motions, praying you'll come around, and he needs you. He needs to take care of you."

"Some days, I want to die," I said, sobbing. "At first, I couldn't stop thinking about living when I was stuck in that barn. Now I wish I'd died."

Bess got up and lay down with me, curling her body around mine. "You are not going to die until you're old, Aly. You've got a full life of living ahead of you."

She stroked my hair as I sobbed, rocking me in her arms until I couldn't cry anymore. We fell asleep like that, our breaths commingling, our bodies curled up together like kittens.

She was the sister I never had, the confidante I'd always dreamed of. Curled up in Bess Wrigley's arms, I dreamed of growing old, like she said. In my dreams, I was gray and Jake was still fit and gorgeous, but his arm was flung around me, holding me close as he kissed my temple.

"Ladies."

The bed depressed next to me. With one eye opened, I saw Jake.

He was a mess. His hair was unruly, thick stubble lined his face, dark circles ringed his eyes, and new veins bulged along his biceps.

He looked terrible, and it crushed me that I hadn't noticed his suffering, being so caught up in my own tragedy and all. Here was this guy I'd thought I was falling for, and despite my being a total nut, he cared for me. Yes, he was bossy, and swept me up into a whirlwind of a romance, going way overboard by moving me to a new place and buying us a dog.

But he'd made me want to live once. Could he do it again? Could I live a full and happy life like Bess said?

"I'm going to go," Bess said in a hushed voice. Sweeping her dark hair behind her ear, she pushed off the bed and stood up, her eyes speaking clearly to me. *Jake is a good man.* She glanced at Jake and nodded before she slipped out of the room.

Jake took her place in the bed. I moved my right leg a little bit, letting the tingles escape. The phantom tingles tickled their way down my missing left leg, and I let them run their course. I knew they weren't there, but I pretended I was whole for one moment.

"Aly, come back to me, babe."

Settling in, he kicked off his running shoes and snuggled closer. "Come back to me. I love you."

I love you?

Trembling, I lifted my hand to touch him but let it fall. He needs you, I told myself. So I lifted my hand again and brought it to Jake's broad back, then drifted it in slow strokes up and down his spine. "I'm going to try to come back, Jake."

Somewhere between declaring I wanted to die and falling asleep, I'd decided I wanted to live. I didn't know if it was what Bess said or my dream that had changed me, but I was ready to live.

"Good," he said, and snuggled closer.

As I stroked his back, I felt a lump under his shirt and panicked. "What is that?"

"It's all good, Aly-cat." He stood abruptly and tugged off his shirt, his movements sending his abs and arms rippling. He turned his back to me and reached over to rip a bandage off his shoulder blade.

I blinked, unsure what I was seeing was real. Tattooed across his shoulder blade was one of those silhouettes of a woman's legs, except this one had one real leg and one with a prosthetic. It should have been ugly, but it wasn't. It was very sexy. Red stiletto fuck-me heels adorned each foot, both the real one and the prosthetic, and underneath, *Legs* was written in a beautiful script.

"You ready to get your new leg, babe?"

CHAPTER TWENTY-NINE

aly

"**S**HOOT!" The bottle fell to the floor, sending bright orange lotion squirting everywhere except where I wanted. Deflated, I slammed my palm into the counter and grabbed my crutches. I let out a defeated sigh as I hobbled over to the stupid bottle, bending over on one foot to grab it, and cursing the fact I didn't put on my damn prosthetic.

I needed a break from that mechanical hunk of junk. Of course, it was top of the line; I had government-employee health insurance. It still stank; it was ugly and foreign. And it wasn't me. For God's sake, all I wanted was to go into the damn bathroom and have some girl time without having to strap on my suit of armor.

With my right leg laid out straight in front of me and my good ole stump there too, I slumped down on the floor and snatched up the bottle. It was the Fourth of July, and I hadn't spent much time outside so I was pale as a ghost. Was it too much to want to look sexy, seductive even, with an uneven body?

I slathered the hideous self-tanning lotion over my muscles

and curves. My right leg had definitely benefited from the grueling workouts; it was toned and firm. My arm muscles flexed as I blended the cream into my fair skin. I was more fit than ever before, everywhere but my left leg. My right quad was sculpted, my calf equally as defined. I could have run a million steps with two legs, and they wouldn't have been this muscular.

I guess one is better than none.

Shoving all of it to the back of my mind, I went back to prettying myself. I'd never been self-conscious before. I used to take care of myself, making health and wellness a priority but not a life mission. Forced to live within a budget in my old life, I'd bought flattering, somewhat sexy professional and casual clothes on sale. Now I lived with a muscle man and was a semi-cripple.

Okay, so I hadn't shoved my inadequacies as far back as I'd hoped. If I wasn't so fragile, why did everyone continue to treat me as if I were?

There was a knock on the door, followed by it opening a crack. "Al, you good?"

"Yep," I squeaked out.

The door opened wider. "Babe? What're you doing on the floor?"

Proud of myself for holding the tears at bay, I pushed up to one leg and leaned against the counter. "I was putting on some cream. I'm good."

Jake didn't waste any time. He stalked across the bathroom tile barefoot and shirtless, his workout shorts hanging low on his waist, and picked me up.

I slapped his back. "Jake! You're getting self-tanner all over you."

"So what!"

Tossing me over his shoulder, he walked me over to the couch in the far side of his—our—bedroom. A throw pillow fell to the floor as he set me down.

"Get it," he commanded Maverick, and the growing puppy gingerly picked up the pillow and brought it to Jake. In addition to a slew of PT people and gym buffs, a dog trainer came twice a week to train Mav to be helpful to me.

It was all too much, but between Bess and Jake, there was no saying "no." Bess steamrolled over everyone at rehab, demanding the best from every social worker and discharge planner in the place. She knew all kinds of lingo from volunteering with addicts, and she tossed it around like confetti on New Year's Eve.

"Why are you smearing this shit all over your beautiful skin?" Jake wrinkled his nose and ran a finger down the gross orange color streaked down my leg.

"I've barely seen the sun, and now we're going to a party."

"Aly-cat," he growled, and gathered me in his lap.

He put his hands on either side of my face and looked into my eyes. I wondered what he saw; his blue eyes were tortured with equal parts understanding and anger.

"I don't like this crap all over you. I want you the way you are. You haven't been outside because you're training."

"Rehabbing."

"No, training for life." He ran his lips over my jaw, speaking into my ear as he added, "With me."

He kissed me; not a rough kiss, but tender, like his touch. We'd made love since the accident, and it was always soft and gentle. I'd be on the bottom, propped up on pillows, and Jake would get me off with his fingers before slipping inside me and riding me slowly. He didn't gather my hands above me anymore, nor did he give me a little spank on the thigh or roughly snag my whole leg and shove it up on his shoulder like he used to. The days of Jake needing to be in charge were gone.

"Stop!" I blurted, creating distance from his lips brushing across mine.

He pulled back his head and raised an eyebrow.

"Stop," I whispered. "Please, take me off your lap."

Afraid of me—as usual—Jake set me down on the couch and walked to the bed. "What's wrong?" He sat on the edge of the comforter, his bare feet restless on the hardwood in front of him.

"You can't keep treating me like I'm a piece of fine china," I said, and he swallowed and ran his hand over his forehead. "You don't want me the way you used to want me, and I don't want to be some guilty project for you so you can feel whole. I know I don't look like a real woman, but I am one."

"Fuck me!" He stood and punched the wall. Plaster spilled onto the floor, sending dust particles afloat in the still air.

"You are not some guilty *project*," he said, sneering on the last word. "You're not any project. Don't be fucking ridiculous. A *project*? Get real!"

With his arms flexed and his amped-up breathing, he looked poised to fight. But not with me. With himself, his inner demons, whomever he wanted to blame for his reluctance.

"Then what am I? You have all this equipment in *your* house, a therapy dog, and me with one leg in your bed. You've moved me twice now. When we first met, you demanded I allow you to be in charge. Now you're all touchy-feely, carrying me all over the place. I'm not a baby, Jake! I'm a woman."

This time, Jake brought up his other hand and punched a matching hole in the wall. "I told Bess I was treating you too gently! I knew I was fucking up. Doc Wells told me too. Al, I don't know what to do. I'm a helpless man. Up until I met you, I barely stayed the night with anyone. My ass was out the door before breakfast."

"Then go back and do that!" I screamed.

"But I don't want to," he shouted, pacing back and forth in front of me as he ran one hand through his hair. Then he stopped in front of me where I sat on the couch and glared at me.

"I want to throw you on your stomach and pull your hands above your fucking head and slam my cock into you from behind. Then I want us to shower—together—and I want to take you out to dinner. But you only have one leg! One fucking leg, Aly! And I don't know how to deal with that other than to take care of you like I've been doing. To me, you're still Aly. But I want you to be my Aly-cat, and I want to plunder you and love you, just like I always did. "

He made his way close and slid onto his knees in front of me, laying his head in my lap.

"But that's my problem, not yours." I didn't touch him when I said it; I just shut my eyes and sucked in a deep breath.

"It *is* my problem," he said, mumbling into my lap. "I could've been there, saved you, found you. Fuck, I could've prevented the whole thing from happening in the first place. Instead, Shirley was there. The person I hate the most."

I leaned back, trying to see his face. "Is that what this is about? Shirley?"

I knew she continued to plague him. The thought of her watching him, keeping an eye on his brother and niece, messed with Jake's head. He hated that she pretended to care, and despised her for rescuing me. He panicked at the thought of letting his anger go, not knowing what to do with himself without it.

If he let go of it all, he'd be absolved. I learned this from Dr. Wells during one of the two times I'd gone with him to see her. He wanted me to go more, but I'd shied away, unsure of what we were or what we were doing.

"The last two decades of my life have been about Shirley," he mumbled. "I never wanted to fall in love and then I did. With you. All I wanted was to forget her and everything she reminded me of, but now she's front and center in my life again, and I hate it."

"She doesn't have to be, Jake." I brought a shaky hand down to the top of his head and smoothed over his buzz cut. He'd cut his long layers when summer came and he was busy, not only with his businesses but with me. The burden.

"So what? She found me and did a good deed. I'm happy and alive. I wasn't at first, but now I am. It doesn't mean I forgive her for past wrongdoings or want to be best friends with her, Jake. I'm just reminded she's human like my dad, or the guys who got to him. I'm reminded to be better. Teach my kids better. That we have the power as people to do good."

He lifted his head to stare at me, his eyes wide. "Kids?" he said, his voice all gravelly. "With me?"

"Yes, Jake. I think so. I hope with you, if I can, but I don't know. I don't want to push you. We can't deny your past, but we need to let it go. You need to let it go. Your past is your past. And your mistakes were those of a little boy, and I know you know that now."

He nodded.

Kids? Where is this coming from?

I hadn't thought about the future much, other than what the hell were we—Jake and me. But suddenly the subject of kids was tumbling from my mouth, and Jake fixated on that one word.

What did that mean? Did he want to make more of a life with me? Would he go back to the old Jake? Would he be able to leave Shirley in the past where she belonged?

"Do you still want to take me from behind?" I asked on a whisper.

"I do. So fucking bad," he said, and grabbed my hand. "But you've already had so much taken away from you. I don't want to take all the power too. Do you get that? I'm trying to be considerate."

"Jake, don't you see that you doing that, being that way, is not being yourself. That you not acting like yourself takes something away from me?" I ran my hand over his short hair, the tiny bristles like smooth velvet on my palm.

"Remember when you told me all that stuff about you?" I asked. "You thought I'd go running for the hills, but I didn't blink. I held your hand and supported you. I've fallen for you from the beginning, just as you are, Jake. All of you—your demanding side, your guilt, your big heart. Ever since the night I met you in jail, you stirred something to life in my heart, but I didn't know it yet. And then you came blazing in with all your crazy ideas, and I was done."

"Aly, I just can't believe it."

"You can."

Jake knelt closer, then reached up and kissed me. His tongue swiped the roof of my mouth and he bit down on my lower lip. Without letting go of my mouth, he brought my hands around my back and pulled me tight, securing me in place as he sucked my nipple through my shirt.

A desperate moan rose up in my throat. Jake brought his hands to the neckline of my tank and he ripped it right down the middle, then unclipped the hook on the front of my bra and brought his mouth back down on my bare breast. When he made contact with my skin, my nipple went hard in his mouth, and I shoved my breasts further in his face.

"No, Aly. I'm in charge." It came out as a growl, a command, a no-arguments-allowed demand.

Yes!

His tongue slid down my belly. It was tighter than before, since all I did was use my core for balance.

"Love this," he whispered as his tongue grazed along my belly button. In a moment of rage, I'd forced Bess to take me to get a belly-button piercing. I had no idea what possessed me. I'd always been such a good girl, and I still was.

But I had discovered there was a tiny naughty side hidden inside me, and I wanted to feel sexy, no matter what. I liked being smart and sassy. It reminded me of the interrogation room where I first met the marvelous man currently kneeling between my legs.

Jake's tongue flicked the small silver circle with a few dark blue beads before he slid off my workout shorts. Now there was nothing between his tongue and my clit. I'd thought about getting that pierced too, but chickened out.

Guess I'm only a little dirty.

"This good, babe?" he asked, his scruff dragging along my inner thigh.

"Yes! Yes, Jake," I said, loud enough the neighbors might have heard.

A load moan floated from my lips as Jake settled right where I needed him. Flicking my spot with the tip of his tongue, he pushed his finger deep inside me, and I pushed against him, wanting more.

He swirled his rough mouth around my soft lips, the friction from his beard increasing my desire, tickling me in all the right spots. It made up for the loss of his longer hair, which used to tease and taunt me.

I came fast and hard on a whimper as Mav's head brushed my leg, and tamped down the scream burning up my throat. The pup was probably being protective, worried that I was hurting. We'd need to leave him downstairs from now on during our naughty time.

"Jake," I said on a sigh, catching my breath.

He focused on my eyes as he stood and dropped his shorts, leaving him ready for me—his perfect V on display, his erection reaching for me, a drop of pre-come slipping out. He snatched me up fast and tossed me onto my stomach on the bed, then climbed behind me and entered without warning.

Thank goodness I'd gone on birth control after rehab. It seemed appropriate with us temporarily living together, but hadn't made a difference until now.

"Yes," I said on another moan. "Don't go easy on me."

He stretched my arms above my head and held them tightly while he drove into me hard. I wriggled a little under him, thinking how delicious it was to feel so much sensation. My whole body tingled as I ran my right toes along the bed, thankful they were there. Then I clenched my inner walls around Jake and was pretty thrilled he was there inside me. A moment later he came on a shout, then toppled on top of me and didn't move.

And *that* was the most delicious feeling of all.

Later that evening, we sat on the deck watching as fireworks erupted above the stadium. We'd skipped getting together with everyone for the holiday, and Jake opted to grill instead. He'd ordered me to sit on the chaise with wine while he made dinner, but I refused. Wearing my prosthesis, I moved around the kitchen without too much trouble, assembling a pie and baked ziti while sipping wine. It was the most normal time I'd spent since the incident, and it felt good.

Really good. Normal, even.

While we ate, I asked about the gym, the deal with the baseball team, the construction, and for a few hours, I felt like Aly. Jake had been giving me small updates over the last few weeks, but I wanted to hear it all. He smiled when I asked about his work with the baseball team, and he downright glowed when he explained Fizzle Cubed was on schedule for its grand opening.

He asked my opinion about the equipment in the basement, if it was quality or shitty, explaining he was thinking of adding a PT department to the new joint.

"How could I say anything was shitty? I have my own private rehab, Jake," I said as blue and red bursts overtook the sky. We moved to the outdoor sofa for the fireworks display. Jake sat and wrapped his arms around me as I leaned back into him.

"Babe, it's helpful for me to know." He pinched my side, and I laughed like I hadn't laughed in a long while.

Maybe it was the wine, maybe it was Jake, or both.

After I gave him my thoughts about the equipment, he asked about the townhouse. He fired questions into my ear, questions too difficult to discuss face-to-face.

"Do you think the stairs are too much? I see you're not sliding down them on your ass as much, but seriously . . . maybe we want a ranch?"

"Jake, I'm not going to stay here forever," I whispered into the night sky, watching as multicolored bursts popped overhead.

He sat quietly, not reacting at all.

Convinced he didn't hear me over the booms, I focused on the fireworks, then gasped as I was whipped through the air. Jake had twisted out from underneath me, lifted me up, and set me back down on my rear. Then he knelt in front of me.

Admittedly, I was confused for a beat—all that sudden flying around—until I realized what he was about to do.

"No! No, Jake! Not now. Please." I yanked at his shoulders for him to get up, and he quickly schooled the hurt rushing over his features.

"No! Jake, don't do that. It's not that I haven't sort of thought about this very moment, before all this." I waved my hand at my leg. "Just not now. I have to get a plan in my head. I'm not even sure if I should still stay here, freeloading off you."

He crept up next to me, pulled me in tight, and pushed my hair behind my ears. His expression relaxed and he kissed my cheek all the way to my ear. When he pulled on the lobe with his teeth, I felt it—everywhere.

"I can accept you're not ready for it all," he said, "but you're not going anywhere. This isn't freeloading. This is two people making a commitment, Aly-cat. I've never done that with anyone, never wanted to with anyone but you. So you're stuck."

I leaned my head into the crook of his neck, and when I ran my hand over his chest, he asked, "Feel that beating? Steady and even? That's how I feel about you. We're steady and even. I know it's been all quick and shit, but I'm in my thirties now. It's about time I had some good in my life, and that goodness is you."

We kissed, my heart not beating one bit steadily. It thumped with pride at Jake's last words. I was his goodness.

He gave my lower lip a gentle bite, then his tongue swiped along my lips and found its way inside my mouth where it brushed along mine. I felt myself scooted back into his lap as he continued to explore my lips and mouth.

As his erection dug into my butt and the fireworks still burned overhead, I came up with a plan.

The next morning, we had the gang over for brunch. Bess joined me by the sink and whispered in my ear, "Happy to see you up and around, Al." With her arm wrapped around me, she gave me a squeeze and asked what she could do to help in the kitchen. I told her to sit down with a virgin Bloody Mary and cuddle her baby girl, who was toddling all around the place.

I was scared to death Maddy was going to fall down the steps or get hurt on a few pieces of PT equipment we'd moved upstairs to be more convenient for me. I made a mental note to let Jake know I loved the place for now, but if we stayed the course, we needed a more family-friendly place.

Then I mentally slapped myself for even thinking that way. What the heck was with me and all this kid stuff?

"Oh, I'll cuddle my baby girl," Bess sang as she scooped up Maddy and kissed her all over her wild hair.

Immediately, I stopped what I was doing and watched, more and more fascinated with the idea of having a baby. Would I be able to do that with my leg? Snatch my babies up and swing them around, covering them with kisses? Would Jake want that with me? Would he help?

A tear slid down my face as I was slicing berries for a trifle. I didn't know why I was so emotional all of a sudden. Then the phone rang, and it was the nursing home where my mom was, notifying me that she'd passed in the early morning hours.

I cried a little after I hung up and explained to Bess what had happened, but Mom was better off. Living without memories was no way to live. I knew that now that I was making them—even if it was only Jake and me.

"What was your momma's full name?" Bess asked.

"Winona West Road," I told her as Jake made his way to my side, running his hand down my arm and kissing my hair. "West was her maiden name. Winona was a family name."

"That's the circle of life, you know. One life out, and another one in," Bess said. "And I think we'll name this one after your momma." She patted her flat belly and smiled like a fool at Lane.

"Really?" I asked.

"Really. We're family." Bess came over with Maddy and held me tight. "Group hug," she told her little girl, and all of a sudden I was crying happy tears while being strangled by a toddler.

And this time, no wimpy little sad tears for me. This time I cried big, full, ecstatic teardrops.

CHAPTER THIRTY

jake
One year later

A LY ran her hand along my back, her fingers gently tracing every inch of the way to my tattoo before heading back down toward my ass. Her touch ghosted over the crack, setting small blazes along the way, burning me up with need from just her soft fingertips. I was flat on my stomach, Aly spread out next to me, her chin on my shoulder, her right leg thrown over mine.

Oh, those legs, they had me salivating that night when we met in jail so long ago. I never wanted a pair of legs to be wrapped around me as badly as I had back then. Or now—even if it wasn't possible. My dick was hard as fuck against the mattress, but I didn't move. No way I was missing out on this moment of Aly touching me.

Keeping my head buried face-first in the pillow, I felt small kisses being placed on my shoulder, up and down the pair of legs permanently marked there. Aly's long hair tickled my cheek as she leaned in and continued to run laps along my spine, taking the time to do wide circle eights around my traps.

"Love you, Jake," she said, her voice hoarse and sultry.

"Love you, Aly-cat," I grumbled, the desire evident in my words.

The patio doors were open, allowing the salty ocean breeze to waft through our bungalow. It was still dark out, early morning before the sun breached the sky, the time I would normally get up to pound some iron at home or the gym. But this was my honeymoon, and I wasn't moving.

"You good, babe?"

"Mm-hmm," she mumbled as she slid completely on top of me, her front flush to my back. Her kisses traced the nape of my neck while both her hands wrapped around the front of me. I lifted my pelvis, granting her access between the mattress and my cock, but she didn't take advantage of it right away. Her fingers tickled my groin area, teasing the seam between my thigh and the promised land.

"Al . . . you're killing me."

"Shh," she whispered in my ear before sucking on my earlobe. "I'm taking my time."

"I got all the time in the world with you now. I got you back safe and sound, and I made an honest woman of you. But if I want to get in you quick, why can't a man get what he wants?" I begged.

Yes, I beg now. Beg for my wife.

All. The. Time.

Her hand wrapped around the target and gave a small squeeze.

"Harder," I couldn't stop myself from commanding, and she obeyed.

I ground into her hand, the tip of my cock hitting the satiny sheets, her warm hand rubbing me tight and rough without stopping.

"I'm gonna come from a handy, babe."

"S'okay." Her words and the sound of the ocean lapping the shore drifted over my ear, tumbling deep into my soul. All she said was *s'okay*, and I wanted to marry her all over again.

Everything with Aly was beautiful, especially after we got over all the hurdles. It was worth it. All of it. I never thought I'd love a woman this way, more than myself. But I did.

When we'd stood together in front of our family at our wedding, and she told me she loved me and whispered, "Jason, I mean all of you, including all your past transgressions," I was done in. She took everything as it came—my moods, my proclivities and wants, and all my fuckups. She was the first woman to call me Jason since my mom, and it sounded right coming off her lips.

My brother and his family, a priest, Hilary, and James, those were the only people we invited. It was a small affair in Lane's backyard. Bess had planned the whole event in five seconds flat with James over the phone. It was simple and sweet, understated and beautiful, just like my wife.

Now, there was nothing sweet about the vixen as she fisted me hard the way I needed. I grunted as I shoved my morning wood within her grip.

Pretty sure I liked her from the first minute in jail. Honest to fucking God, I was that kind of sap now. I didn't know it would be like this when I walked out of the jail cell a free man on Christmas morning. When we kept running into each other, I'd thought maybe she would rescue me from a life of selfishness by letting me do something noble, protect her or save her, or some shit like that.

Instead, she needed me to protect her forever, and it almost cost her life and my soul. It did cost her leg and my sanity while she was missing.

My balls rose up, full and ready, and I tried to distract myself by thinking of a barbell hitting the mat. She felt too good, and I wasn't ready to blow my load.

Doc Wells was helping me accept that Aly's kidnapping wasn't my fault. Sometimes Aly and I went together to see her; other times, I went by myself. I was slow when it came to these things, but Aly took all of me, including all my past transgressions, just like she'd promised at our wedding.

"Fuck!" I blurted. Her hand was soft and supple from the day before. We'd waded in the ocean, Aly in my arms, the salt lapping all around us, and the sun kissing our skin.

"Maybe I'll do this every morning when we get back, keep you home from the gym," Aly teased, slowing her pace up and down my cock, running her finger over the tip and then squeezing me hard.

I didn't answer, just let out a loud rumble as I came all over the thousand-dollar-a-night bed.

Fucking show her what she did to me.

Shifting my hips up and knocking Aly off-balance, I flipped us around. I wiped my sticky hand on the blanket, gripped the sheet, and cleaned myself off, promising myself I'd leave a tip for housekeeping later.

I ran my hand over her shiny red hair and down her smooth back. "If I miss the gym, babe, the body goes to hell. Don't think you'd like that."

She rolled her eyes, and I smirked.

"Probably not," she admitted, and leaned in for a kiss. Before I could take her tongue, she pulled away and added, "But I'd love you no matter what, Jake. Want you any way I can have you. Tight body or not." And then she let me have her tongue.

She meant it.

I'd witnessed the way she'd handled Shirley. We couldn't ignore the fact that the woman had saved Aly; that would be both rude and cruel. So we'd thanked her profusely, and Bess had even sent flowers from me. I would have never thought of that, let alone actually done it, yet that was all I could give her. But Shirley wanted more; she wanted all of us—Lane, Bess, Maddy, Aly, and me.

Aly had left it up to me, watching for clues I had changed my mind before she stepped in and put her foot down. Her intervention had started when Shirley called Bess, wanting to come to the wedding and see the ceremony. That was when my girl took charge. She'd picked up the phone to call Shirley and told her no. It was a simple *no*, and that was all she said. No explanations or long guilt-ridden conversations that would have been awkward for both of them.

She told me she'd ended the call with, "Shirl, we know you're there. We know where you are, and we know you're trying to care, but for right now, it's always going to be *no*. If we change our minds about having you be a part of our life, we will come to you."

Aly interrupted my foggy memory by saying, "Babe, I love you no matter what. You know that? Any way you come."

I nodded. I knew it.

"Best thing I know. The only thing I know," I told her, kissing her neck. I traveled my left hand down her rib cage, tickling her hip and caressing her thigh until it ended.

"Jake, let it. We're having a moment, and I don't want to ruin it."

"Nothing's ruined. It's better. You're here." A shudder rippled down my spine at the thought of her not being here.

"With half a leg," she said.

"One and a half is better than none," I protested. "Look at me." I grabbed her chin and forced her to face me. "To me, you're always going to be all legs, and now the one you have is looking pretty fine from PT."

I winked at her and she gave me half a smile. When I tickled her rib cage, she gave me a full smile.

It hurt, and I knew it. Her leg ached, her heart was pained, but it didn't make a difference to me. She was my tough Aly-cat, learning to walk with a prosthetic and training to do a 10-K with a hand cycle. Her arms never looked so amazing, but with Aly it didn't matter, because her beauty came from within and shone through all that shit.

"Babe, can I continue seducing you?" she asked, and my body rose to the occasion.

"Yeah, I'll be quiet now."

Her hand came around the nape of my neck and pulled me close. She licked the seam of my lips and I let her inside, her tongue sweeping my mouth and brushing against mine.

The silk of her nightgown rode up and bunched under my hard abs, bringing to life the tiny hairs scattered over my body. I wanted her bad. I was desperate to take control, but I'd let her have her way for a while. Her nails scratched my back up and down, down and up, small circles, then big ones. She brought her right leg around my back and dug her heel into my ass to press her cunt against my cock, which was ready again.

My tip rubbed her clit and she let out a long purr, which was my undoing. Grabbing her arms, I pinned her hands above her head and snatched the leather ties from the nightstand. After I secured her hands in place and tied them to the wrought-iron headboard, I began my descent to her pussy.

"Jake, I was in charge," she grumbled as my tongue lapped up her creamy skin.

"Not anymore," I replied, and bit down on one of her nipples.

I blew my hot breath on the sensitive point, allowing my tongue to love it gently. Then I bit the other one, repeating the same tenderness I had a moment before. Her nipples stood at attention on her chest, pink and reaching for my mouth.

"Gorgeous. Fucking stunning."

"More."

"Who's in charge? Not you, Aly."

"I want more," she said.

Of course I gave in, bringing my mouth down again on her tit. I sucked it until she was squirming and screaming. Finally, I was on the move again, dusting her flat stomach with kisses and making my way to where she wanted me to be. When my tongue grazed her clit, she arched right up into my mouth.

The ocean air swept in from the window, coating our skin with salt. We were in Grand Cayman, but we might as well have been in some basement in the middle of Kansas, because I had no intention of leaving the room. At least we were enjoying the breeze.

"Jake, don't . . ." Aly whimpered when I quickly moved my tongue from her clit. "I want it back," she begged.

I didn't answer. My mouth wandered to the crease where her thigh met her groin, and did a little exploring in the small cavern of sensitive skin. I sucked hard when I made it up to her hip bone, leaving one hickey and then another.

"Please."

That was all she had to say from her sweet mouth, and I was sucking the hell out of her clit, my finger dug deep inside her. I was done teasing, over being gentle, my control snapped. Her hips smacked my face as she tilted off the mattress. Fuck, her glutes were strong as hell when she wanted me to dine on her pussy. She kept her right heel digging into my own glutes, and I was pretty sure my cock was going to snap from the pressure.

I slid a second finger inside her, using the two in synchronicity to find her spot—*the* spot—and put pressure while I dragged my tongue hard over her clit.

"Oh God, Jake," she wailed as she came hard and fast all over my face, her juices tickling the stubble along my jaw.

I sat up and swiped my hair out of my face. It was long again. I hadn't buzzed it since the night Aly made me take charge again. There were fireworks that Fourth of July, and not just in the sky. I shaved it back then so I didn't have to bother with it, but my girl liked her guy's locks to be long enough to pull on. It was nothing but a quick trim these days when I went for a haircut.

"You want your hands back or you want to keep them tied up like a good kitty?" I asked as I propped myself over Aly's sweet and sweaty body.

"Leave 'em," she said.

I didn't need any further talk. I just dove inside her body, my cock hitting the back wall of her pussy fast and furious. After a few pumps, I slowed the pace, dragging my length back and then leisurely sliding inside my most favorite place. We did this dance for a while, fast and slow, slow and fast, before Aly said, "Need my hands."

I rubbed her wrists after reaching up and untying them, never slipping out of her. She fisted my hair and brought me in for a kiss, running the tip of her tongue along my mouth, prying it open and entering without warning.

"Faster." She breathed the word inside my mouth, and I felt it rumble all the way down to my chest.

"Fuck!" I shouted, a loud growl escaping as I came hard inside my wife.

I tumbled off her and trotted off to the bathroom, my dick loose and rubbing my thigh. When I came back with a cloth to wipe Aly with, she was sitting on the edge of her bed, fastening on her prosthetic. "What are you doing, babe?"

"I just wanted to feel complete when you came back."

"You are," I told her. "You're always complete."

I knelt on the floor in front of her, taking her hands in mine and slipping off the prosthetic. I set the piece of metal and fake flesh to the side, bent my head, and kissed her stub. I knew she missed her leg. She couldn't run stairs anymore. I owned a gym, exercised for a living, and that was something she'd always struggled with—the women all around.

"Aly, there's no one but you for me. Not yesterday, today, or tomorrow. This"—I ran my finger along the scar where the doctors severed her leg to save her life—"this is nothing but another piece of your beauty. How you held on and survived for me, so we could live life together."

Her eyes were pained as she looked up at me. "How will we have babies with me hobbling around?"

I knew she thought about it a lot. Since Bess and Lane announced they were pregnant with their second, Aly had mentioned babies here and there.

"What? I don't know, but we'll figure it out. I promise."

"How do you know?" she asked as she ran her hand down my face.

"I just do. What are you trying to say?" I brought my hand under her chin and lifted her eyes to meet mine. My knees dug into the floor, my forehead rested on hers, and my heart beat at a furious pace.

"I'm pregnant."

For a single millisecond, my heart stopped and my throat went dry. Then I remembered this was Aly, and we were meant to save each other; that with her I felt I deserved life, and now we had created life.

I grabbed her cheeks between my hands and kissed the fuck out of her face before I lifted her off the bed and up into my arms. "We're going to be parents?"

"Yes." She nodded, her eyes shining.

"Do you think I'm going to be okay? A good dad?"

Another nod from her. "But what about me? And this?" Her gaze wandered to her stump.

"I'm not worried, Aly-cat. I'm never worried when it comes to you."

I could see her swallowing back tears, and I didn't think we deserved that on our honeymoon—or ever—so I begrudgingly carried her outside the hotel room and onto the balcony. I set my wife, the soon-to-be mother of my child, into a chair, and I pulled up one right next to her.

Hand in hand, we sat and watched the sun rise. If this was what absolution felt like, I liked it.

No, I loved it.

EPILOGUE

jake
Another year later

OH my God, there were kids and dogs everywhere. Maverick rolled in the grass with Lucky, Bess and Lane's new golden retriever puppy, and Luna, our new chocolate Lab pup, while Brooks staked out a quiet spot so he could keep a watchful eye on everyone.

Maddy was running through Lane and Bess's backyard with a kite flying behind her, helped by James, who was all dolled up in linen pants and a dress shirt and carrying the baby he'd recently adopted, Cliffie. He couldn't let Bess have one up on him with her gorgeous family; he wanted one too. He'd finally settled down with a man named Zach, who worked at the hotel where Bess used to work. The two of them gave a baby left at the local church a second chance. Now they were permanent fixtures in all of our lives. Weston toddled behind all of them, desperate to catch up to his big sister, chanting his favorite word for Maddy, "Ma, Ma, Ma."

And under the tree, next to calm Brooks, my beautiful Tabitha slept in a Pack 'n Play, her tiny pink-covered bottom facing up, the mass of red curls matted on her head, her back rising and falling with each breath. I didn't miss a one; my heartbeat was in sync with that little baby.

When Tabitha was born, I decided to take a final stand with Shirley. The tiny person placed in my arms right after she was delivered deserved a whole me, and it was about time I punched the past in the gut.

I knew Shirley had wanted to reconcile and be a part of our lives, but that was never going to be possible with me. I'd gone to see her and thanked her in person for returning Aly—I even gave her a gentle hug. She'd thought it meant one thing, but it actually meant the opposite. I'd explained how I needed to leave her in my past with all the other crap. I was moving forward, and I couldn't do it with her hanging around. I had a new family that was depending on me, and they kept me grounded in the present. To maintain that, I needed to give up my fight with what happened.

I asked her to be happy for me and understand, and if she couldn't, Lane and I would be taking legal action. She'd been upset and disappointed, but after her husband had urged her to cooperate, she'd agreed and stayed away.

Aly supported me in whatever I chose regarding Shirley, but I'd obviously pick Aly and Tabby any day of the week. No contest. With them, I permitted myself to go forward, to stop internalizing my anger. It wasn't exactly perfect absolution, but more a new beginning, "starting over" or whatever Doc Wells called it. I'd come out the other side of whatever hell I'd resided in for so long.

Surrounded by my small circle, I felt confident in my purpose. Like today.

Lane was wearing some designer getup as he manned the grill, and looked as ridiculous as he usually did when I caught him venturing into the outdoors around their house. Bess and Aly came out the back door carrying various salads. Bess was pregnant again; my brother really needed to keep his dick to himself or wrapped the fuck up. Aly's cheeks were slightly pink from the sun, her curves still a little rounded from having a baby, but her limp was now barely noticeable. She wore yoga pants despite it being summer because she still preferred not to put her prosthetic on display. I thought she looked gorgeous either way.

Pregnancy had been rough. The hormonal surges weren't easy to begin with, let alone when you're missing half a leg. But ever since Tabitha was born, Aly had been good. *Really good.* She'd worked for the last year for me, trading in defense strategies for business law. Apparently, while she was home recuperating from the whole incident, she took an online course on business malpractice and how it pertained to exercise facilities. That had been her grand plan, and I'd loved it the moment she'd shared it with me.

Aly had decided she was better suited for contract work. It was objective and clear-cut, and rarely resulted in abductions. Now she headed up my legal team. Actually, she was my legal team, but had been on maternity leave, taking a few months off to be with Tabby. I was her boss; she could do whatever the fuck she wanted.

"How do you want your burgers?" Lane called out.

"Cooked by a real man, not one in some Prada shit!" I yelled back, surreptitiously giving him the finger, to which he responded by mouthing *fuck you* back to me.

"Lane, why don't you let Jake handle the grill?" Bess asked, laughing.

"Oh yeah, I want to see you behind that hot, smoky grill!" Aly chimed in, turning her grin toward me.

"Both of you, stop! I'm perfectly capable of grilling," Lane said in his own defense before turning his attention back to his burgers.

Aly came over to where I was sitting and drinking beer, and sat on my lap. I rubbed my hand up her leg and let my thumb graze the crease between her thigh and that sweet, sweet pussy of hers.

"Want to go upstairs for a quickie?" I mumbled into her long red hair. She was wearing this gauzy, see-through white tank, and her hair was all wavy and wild. I wanted to yank it back and fuck her from behind. "Or we could take a quick ride in my new car and stop for a little nooky?" I teased her.

I'd kept the Hummer for the car seat and dog crap, but I did buy myself a hot date car. It was a fast little Porsche convertible in cherry red—my favorite color, by the way. Lane had tried it out this past week, and wanted one himself. Maybe I'd get him a little present for helping me get to where I was in my business.

"Al, you hear the big plans?" Lane called out.

Shit.

She raised one of her eyebrows. "Um, no. Do tell."

Lane paused from flipping the last burger and scowled at me. "Jake, what the hell? Why do I have to be the one?"

"Because you have a big fucking mouth," I shot back, frowning back at him.

"Jake, Maddy can hear you and repeat after you," Bess said, scolding me.

Aly poked my arm, definitely not letting this go. "Lane, Jake? Bueller? Anyone? Can someone please tell me what's going on?"

Lane shot me a shit-eating grin before he focused on Aly. "You're sitting on the lap of a mogul, Al. My brother just stroked a deal with the biggest luxury hotel chain in the country to franchise his gyms in every single location. That's right . . . Fizzle To Go will be in almost every major city soon, so when you travel, you don't have to miss your gym at home."

Her eyes huge, Aly turned in my lap to gape at me. "Babe? Why didn't you tell me?"

I ran my hand over her cheek. "I needed to make sure it really happened. I still don't believe it, but it looks like I need you to come back to work and go over the papers and actually hire a legal team. Lane's guy has been filling in, and I need my main girl back."

"Seeing as how I totally took advantage of my maternity leave, I get it." Aly wrapped her arms tight around me, hugging me in only the way she could. "How did this happen?" she whispered. "It's like a dream come true!"

I shrugged. "Well, the baseball team was traveling and didn't like the hotel facilities after using mine, so they may have suggested to one hotel to check my shit out."

"Jake!" Bess yelled at me again.

"Okay, Bess, I got you. I'm watching my language."

"You have a baby now too, so clean up your act."

I nodded and went back to my wife, whose ass was rubbing my chubby. "Let's go celebrate upstairs."

She smacked my chest. "Later, after Tabby goes to bed, I'm going to give you a little congrats present, but not now."

"Promise?"

We were interrupted by the dogs barking at a squirrel scampering up a tree, and the puppies going wild trying to climb up right behind it. Whining ensued when they couldn't catch the damn thing. Then crying followed, which was my cue to grab my baby girl. I knew it wasn't bad for her to cry for a minute, but not my Tabby.

"I can get her, babe," Aly said, hustling behind me.

"I was just going to bring her to you."

She stopped and hooked her hands on her hips. "That's not it, and you know it. You just can't stand her crying for an extra second, and you're the fastest one here."

I nuzzled Tabby's hair as I lifted her, inhaling her awesome baby smell. "Okay, yeah, but so what?"

"No one is ever going to live up to her softie of a daddy, Jason."

I shrugged. "And that's a bad thing?" I asked, knowing no one was ever going to be good enough for this little girl.

When I handed Tab over to Aly, she situated the baby's head under her shirt. Of course, I stood guard to make sure no one saw boobage. My boobs.

"By the way, I'm not a softie," I told Aly as I stroked a finger down her cheek. "I'm a bad-ass bodybuilder, Aly-cat, and don't you forget it."

"You're just like your brother," James chimed in. "You were all hard until you met a woman, and then you went soft like mush."

"Isn't it time for Cliffie to get a bottle or something?" I said, and shooed him away.

James just laughed and snagged a wine spritzer or some other girlie drink from the cooler next to me before walking off.

"You know I'm tough, right?" I asked my wife as I plopped down in the chair next to her, running my hand over Tabitha's back under Aly's shirt.

"Yeah, babe. You're big and tough on the outside, but neither of us were survivors until we met each other. We're our own little fairy tale, meant to be together. Beauty and the Beast."

Isn't that the truth? I leaned in to kiss the top of her fiery red hair, trying to get a quick look at those gorgeous tits of hers.

Maybe later.

THE END

EXCERPT

Read more from Rachel Blaufeld in *Electrified*, Book One in the Electric Tunnel Series.

electrified

CARSON GRAHAM shifted into fourth gear as he hightailed it away from the club toward his hotel. Why did he keep coming back to Vegas? Who the hell knew. If there was one thing he didn't have any trouble finding or getting, it was willing women.

He knew women weren't really "things." They were interesting, often complicated creatures, and he both appreciated and respected them. He just happened to like women in his bed who came with no strings. It was the twenty-first century, after all, and there were plenty of women who liked that kind of deal.

He had never settled down, and he sure as hell wasn't about to start now. At closer to forty years old than thirty-five, he felt the bachelor life suited him just fine. Or maybe it was that he only deserved the single life. His particular circumstances hadn't exactly set him up for success in the relationship department.

Picking up a little speed, he changed course and steered toward the mountains, needing more time to clear his head.

It would be great to be on his motorcycle right now, to be able to lean into the steep and winding curves, but it was back in his garage on the East Coast, grounded—just like his life at the moment. The sports car he'd rented here in Vegas would have to do.

As he shifted the engine into fifth gear the car jetted forward, allowing the tension to bleed from him with the increased RPMs. He was trying to drive away from the pull as fast as he could; the pull coming from an insanely gorgeous stripper he was lusting after in a big way.

There was something magnetic about Sienna Flower, dragging him in deeper and deeper. More than her sleek, toned body and her sensual moves when she wrapped herself around the pole, there was a draw deeper than the physical. Carson wasn't a hard-up kind of guy. He never got like this over a woman. Ever.

Growing up without a mom, he was fairly certain there was nothing lasting about "love." If a mother could actually up and leave her child without any notice, like his did, there was no such thing as forever. His dad had done the best he could to be everything to Carson, but the fact remained: When a six-year-old's mother left and never came back, that fucked with a kid.

It fucked with a grown man too. As a result, Carson never considered love an option.

Lust, a few cocktails, dinner out, and then a good roll in Egyptian cotton sheets—that was Carson's modus operandi. He definitely didn't have any delusions of long-term love.

In reality, his thoughts on the subject of love didn't really matter. His lifestyle and career didn't allow for love; at least, that was what he told himself. After joining the FBI, he traveled all the time, leaving at a moment's notice on any number of classified assignments. He was wise enough to know the FBI lifestyle didn't lend itself to successful relationships, so he never pursued them. If he were honest with himself, he might admit maybe that was why he originally chose to take the FBI job, but who wanted to look that closely at their own motives?

He certainly couldn't be hunting down a suspect in a different time zone while pretending to be at a sales conference in Orlando when he called home in the wee hours of the night . . . or morning, depending on where he was.

Eventually all the lies, fibs, or whatever you wanted to call them caught up in a field agent's relationship. As a man who avoided conflict in his personal life for fear of being deserted, he knew the lying would eat away at him.

After cracking a high-profile missing person's case at the FBI a few years ago, Carson had struck out on his own. Going solo, he built his own firm, still traveling and having a grand fucking time doing what he did best, which was remaining uninterested in a long-term relationship. Now he was an independent private investigator, making his own rules, and it suited him just fine. His reputation followed him and he took the cases he wanted—except for this current bitch of a case—which allowed him to have a good time living life.

To most people, he introduced himself as a bounty hunter or some shit like that. No need to have every Tom, Dick, and Harry asking him to take this or that heartbreaking case. Carson worked, traveled, and enjoyed the finer things life offered. He liked getting paid too much to take on pro-bono cases.

Although his recent case was starting to feel like one . . . that and a big, annoying crock of shit.

A vibration in his pocket partially dragged him out of his funk. Holding the wheel steady with his knee, Carson pulled the phone out of his pocket and hit ignore. Speak of the devil who got him involved in this crap. His best friend, Alex. He should have answered; the guy's family had practically raised him. He owed him that but he wasn't in the mood, since it was Alex's fault that he'd taken this damned case.

Guilt overtook him as he traveled the long, dark desert road, and Carson dialed his friend back.

"Hey man, what's up?" He focused on the open road ahead of him, the mountains bleeding into the skyline, the moon lighting his way.

"Not much. Just checking in. Making sure my oldest friend is still alive and causing trouble wherever he may be at the moment."

"Yeah, yeah. All good here. Kicking around out west, trying to solve that shit case you sent me. Taking a much-needed break in

Vegas as we speak." He pushed his speed a little more, feeling the car purr.

"Way to make me jealous. I'm stuck at home watching the baby while my wife is out on a girls' night out, and you're probably on your way to getting laid. What's wrong with this picture?"

"Nah, Alex. You go be with your baby and let your wife have a good time. You're not missing anything. Except for a few strippers." He laughed out loud.

A small chuckle came from the other end. "I'm gonna get you for that one. Have some fun for me, will ya? Keep me updated on the case. I know I can't be much help, but if you need anything, let me know."

Carson chuckled. "I wish you could help with the case. It's turning into one hell of an adventure. I'm trying my best to help out your relative's friends, but for the first time I just don't know. Hell, listen to me rambling like I'm a spoiled bitch. Forget it, man. Go love your baby."

"Okay, but stay in touch, Carson. Don't go MIA so often."

"I hear ya."

As he disconnected, he thought about Alex's comment. Going MIA, doing his own thing, was part of who he was.

His current personal life lined up with his new career perfectly. He had a few women around the country who knew the 411 when it came to him. Lavish times with no commitment; that was how he rolled. Period.

Now here he was, rushing back to Vegas every weekend. Why? What the hell was the draw? Carson sighed because he knew damn well.

Sienna Flower, adult entertainer with moves that would ignite a dead man, and eyes like a virgin, making him feel like a young kid all over again.

Christ, he had a problem.

The case he was currently working was burning him up and playing with his mind, besides displacing him to the West Coast. Although the job was lining his bank account—even at his lowest rate—it was taking much longer than he expected. He needed it to be over.

Am I losing my touch already?

He sighed and turned the car back toward the Strip while something nagged at his gut over this assignment. There was something odd, some piece of the puzzle missing, which was why the case was taking longer than expected.

What was wrong with him that he couldn't find it? What was he missing?

It was a first for him, and he didn't like it. Not. One. Fucking. Bit. Which was why he found himself running off to Sin City every weekend.

He needed to let off steam, and where better to do so than Las Vegas? It was an occupational hazard of his . . . letting loose. Going back to his FBI days, Carson always needed a little fun, a tiny walk on the wild side to let go of the stress of the job. Otherwise, he lived and breathed his cases, working late into the night to solve them.

He needed a good time to release the pressure, which he currently was finding at the Electric Tunnel, but the pressure only mounted more after visiting the club. What originally started out as a method to clear his head and make way for him to solve the case, was clouding his judgment even more.

Sienna Flower had happened . . . that was what.

His latest client—or *clients*, since it was a married couple—was able to pay him. Yeah, they were making good on his rates, but their friends raised the funds, not them. They were willing to keep transferring money to him, yet he didn't like the eerie feeling that had begun to dog him. They were lying to him. Withholding information, at the very least.

For the first time ever, Carson was considering giving up the case. The only thing that stopped him was the worry that nagged him over the missing person he was hunting down.

Shit, I'm going soft.

He was turning into an emotional cream puff, which was a bigger occupational hazard than having a grand time in Vegas.

Originally, he'd needed a respite from the bone-deep worry that something was terribly wrong with the case, so he started heading to Sin City for the weekends. Now, his gut was messed up from the case *and* his head was fucked up from a stripper.

The family who had hired him was pretty certain their missing relative had fled out west or thereabouts. Why were they so convinced of that theory? Carson had been stuck scouring small towns for the last month and a half. He didn't like small towns with strange people all up in each other's business. Almost as little as he liked the case.

He was starting to need his weekly adventure to Vegas by Tuesday of each week. It was a place where he could disappear and enjoy himself for forty-eight hours. After all, he was still a man with baser needs.

The problem all began when he went to check out the infamous Sienna Flower the first night he got to Vegas. He hadn't been able to tear himself away from her image, nor enjoy himself at all since that night. He couldn't figure it out. He'd had many women over the years—gorgeous, seductive, exotic women when he was traveling—and now he was stuck on some Vegas showgirl. No, not a showgirl. Exotic dancer.

Carson downshifted the car as the lights of the Vegas Strip came into view, rolling around what little he knew about her in his head. Nothing about her made sense. She'd arrived on the scene a few years back, and before long became the biggest thing Vegas had seen in years. She didn't do private rooms or parties. Ever. Asher Peterson, king of the adult dance club world, pulled her from lap dancing after only a year of dancing at the Tunnel. Now all she did was grace billboards, shake her ass onstage, and bring millions of dollars into the club.

He knew all this from Google. Fuck, after the first night seeing her, he couldn't get her tits, firm ass cheeks, and electrifying eyes out of his mind. He'd Googled her like a horny teenager, and decided she must have been a local Asher had taken a liking to.

Were they romantically involved? Was Asher tapping that?

And why was he even thinking about Sienna's potential bed

partners? He was fairly certain that wasn't a role even he could fill.

Do I want to?

Unfortunately, Carson had developed a nasty habit of heading to the Tunnel every Thursday through Saturday nights for the last month. Tonight was no different. He went to see Sienna dance. Then he left to go back to his hotel to either pick up someone in the hotel bar or jack off. Lately, his preference was to stroke himself to recent memories, those of a striking, gorgeous, naturally curvy woman with a heady combination of innocence and salacious moves.

He might as well have been in high school all over again, lusting after the prom queen, not knowing what to do about it other than rub one out.

This evening was different, though, because he had felt Sienna lock gazes with him. She looked right out at him as her act ended. She was smiling, but he could see right into her eyes. She was examining him back as if she wanted to know more about him.

It was disturbing on so many levels. He was a private eye. He should be able to read people. Yet she seemed to be reading *him*, looking deep within him.

He couldn't begin to figure out Sienna Flower, and now she was trying to figure him out? The thought made him harder than he normally was when he exited the club. Tonight he was practically limping as he walked out.

He needed to get laid, stop coming back to Vegas, and leave his thoughts of Sienna Flower at the door.

Of course, he knew he'd be back at the same place tomorrow night with his eyes homed in on one stripper, his dick standing at attention. Weeks ago, he'd paid the concierge at his hotel extremely well to keep him on the weekend list for the Tunnel. Open ended. No need to waste that.

Leaving his rental sports car at the front of his hotel with the valet, Carson bypassed the gaming tables and slot machines and went straight to his favorite bar for a drink. He grabbed a seat at the far end of the bar and nodded at the bartender, Victor, who now viewed him as a regular and brought him a drink without his even needing to order. Top-shelf Scotch on the rocks.

Fuck, he was officially a Vegas groupie. The valets knew him, the bartender knew his drink and had it ready as soon as he stepped foot in the lounge, the front desk gave him the same room each weekend, and he was lusting after a woman who starred in Lord only knew how many other men's fantasies.

If his FBI buddies caught wind of this, they'd never let him live it down. Most of them were settling down, either resolving themselves to living double lives, or trading in their FBI badges for white-collar jobs. Not Carson, he was living the dream. Fast cars, motorcycles, big money, booze, high-end escorts—or dancers, depending on how you looked at it—and his current bullshit case.

He needed to relax and get a handle on all this shit. Carson caught Victor's eye and then lifted his chin, smiling when Victor made his way over to him.

"Hey, Vic, how's it shaking? You got any cigars back behind the bar, or do I have to move my ass to a special bar to smoke one?"

Victor chuckled as he wiped his hands on a bar rag. "You're in luck, buddy, this is Vegas, where anything goes. I just happen to have a few select ones in a humidor under the bar. Let me grab it and you can pick your poison."

Moments later Carson inhaled deeply, Scotch in one hand, a fresh cigar in the other, his view on the casino floor. Actually, he was relaxing for the first time all week, coming down from his dark mood, and found himself not wanting another woman. He wasn't even sure if he wanted to take care of himself either, which was new.

Surprised at that revelation, Carson decided he was content to only finish his drink and cigar before heading upstairs to go straight to sleep.

There was always the promise of tomorrow night, and Sienna locking eyes with him again.

ACKNOWLEDGMENTS

These thank-you lists keep getting longer and longer. In an effort to not write another book, I'd like to thank a few people, none of whom I could do *any of this* without . . .

My editor, Pam Berehulke, and her swift red pen.

Sarah Hansen and her way more than Okay Creations.

Neda Amini, the sweetest everything to me, chief hand-holder and master-minder.

Robin Bateman, Terilyn Smitsky, Jennifer Wolfel, and Virginia Carey, who together are my personal cheering squad, and the ladies who tell me when I have food in my teeth or write shitty dialogue.

Milasy Mugnolo, Michelle Rodriguez, Erin Noelle, Christy Pastore, Fabiola Francisco, and Debra Doxer, for my daily dose of confidence or commiseration.

Emily Tippetts, Stacey Tippetts and Tianne Samson for formatting and endless advice.

EXTRA-SPECIAL THANKS GO TO . . .

My family. Seriously, you never know what you're going to get with me. I may be showered and ready to leave the house or holed up in my robe for days. I love you.

You too, Mom!

Nicole Snyder, who keeps me from going over an unorganized cliff.

My other mother, Susan Ward, who entertains me with her analysis of sales trends and hysterical quips.

My "F the noise" girls. Keeping it real, all day, every day.

The wonderful members of *The Electric Readers* group on Facebook for their energy and tireless support.

The bloggers who tirelessly sit behind their laptops, helping books find new readers.

Stacey, who has the patience of a saint when it comes to the alpha males in my head.

And my friends at home who hold my hand, allow me to cry on their shoulders, and drink California chardonnay.

ABOUT THE AUTHOR

Rachel Blaufeld is a social worker/entrepreneur/blogger turned author. Fearless about sharing her opinion, Rachel captured the ear of stay-at-home and working moms on her blog, *BacknGrooveMom*, chronicling her adventures in parenting tweens and inventing a product, often at the same time. She has also blogged for *USA Today*'s "Happy Ever After" feature, *The Huffington Post*, *Modern Mom*, and *StartupNation*.

Turning her focus on her sometimes wild-and-crazy creative side, it only took Rachel two decades to do exactly what she wanted to do—write a fiction novel. Now she spends way too many hours in local coffee shops plotting her ideas. Her tales may all come with a side of angst and naughtiness, but end lusciously.

Rachel lives around the corner from her childhood home in Pennsylvania with her family and two dogs. Her obsessions include running, coffee, icing-filled doughnuts, antiheroes, and mighty fine epilogues.

If you liked this book, feel free to leave a review where you bought it or on Goodreads.
Send me e-mail when you do, and I will thank you personally!

Please connect with me on:
www.rachelblaufeld.com
Facebook
Twitter